BREATHLESS ON THE BOULEVARD

THE BACHELOR NEXT DOOR - BOOK THREE

PAMELA FORD

AINE PRESS

BOOKS BY PAMELA FORD

BACHELOR NEXT DOOR SERIES

Love on the Lane

Dancing on the Drive

Breathless on the Boulevard

Romance on the Road

Kissing on the Corner

CONTINENTAL BREAKFAST CLUB SERIES

Over Easy

Fresh Brewed

Honey Glazed

OUT OF IRELAND SERIES

To Ride a White Horse

A Rush of White Wings

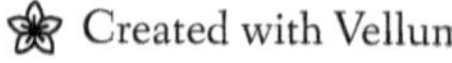 Created with Vellum

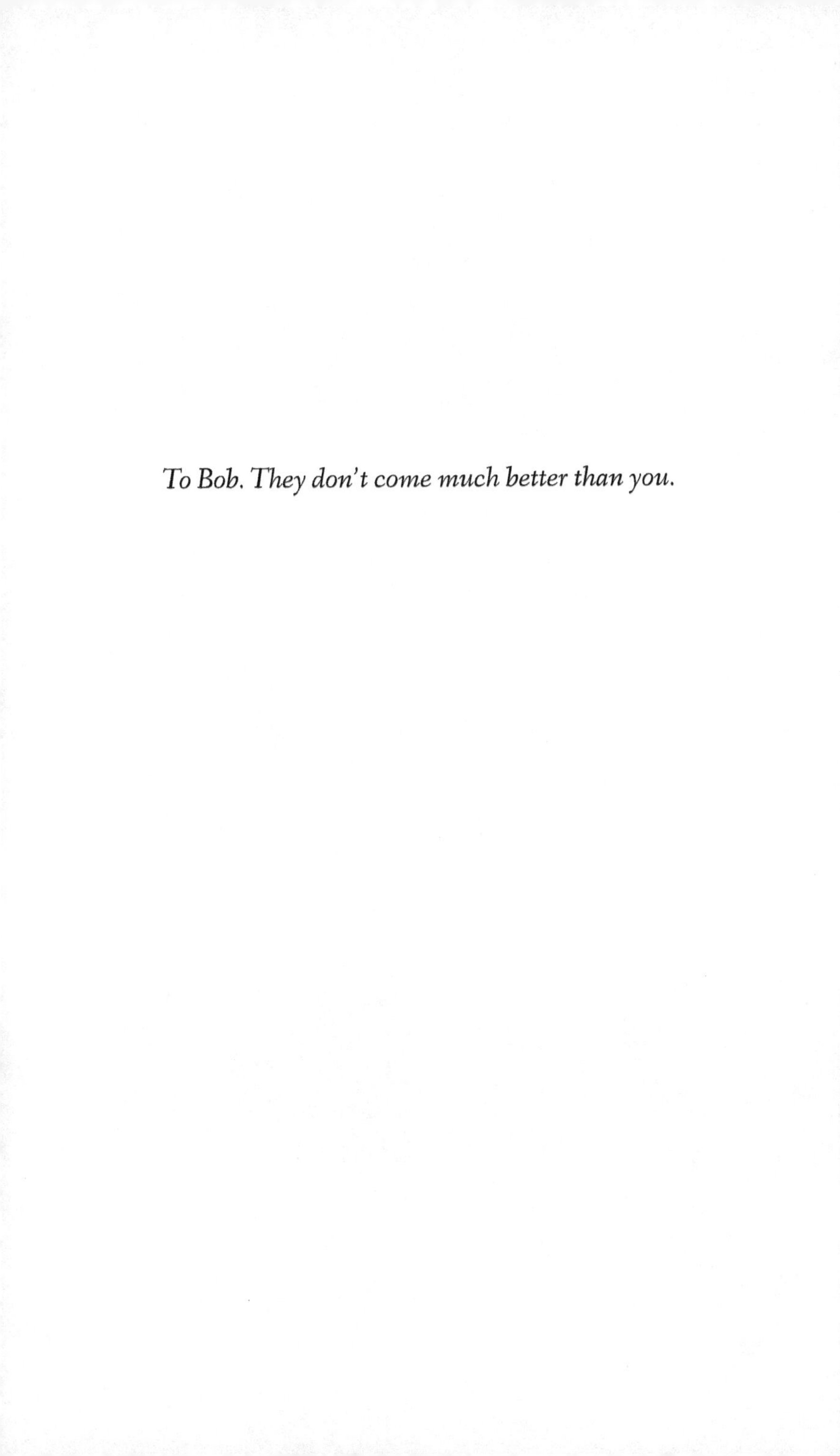

To Bob. They don't come much better than you.

1

————

Nora Clark knew she was in trouble the moment she heard her sister's voice on the phone. "Tell me I just misunderstood you," she said. "Tell me this connection is so bad you didn't really say what I think I just heard."

"It's the only answer," Tess replied. "You have to take my place."

"Don't be ridiculous. We're not kids anymore. This isn't a game." Nora tightened her grip on the phone, paced across her small kitchen, and looked out at her tiny San Francisco backyard. She'd been supporting her sister for two years as she tried to build a personal shopping business. Now Tess wanted Nora to *be* the personal shopper?

Enough was enough. "Look, Tess, when your new, important client wants you to do a rush job for her son, the correct answer is, you get off that cruise ship and come home."

"I'm on the Inside Passage, remember? Alaska? Open water. Icebergs. You don't just jump off cruise ships up here. Besides, I can't desert Liza. She only came along because I begged her to." Tess's voice turned pleading.

"Please, Nora ... I can't afford to lose this account. Camille Lamont is such a famous author. She's so connected, she could totally make my career. I can't say no."

"This is *your* business, not mine," Nora said through gritted teeth. "If you want to help ... this guy—"

"Erik. His mom said his name is Erik."

"If you want to help Erik, you need to figure this out your—"

"I'm trying to. But I'm telling you, there's no way off this ship except via emergency helicopter. And I doubt that shopping counts as an emergency. Please, Nora. He'll never know you're not me. We're completely identical—"

"Tess, this is beyond stupid—"

"No, no, it's smart actually. Think about it. If I make Camille happy, she'll give me referrals, referrals mean I make more money. And more money means I get out of your hair—not to mention your house—sooner." Tess paused. "Maybe then you'd have time to date."

"Tess!"

"Nora!" Her sister mimicked her annoyed tone.

"Okay, fine, I'll go to the appointment ... and explain that you're on a seventeen-day cruise—"

"No! What will Camille think when she learns I sent someone who knows *next to nothing* about personal shopping to meet with her son?" Tess groaned. "I can see this account waving goodbye already. You have to be me. Just pretend you're me."

"Absolutely not. Either tell her the truth or come back to San Francisco and meet with her yourself," Nora said as evenly as possible. "It's called re-spon-si-bility."

"We're practically in grizzly territory up here. Probably polar bear, too."

Nora let out a snort. "I doubt the bear populations will

be attacking you at the next port of call—or the airport, for that matter."

"Nora." Tess's voice dropped low. "When Keegan called off our wedding, I thought I would die. I need this cruise. Even *you* said it was a good idea. The Lamont account is important to me, but I'm just not up to it yet. I've only been on the ship one day. What kind of a respite is that?"

Nora dropped into a kitchen chair as she tried to reason everything out. Tess had really hit bottom when Keegan dumped her. And though Nora had never been able to understand her sister's devastation over losing that idiot, she'd agreed that time away might help Tess heal. Especially since their cousin Liza—the epitome of responsible—had agreed to go along. Maybe she'd rub off on Tess. Besides the cruise had already been paid for—it was supposed to have been Tess and Keegan's honeymoon.

Still, that didn't mean Nora taking her place was a good idea. "Tess, we may look the same but that's where the similarity ends. I'm a physical therapist. You're a personal shopper. You're loose and carefree. I'm ... not."

"I'll say."

"What?"

"Sorry. Sorry."

"Anyway, pretending to be you, even for one meeting, is like ... expecting apples to be oranges."

"You didn't used to be an apple. You just became one over the years."

"I did not." Indignation rose up inside her.

"Then why do you keep staying in that hospital physical therapy job when you hate it? Come on, I know your complaints by heart." Tess's voice took on a singsong quality. "Once people have surgery, all you do is make sure they can use a walker and get out of a chair, and then—boom!—they're gone. Discharged. You never get to see rehab through to the end."

"It's important work," Nora said.

Tess kept talking. "And what about that new sports medicine rehab center the hospital's opening? They have to hire someone—have you even applied yet?"

The truth in her words irritated Nora more than the know-it-all tone of her voice. "Tess, when people grow up they discover you can't have everything. You become—"

"Dull. But you don't have to."

Nora slowly counted to ten in her head. "Whatever. My pretending to be you is still beyond stupid. Switching places is something you do when you're seventeen."

"Or something you do when your sister really needs your help. This isn't about Erik Lamont and you know it. It's about keeping his mother happy. If she wants me to do a quick job for her son, I can't *not* do it." She let out an exaggerated sigh. "Nora—she'll hire someone else."

"Couldn't you just call her and explain that—"

"Nora? Hello? Hello? I'm losing you."

"Tess? Can you hear me?"

Silence greeted Nora's words, and she raised her eyes to the ceiling in frustration. Pressing redial, she kicked into her spiel again as soon as Tess answered. "Just tell Camille you're on a long cruise in Alaska. Surely she'll understand that people take vacations." She pressed the fingers of one hand to her forehead.

"I don't want to risk it—she's too new a client. How hard could it be to take my place just this once? Help me out with Erik Lamont." Tess let out a laugh. "You never know, he could be cute ..."

"Not even funny." Nora stood, unable to stay seated

long with the conversation twisting and turning the way that it was.

"Why do you always discount the possibility of meeting another man? Kevin died five years ago—"

"How did we get from me impersonating you to my getting hooked up with some guy we don't even know, and for all we know is an unemployed loser living off his mother or still in high school or something? Tess, sometimes you're like a broken record."

"So will you take my place?"

Nora huffed. "New song. Same broken record. No. How could I? What if his mom notices the difference?"

"Why would his mom be there? You're shopping for him."

"Well, his mom made the call. Really, Tess, I'd help you if I could." She felt a tugging at the back of her shirt and turned to smile at her five-year-old son.

"Mama," Danny said. "I think I found a new daddy— the right one. Come." He pulled her with him toward the living room.

Tess kept talking into her ear. "Yeah, well, what happens if I tell his mother I can't do it?"

"Hold on a minute, Tess." She looked at Danny. "What?"

"I found a new daddy on TV." His brown eyes shone with earnestness.

"You can't just find a daddy on TV. It's not that easy."

"But you said if I found one to let you know."

Nora sighed. Whatever had possessed her to say such a thing to him?

"He's really nice." Danny pointed at the television where Mr. Rogers was cutting construction paper with scissors and talking in his perfectly calm voice.

"Mr. Rogers? Oh, Danny, Mr. Rogers is—" *Dead.* "Uh—married already. Tell you what, sweetie, why don't you go get a cookie and I'll be off in a minute." She watched him dash into the kitchen, then turned her attention back to the phone.

"Something wrong?" Tess asked.

"He's looking for a daddy again. Found one on TV that he thinks is just right. *Mr. Rogers.*"

"God, he's really getting determined about that. Maybe you should sign up for some online dating—"

"Stop."

Danny hopped into the room munching on a cookie and she went back into the kitchen.

"Okay," Tess said. "So I was saying, what happens if I turn this job down and Camille finds some other personal shopper who is ready and willing to help. Then she thinks, *Wow, I like this new on-the-ball shopper girl who's available whenever I need her. I think I'll give her all my business.* Just like that, I'll have lost my biggest account. All because I didn't meet with—"

Suddenly, silence was all Nora heard, and she knew the connection had dropped again. "Damn!" she muttered. She set her phone on the counter and stared at the cupboard, noticing for the first time all the dried milk spatters on the dark wood doors.

How did all this milk splash up here? And how could she not have seen it before? She grabbed the dishrag from the sink and began to wipe off the doors as she debated whether or not to call Tess back.

Her head felt like it was going to burst. She knew this account was crucial to Tess's success, to Tess making enough money to support herself, *to Tess ever moving out of*

Nora's house. She exhaled. Which meant, keeping this account had to be as important to Nora as it was to Tess.

She picked up the phone and pressed *redial.* Her sister answered on the first ring: "I don't know how much longer I'll be able to get a signal out here."

"Look," Nora said. "There's not much I wouldn't do for you, but this ... this ... I wouldn't know the first thing about what I'm doing."

"It's not that hard." There was hope in Tess's voice. "Liza agrees."

Nora looked down at her T-shirt and leggings and felt ill. "For God's sake, I don't know anything about style, let alone being a personal shopper."

"I'll talk you through it—"

"You're on a cruise ship with crummy cell phone connections." Kneeling, she attacked the spatters on the lower cupboard doors as if the forcefulness of her effort would erase her frustration.

"There's always ship-to-shore radio."

Nora groaned and sat back on her heels. "I'm sure that's a reasonable price per minute. Let's just look at this realistically. What if he figures out I'm not you? What if his mother comes along on the spur of the moment? What if I do a really bad job and you lose the account anyway?"

"Nora! We don't have any other choices."

We? She pushed herself to standing and went into the front hall to inspect her reflection in the full-length mirror. Pulling her dark hair out of its ponytail, she shook it loose around her face. Yeah, she could pass for Tess without a problem.

The thought made her stomach take a flop. She wasn't actually considering this ridiculous idea, was she? No way. Absolutely not.

"Nora?" Tess asked.

"One meeting," she answered. Omigod, what was she thinking?

"Right. Two at the most."

"Two? When did this happen?"

"If you have to buy him something, you're going to have to deliver it," Tess said. "No biggie. He tries it on, you say it looks great, you're out of there in, like, twenty minutes."

"You'd better be right. Okay. Two meetings at the most." Nora felt the room begin to spin. "And you'll talk me through everything?"

"Everything."

Lightheaded, Nora sank down onto her couch. Across the room, Danny sat cross-legged on the rug in front of the TV, still enthralled by Mr. Rogers.

"But ... what if he *is* cute?" Nora whispered. "And he wants me to buy him—" her voice dropped lower. "—pants. I don't have to measure his inseam or anything, do I?"

Tess barked out a laugh. "No. He should know what size he wears. If in doubt, get a couple of sizes and have him keep the one that fits best."

"I have to tell him which pants fit him best? Some guy I don't even know? What if he's cute? What if he's, ahem, *built?*"

Tess laughed harder. "You just say they look *fabu* and get out of the house before he takes them off and asks you how his briefs fit."

"No way. I can't do it. I can't. Really, Tess, I am not ready for this—"

Tess's laughter reached hysterical proportions before she pulled herself together. "I'm kidding. You really do need to get out more. Clients *do not* come on to the personal shopper. It just isn't done."

"Right. I know that." Nora let her head fall back against the couch.

"So, will you do it? Just this once ... just switch places one more time."

She knew better. She really did. "Oh, Tess, how many times did we change places and have it backfire—"

"And think of all the times it didn't ... Nora?"

She hesitated even though she knew she didn't have a choice. Not really. Not if Tess was going to get what she wanted so that Nora could get what she wanted. She hesitated, even though she knew she was going to say *yes*. She drew a breath. "You have to promise—"

"Anything. Anything you want."

"*Never* to ask me to do this again."

"Never?" Tess sounded shocked.

"Never."

"Never is really an absolute. I mean, what if it's mutually beneficial? Because there are times when—"

"No." Nora said in a voice, firm and strong.

"Wow. Okay. But, just in case you're wondering, I'll still be you sometime if you want me to—"

"No, no, no. After this time, *never again*. Never."

"Okay. I think I got that," Tess said.

Nora closed her eyes a moment and hoped she wasn't on the verge of creating another massive complication in her life. "Now what do I have to do to be a personal shopper? You're going to have tell me more than just what questions to ask the guy—you're going to have to dress me, too."

As Tess's laughter came across the airwaves, the phone cut out again. Nora hit redial, but the call didn't connect. She tried again and got Tess's voicemail.

"Just great," she muttered. "I'd better not have to make this up as I go along or we're both going to be in big trouble."

2

———

"I'm not meeting with a personal shopper." Erik Morgan scowled at his mother, working at a computer at her large mahogany desk.

"Why not?" She spun her desk chair around to face him.

"I don't have the time. I don't have the inclination. I don't want some strange woman that involved in my life."

"She doesn't get involved in your life. She just shops for you. Or with you." His mother smiled calmly and he knew manipulation was running rampant beneath her perfectly coiffed blond hair. "Whichever you prefer."

Erik rolled his eyes. "Is this why you asked me to come over today? To talk about personal shopping? Not to check your knee?"

"I want you to check my knee, too. This replacement they put in doesn't seem to work that well yet." She rubbed her knee.

He knelt by her chair and checked her leg for swelling, then used his hands to straighten and bend her knee a couple of time. "Your range of motion is still limited. Let me see you go up the stairs." He stood and took her hand to help her up. "Are you doing the rehab exercises? And walking, like you're supposed to?"

They moved slowly toward the wide curving stairway in the marble-floored foyer. This house was way too formal for his taste; he was glad he hadn't grown up here.

"It's hard to find so much time to exercise," his mother said. "I've got a deadline. I've got to get this next book written and the words aren't coming easily. Maybe it's from going under the anesthetic. Doesn't that have some sort of effect on brain neuron connections?"

For a bestselling author, sometimes his mother was really a ditz. "Maybe on you."

She gasped, and he held in a grin. "Really? Is it permanent? How will I ever finish this book?"

"Mom, no—"

"It's not permanent then?"

"It doesn't happen at all. I just said that because you're driving me crazy." He frowned as he looked at her left leg. "A knee replacement isn't going to finish healing unless you help it along. I know it's been five weeks, but you've got to get up and walk."

"Honey, isn't there some other way—"

"No." He tried to stay patient. "That knee is going to freeze up if you don't work it. If all you wanted for a leg was a bent stick, we could have given you one in the first place and it would have cost less." He gestured at the stairs. "Let me see you climb."

"Now, Erik, there's no reason to get testy." She took hold of the banister and started up the stairs, one step at a time. "I'm doing most of my exercises. I just wanted to double check because I really have to get this book finished."

Patience. "Some isn't good enough. Look at you on the stairs—you don't have the strength to go step-over-step yet."

"What are you going to wear to the party?" she asked over her shoulder.

He watched her knee. "Promise me you'll do all your exercises even if you have writing to do."

"We'll talk about it. Now, what are you wearing to the party?"

"What party?" he asked irritably.

His mother sighed. "And you wonder why I want you to use a personal shopper?" Halfway up the stairs she turned around. "The one my publisher is throwing—"

"Oh, yeah. Fifteenth straight book on the *New York Times* bestseller list."

"And you have an outfit to wear?" She continued down the stairs, her eyes never leaving his face.

"An outfit? Sounds so ... matching."

"Erik—"

"Mom—"

"Don't *Mom* me. You spend all day in scrubs and the rest of the time in jeans. It's time you start dressing like the grown-up you are."

He folded his arms across his chest. "I have other clothes, trust me—"

"I don't trust you. Not since you showed up for dinner at the Cavanaugh's dressed like you were going skiing." She stepped off the bottom stair and took the hand he held out to her.

"That's because I was coming *from* skiing. I just overestimated how long we'd be out there."

"Well, you had the appearance of someone who ... doesn't know how to dress appropriately for the occasion."

He snorted out a laugh. "Mom, I'm a doctor. Everyone

knows I can buy clothes if I want them. Who the hell cares what I wear as long as I can fix their bodies up good as new —or almost good as new."

"Well, Mary Jean's niece cared. She wasn't impressed at all, even if you *were* on the Olympic ski team once upon a time."

Oh, wait a minute. He'd thought something was strange about his mother's obsession with his apparel. Now he knew what she was up to; she was matchmaking gain. "Mom, I don't want to meet anyone at this party."

She started back to her office. "I don't know what you're talking about."

"Don't invite anyone who might want to introduce themselves to me, either."

"Erik, I wouldn't dream of interfering in your love life."

Ha! He held up a hand. "Just so we're clear. No more daughters of friends, friends of friends, acquaintances of friends ... I'm tired of meeting plastic women who just want to land themselves a rich, successful husband."

A pensive expression crossed his mother's face as she lowered herself into her office chair.

"Now what?" he asked against his better judgment, knowing full well that the master manipulator was just getting started.

His mother rubbed her knee.

"Does your knee hurt?"

"Only when I get into disagreements."

Erik laughed.

"Now, sweetheart," she said. "About that promise to do my exercises ... I think I would feel so much more inclined to do them if I could remove the worry that you had something appropriate to wear to the party."

"Fine, put your mind to rest. I do." *Khakis and a polo.*

"What?"

"What do you mean, *what?*" He shoved his hands into his jeans pockets.

"What are you going to wear?" she asked calmly. "Not old khakis and a worn polo."

He exhaled silently. "I'll buy something."

"When?"

"Soon."

"I've heard this before. And it's not good enough. My shopper can take care of everything. Then I can do my exercises in peace knowing that your outfit is taken care of … and my brain neurons can reconnect so I can write the rest of this book."

If his mother hadn't succeeded as a novelist, she would have made a great lawyer. Juries wouldn't even know what hit them.

"Mom! I don't need a personal shopper. What's next? Should I have my nails buffed? My chest hair waxed?" He held up both hands. "Okay, I'll go shopping and buy some clothes. I'll even ask the clerk for help—if I need it."

"Don't be silly. There's no reason for you to go this alone. This is the same shopper I use. You'll like her. First, she'll interview you." She rummaged through the papers and notebooks on her desk. "I have an extra card here somewhere," she said. "Then she'll shop and bring what she bought to your house. You try it all on and keep what you want. Or in your case, you keep what she recommends so your clothes match. It's jolly fun."

"Jolly fun? Are you going British?" he asked grumpily.

His mother chortled. "So, what do you think? Should we make a deal? I'll force myself to get up and walk. That will make you happy. And you'll force yourself to meet with my personal shopper. That will make me happy. Do we have an agreement?"

At least this was better than her playing matchmaker and trying to set him up with one of her friends' daughters. "Fine. What's her number? I'll give her a call."

She waved a hand at him. "No need to call. It's all set up. She'll be at your house tomorrow night at seven."

"You already made the appointment? Mom, what are you doing?" No wonder his sister moved halfway across the country. He'd been the stupid one to move back when he finished his residency.

"I thought about having her meet you here since I know her already, but she'll probably want to take a peek at what you've got in your closet."

"She's going to go through my clothes?" he asked, appalled.

"Well, how else do you think she'll help you?"

"Mom! Why do you do these things?"

"I checked your schedule at work—"

"You checked my schedule?" He was so dumbfounded, he couldn't think of anything to say for a moment. "The Giants game is on tomorrow night. I'm not—"

"Talk fast then and the meeting will be over sooner. Now where is that business card?" She shuffled through her papers again. "The thing is, Erik, the party is Saturday. In order for her to have time to shop, you have to meet tomorrow night."

"And I sure wouldn't want to miss an opportunity to work with Miss Personal Shopper."

"Now, Erik, that sounded a bit like an arrogant orthopedic surgeon talking."

Arrogant orthopedic surgeon? Hell, he felt like a fifteen-year-old kid right now. "But, Mom, really, she's going to go through my clothes?"

"Have you got something to hide?"

He almost choked. "No. But it's sort of personal."

"That's why she's called a *personal shopper*. Now, sweetie, I'm sorry but can't find her card, and I've got writing to do and, you know, knee exercises. I hate to push you off like this, but I don't have time to chitchat the night away even if you do." She turned back to her computer, fingers poised at the keyboard. "If there isn't anything else, you really should get on your way."

He really should get on his way? That's what he'd been trying to do when he left work and got an urgent call from his mother insisting he come over immediately. "Great idea. By the way, they say blueberries are good for brain development and neuron connections."

"Really? I'll be sure I get some."

He waited a long moment, but his mother didn't offer the information he needed. "Okay. I give up. Who am I expecting at seven tomorrow night?"

"Tess. Tess Carlisle. Her company is called The Shopping Goddess. You'll like her."

3
____

This was ridiculous. Absolutely insane. And the worst of it was, she'd agreed to participate.

Nora inspected herself in the bureau mirror, her dark brown hair now trimmed to shoulder-length and highlighted with natural-looking streaks of red like Tess's. Thank goodness her sister's hairdresser had been able to squeeze her in over the lunch hour. Although, in order to get the appointment, she'd had to lie, saying she needed the same style as Tess because the two of them wanted to play a prank on some old friends.

She shook her head. This was the whole problem with taking each other's places—it always ended up accompanied by a string of lies, and most of the time ended up in a disaster.

She went into the hall and peeked down the stairs to make sure her son and the babysitter were occupied, then quickly dialed her friend Margo Evans—the only other person besides Tess who knew what she was about to do. "I feel like a fraud," she whispered into the phone as soon as Margo answered.

"Well, technically, you are."

"Thanks. I feel so much better about this now." Nora frowned at her reflection in the hall mirror and put a hand to the V-neck of the persimmon-colored sheath dress she'd pulled from Tess's closet. "You should see me. I'm wearing Tess's clothes—"

"I bet you look incredible. Like something out of a fashion magazine."

"I may be a bit overexposed on top."

"Put on a necklace," Margo said with a laugh.

Nora nodded. "I hope I can pull this off." All she needed was to slip into Tess's nude stilettos and she would be completely transformed. She hoped she'd be able to balance on those toothpick heels.

"Just remember what we talked about. Get in there, find out what the guy needs, and get out. Say as little as possible, don't talk about yourself and, rule number one, *don't talk about his mother.* The shorter the meeting, the better."

"Right." Nora glanced at her watch. "I better finish getting ready or I'll be late. Wish me luck."

"Good luck. You'll do great. You're coming for coffee group tonight, aren't you?"

"Yeah—unless this interview takes too long. And if that happens, you'll be able to find me at the nearest corner tavern drowning my sorrows!" She shut off the phone and didn't move for a long minute, wondering for the thousandth time how she'd let herself get roped taking Tess's place. And even worse, how she'd agreed to a meeting on the one night of the week she actually had something fun to do.

She thought back to how their coffee group had evolved. First, it had just been her and Margo—two friends, both single mothers, meeting to talk, to bounce thoughts off one other, to help each other through the ups and downs of raising children. Then, Nora got to know Selena, another single mom, and brought her along one night; and Margo invited Rosie, an old high school friend who was raising a son alone. Before long, they'd made their group official—meeting every Thursday night for coffee, conversation and camaraderie at Margo's Bistro, a quaint coffee shop near the beach.

She went into Tess's bedroom to get a necklace, looked in the mirror as she put it on, then made a face at the image of her sister she saw there. Thank goodness Erik Lamont had never met Tess, because that was really the only thing that would save them.

Closing her eyes for a moment, she tried to quash her fears. A little *saving* might not be the worst thing right now, if only she had any idea who to ask for help. Her grandmother would have pulled out the name of some obscure saint qualified to assist in this particular situation. There were hundreds of saints, each one with a different specialty. But who could possibly be the patron saint of people trying to pull a fast one?

If only she'd paid better attention during her parochial grade school days. Then again, maybe one of the more well-known saints would be willing to pinch-hit just this once. Like, oh, how about Saint Christopher, the patron saint of travelers? She made a face. Not the best match—or choice. Didn't they de-saint him anyway?

She knew she had to get going, but stalled longer. Who was that saint, the one her grandmother always said answered her prayers?

St. Jude.

"Oh, yeah," she said aloud. "The patron saint of desperate causes. Rather a good fit if I do say so myself."

She ran a brush through her hair and muttered under her breath, "Please, Saint Jude ... get me through this meeting and I promise never to do this again."

She stopped with the brush halfway down the back of her head and raised her eyes skyward. "And, if by chance you happen to be hanging out with any other saintly types up there whose area of expertise might better match my situation, feel free to ask their assistance."

Clearly, she was really losing it now. This was all Tess's fault.

She'd tried to reach her sister several more times last night, but only one call connected—and then only long enough for Tess to tell her to conduct an initial client interview. Then Tess sent a series of text messages that only served to make her more confused than ever. So, at ten-thirty she'd gone digging in her sister's computer and found a client assessment form and half page of notes titled, *Becoming a Personal Shopper*. That was it. She'd printed the form and read the notes, and that was now the sum total of her knowledge about personal shopping. Everything else she'd have to ad-lib.

No wonder her stomach was knotted and nauseous. She opened the leather briefcase on her bed and double checked to make sure she had a pad of paper, the client assessment form, and multiple pens. One could never be too sure. She may stumble through this meeting tonight, but at least she'd have something to write on and write with.

She stepped into Tess's stilettos and her confidence wavered even more. She didn't feel like a personal shopper, she didn't feel like Tess. What she felt like was Nora in Tess's clothing, like the wolf wearing only a partial sheepskin, like the emperor in the nude.

Well, not quite that.

Maybe what she needed to boost her self-esteem were some affirmations—lots of affirmations. "I am Tess," she said to her reflection. She wobbled across the room on her heels, smiling and nodding at nonexistent people. "I *am* Tess. I am a personal shopper. I love to help people fix their wardrobes. I love to shop. How can I help you? I *love* to shop. You look *fabulous* in that. Want to try on something else?" Suddenly she felt like a talking Barbie doll. The shoes didn't help, either—they were exactly like something Barbie would wear. Poor Barbie—her feet probably hurt all the time.

Nora checked her watch. It really was time to go. As long as she didn't have to walk too far, she should be all right in these shoes. Her stomach churned with anticipation and she took one last look at herself in the mirror, wishing she was already coming home from the meeting instead of just leaving for it.

Finally she drew a long slow breath and exhaled, then went into the living room where Danny and the babysitter were mesmerized by some television program. She bent to kiss her son on the forehead. "You go to bed when Ashley tells you, and I'll come in and kiss you again when I get home, okay?"

He nodded. "You look like Auntie Tess."

Good. "That's because we're twins. See you later, sweetie." She ran out the door before Danny could take his thought process a step further and ask, in front of the sitter, why she was wearing Tess's clothes.

———

The guy had good taste, she had to hand it to him. Nora parked on the boulevard in front of a gorgeous Colonial

Revival row house in San Francisco's Russian Hill area, an elegant old home with curved windows and a columned portico in front.

Good taste. And money, obviously.

All from his mother, she bet. He was probably a freeloader living off Mom's royalties. Camille Lamont probably bought him the house and paid all the utilities. No doubt that was it because, truly, how many adult men allowed their mothers to hire a personal shopper to work with them?

Very few. *Or none.*

So he was a momma's boy.

The thought gave her self-confidence a boost and propelled her out of Tess's BMW and up the walk. Probably a nerdy momma's boy at that. Nothing she couldn't handle.

She carefully climbed the steps to the front door, holding tight to the rail so she didn't fall off her shoes. Then she pressed the doorbell and waited for Erik Lamont to answer. A soft breeze slid over her bare arms, and she gazed down the boulevard toward a view of San Francisco Bay in the distance.

She felt a prickling under her arms and tried to control her nervous anticipation by thinking about the weather. May was so beautiful. The rains were past, the summer coolness and fog had yet to arrive, and the hydrangeas and tulips and rhododendrons were nearly at their peak. She closed her eyes and turned her face toward the sun. A wave of exhaustion rolled over her; she'd been up half the night worrying about this meeting. The memory caused her apprehension to multiply.

This was no good. She had to be self-assured in front of this guy. Tess certainly wouldn't be nervous—not with her experience level. Nora drew a breath to calm herself. Maybe she could employ the same strategy they tell you to use when you give a speech—picture the audience in their underwear. That might work. The moment Erik Lamont opened the door, she would simply envision him in his underwear. That should clear out any nervous energy—

"Something going on down the block?" A man's voice jerked her back to reality. She spun round. *Remember, picture him in—* "Ah, no, just looking at—" *his underwear* "—the Bay." Dr. Erik Morgan. Orthopedic surgeon at the hospital where she worked. Former Olympic skier. Dark brown hair. Gorgeous blue eyes. *Picture him in ... his ... briefs.*

Her cheeks began to burn. This was not turning out to be a good plan at all.

"Ah—ah—" She looked at him, dazed, then glanced at the house numbers in confusion as she tried to force the vision of Erik Morgan in his underwear out of her mind. Somehow, she'd come to the wrong place—or something. "I —I'm not sure I'm at the right house. I'm supposed to meet Erik Lamont." *You know, that nerdy momma's boy.*

"That would be me. Although I go by Erik Morgan. Lamont is my stepdad's last name." He grinned. "You must be my personal shopper."

Him? Her heart plummeted into her stomach. She tried not to gape as she attempted to make sense of this development. *She had to dress Erik Morgan?* A picture of him in his briefs, like an undressed paper doll, flashed into her mind.

Omigod. She wrenched her gaze away and glanced down the boulevard, breathless.

What had she gotten herself into?

"Come on in," Erik stepped back to let her into the

house. A medium-sized puppy bounded up to meet her, his long-haired black body accented with white and brown across his face, chest, and legs.

"That's Willa," he said. "She's a Bernese Mountain Dog."

"She's going to be big," Nora managed to get out, her brain still stuck on *Erik Morgan. Dr. Erik Morgan.* He worked out of the same hospital as she did. The minute he recognized her, this whole thing would be over.

"You want something to drink?" he asked.

"Water would be fine." She tried to swallow but her mouth had gone totally dry. *Water would be incredible.*

He disappeared toward the back of the house and returned a minute later, handing her a bottle of Ice Mountain. "I have to admit, I've never used a personal shopper before," he said. Barefoot, and in shorts that showed enough of the legs that once made him a world-class skier, he led her into a living room casually decorated with a mix of antique and new furnishings. A big blue, red, and gold patterned oriental rug covered the hardwood floor.

"Oh, well, lots of people haven't." She perched on the edge of the tweed sofa and tried not to notice the muscles in his legs. Opening her bottle of water, she took a big drink while he dropped down into a comfortably worn leather club chair.

"Do you do a lot of work for my mother?" he asked.

No way were they getting into a conversation about Camille. "Oh, a bit. But it's against my policy to discuss one client with another, even if it is a relative. I hope you understand."

He squinted at her and cocked his head, his dark hair falling boyishly onto his forehead. "Don't you work at Community Memorial?"

Her stomach flopped in panic. "Oh, no," she said brightly, trying to act unconcerned even though her heart was beating like a jackhammer. "You're probably thinking of my sister. We're twins. She's Nora, I'm Tess, but most people can't tell us apart." She mentally cringed at how high and chirpy her voice sounded.

"Oh, that's it. Physical therapy." He pointed a finger at her. "You really look a lot alike, but her hair's different than yours ..."

Not anymore. What were the odds that Tess's client would be someone Nora saw at the hospital, someone who actually knew what she looked like? She decided to sidestep future questions before any arose. "Our hair used to be different, but now, um, Nora got her hair done like mine, so I guess we're pretty much identical." She reached down to pet the dog so she wasn't looking Erik in the face as she gave voice to that falsehood.

"Hmm, maybe I'll stop over in PT and give her a hard time about moonlighting as a personal shopper." He smiled.

What? Omigod, she couldn't possibly interact with him as both Tess *and* Nora. How would she keep anything straight? Leave it to her sister to drag her into the worst possible situation ever. She could feel a world-class headache kicking in. Time to get this show on the road. "I guess we should get started ..." *And over with.*

She bent to her briefcase and pulled out the interview form and a clipboard. Her hair slipped forward into her face, blocking her vision, and she shoved it behind her ears. She missed her ponytail—it did such a nice job of keeping her hair out of the way. "First of all, I have to ask a few questions about your apparel needs, preferences for style and color, that sort of thing."

He settled back in his chair as if he were enjoying himself immensely.

"All right?" she asked, somewhat disconcerted by the playfulness in his expression.

"Ask away."

"Let's begin with why you're hiring me. Is this a general wardrobe overhaul or do you just need something for a special occasion?"

"Hmm." He looked at her for a moment. "Why I'm hiring you, huh? Well, this meeting is the result of a bargain I struck with my mother so she would do her rehab exercises for the knee replacement surgery she had a month ago."

"Oh." Nora scribbled a few words on the paper just to look like she knew what she was doing.

"She's afraid I'm going to wear something to an upcoming function that will embarrass her."

"Really?" *Interesting.* "What kinds of clothes do you ... lean toward wearing?"

"You don't have to go through my closet, do you?"

The paperwork in Tess's files had mentioned something about checking out the client's existing wardrobe. Imagine going through Erik Morgan's drawers ... ah, dresser.

Hate started up her cheeks again.

4

———

"Oh, no, I don't think that's necessary," Nora said quickly. "Not when you just need help for one specific occasion."

He seemed as relieved by her answer as she was. "So, what type of event is it?" she asked.

"A party." He kicked his bare feet up on the footstool. "My mom's hit the *New York Times* list for the fifteenth time. Her publisher is throwing a big bash to celebrate."

"Wow! That sounds exciting. But, wouldn't you just wear a suit?" Though he'd probably look great in one, personally, she liked the shorts and T-shirt ensemble he had going on right then.

He frowned. "Suits I've got."

She restrained the urge to ask, *Then what do you need me for?* and instead asked, "So ... do you need help choosing a new one?"

"The party's at Corinthian Yacht Club—it's not really a formal event. I think the invitation says *casual chic.* Whatever the hell that is."

Tess had talked about all the confusing dress codes in

the past but Nora hadn't paid a lot of attention. Working as a PT, she pretty much adhered to one dress code—comfortable—so Tess's ramblings had gone in one ear and out the other.

She wrote *casual chic* on the paper and underlined it three times for emphasis as she tried to decipher its meaning. Tess had mentioned office casual, smart casual, business casual, black tie, semiformal, dressy casual ... She wracked her brain. Casual chic didn't ring a bell. When she'd agreed to do this meeting, she sort of assumed the client would be giving her more direction than just two words: *casual chic*.

Erik was watching her as if expecting her to say something, so she opened her mouth and began to speak, hoping even a part of what she was saying was correct. Or, at the least appeared to make some sort of sense, since this guy didn't know what casual chic was either.

"Well ... casual chic is really not as complicated as it seems. Not a bit." She sat back and crossed her legs, gesturing with the pen. "We all know what casual is ... well, weekend kind of casual ... blue jeans and ... such. And of course, there's business casual which is a step or two above that. Khakis, polo shirts, the like. Then you see, casual chic is ... is ... simply a few more steps above that." Her body began to prickle as she broke out in a sweat. "Casual chic is more *chic* kind of clothes, dressier ... but still casual. In the casual family, that is." She splayed a hand across her chest in an effort to present a confidence she didn't feel.

"Okay, as long as *you* know what you're doing," he said. "What kind of clothes do you recomm—"

The ringing of the doorbell cut short his question, and he excused himself to get the door. The dog followed right behind him.

Nora let out a sigh of relief. *Casual chic?* She had a vague idea of what *she* thought casual chic was, but until she looked it up online or talked to her sister, she didn't want to take any chances with the definition. All she knew was that she needed to get out of here as soon as possible.

From the front door came a female voice, "I was just in the neighborhood and thought, why not stop and say hi to Tess?"

Moments later, a blond, impeccably dressed older woman limped into the room using a cane. Nora's blood ran cold. *Not Camille Lamont.* Please God, this couldn't be Camille Lamont.

The woman *knew* Tess personally. She'd never be fooled by this charade. And, oh shit, what did Tess call her? Ms. Lamont? Mrs. Lamont? Camille? Goddess?

The woman hobbled over and Nora stood.

"Tess! I'm so glad you could fit Erik into your schedule."

Nora frantically tried to think of something personal shopperish to say, finally settling on the only thing that came to mind. "I'm happy to be able to help."

"So now you've met Erik. He lives in blue jeans. And shorts. And scrubs. How is he going to catch the right woman when he's always wearing T-shirts that have writing on the front?"

"Tess, do you have a problem with what I'm wearing?" Erik asked.

Nora gave him a quick once-over, as if she hadn't already. He looked pretty good—more than pretty good actually. And what was wrong with T-shirts with writing on them anyway, especially when they had muscles the likes of his underneath? She shook her head. "But, I'm sure we can come up with something else for the party."

Erik took a step toward his mother. "Okay, Mom, it was

nice of you to stop over. Good to see you up and about on that leg—"

Camille didn't move, and Nora could tell the woman was giving her a serious appraisal. Oh, God, could she tell the difference?

"Tess," she said. "I do hope you're feeling better now that some time has passed ... since your engagement ended."

Nora struggled with how to respond. *What would Tess say?* "Oh, I'm fine," she said brightly. "We just weren't ... compatible. Now that I've had a little time, I realize the breakup was a good thing."

"Well, remember what I told you ..."

Nora hoped her expression didn't look too blank. *What? What did you tell Tess?*

"Sometimes the right person is standing in front of you and you don't even know it until you clear away the other debris." Camille patted her on the arm.

Nora nodded. "Oh, right. That's great advice." Her grandmother used to say something similar: *Don't look so far and wide you miss out on the bachelor next door.* But no way was she going to prolong the conversation by bringing that up.

"Mom." Erik's voice held a note of warning. He glanced out the window. "Thomas still has the car running outside."

"Yes, I know, he always leaves it running—"

"I thought you were distraught over carbon emissions—"

"Not for me, sweetheart. I worry about those sorts of things for you. As your mother, it's my job to worry. I've just always been relieved you gave up skiing and got into medicine—that took quite a load off my mind."

Erik gave a noncommittal grunt and Tess looked at him curiously. What was that supposed to mean?

"Tess, thank you so much for squeezing Erik in on short notice," Camille was saying. "Please, just dress him well."

From behind his mother, Erik grinned at Nora and shook his head. Their eyes met and she felt the connection of shared understanding. A shiver of attraction slipped up her spine.

"Okay, Mom, so if that's all ..."

"Just one more thing, Erik, and I'll be on my way. What I really stopped by for was to see if Tess could come to the garden club meeting Tuesday night and give a short talk about what she does." She turned her attention to Nora. "Tess?"

Nora felt her breathing grow shallow. "How nice of you to think of me."

"I've told some of the women about your services and I think you may be able to get some new clients that very night."

"I—I'll check my calendar—" *Nope. Speaking to the garden club was never going to happen unless, by some miracle, Tess got off her cruise ship and back to San Francisco before then.*

Camille touched a hand to the back of her perfect hair. "The scheduled speaker canceled suddenly. So I do need to alert the chairperson right away so she can change the program," she said. "This really is a wonderful opportunity, you know."

Yes, it was. *For Tess.* Nora took her phone out of her briefcase and opened the calendar app. Tuesday was wide-open; she'd known that before she even looked. She shook her head and said in a disappointed voice, "Oh, I do have something at that time ... but I'll can check tomorrow and see if it can be rescheduled." She thought she might be sick. Tess was relaxing on a seventeen-day cruise ... while Nora was stuck battling fires as she tried to hold her sister's life together for her. She should never have agreed to switching places.

"Please do. As soon as you know either way, just let me know."

Erik took his mother by the elbow. "You're really inhibiting the progress here, Mom. Tess and I were—"

He winked at Nora and she caught her breath. "Just getting started," she finished, almost breathlessly. *Get a grip,* she told herself.

Camille looked from Erik to Nora and back again. "I suppose I should get going." She kissed her son on the cheek. "Tess, do your best with him. He can be stubborn and, well, he doesn't put a lot of stock in what he wears, so this could be a challenge."

Nora nodded. *Go. Please go. Before you think of some other way to torture me.*

Camille's brows drew together. "You're quiet tonight, Tess. Are you feeling all right?"

Before she could answer, Erik began to guide his mother toward the door. "Mom, nice of you to stop by. Tess and I are already well into this shopping thing, and neither of us has a lot of time to spare. Thanks for stopping."

He closed the door behind her and turned back to Nora, his expression apologetic. "Sorry. You know what she's like."

No, she didn't, but she wasn't going to admit that. "But we all have our quirks. I really like your mother," she said. "Now, should we get back to work?" So *I can get out of here before some other disaster takes place.*

Over the course of the next half hour she interviewed Erik and completed the assessment questionnaire detailing his lifestyle (laid-back), his personal preferences for style and color (casual and blue), his favorite designers or retailers (none in particular) and his budget (pretty much wide open, which meant, pretty much her entire year's salary and more, if necessary).

After filling in the final section on the sheet, she sat back in her chair, immensely pleased with her progress. She'd come here tonight knowing next to nothing about what she was doing, and she'd done all right. Better than all right—she'd done great. This personal shopping thing wasn't nearly as hard as she'd expected. Best of all, she'd be out of here in time to get to her coffee group.

"What's next?" Erik asked.

"Shopping," she said with renewed confidence, feeling more relaxed than she had all evening. Tess always offered clients the opportunity to accompany her on buying trips, but few, if any, actually took her up on it. "You can come with me, or I can pick out several items and bring them back for a private fitting." She met his eyes ... and for a moment, the image of him in his briefs jumped back into her head. The heat of a blush started to rise on her cheeks. Oh, God, that little confidence builder had been her dumbest idea yet.

"It's up to me about going shopping?" He rubbed a hand across the day's growth on his jaw.

She bent over her briefcase to put the clipboard and papers away. "Don't feel bad if you'd rather not. Most people use a personal shopper because they don't want to shop. I know you're busy and—"

"No, I'll come."

"Great, so I'll pick out—what?" *What did he just say?*

"I'll come along. It seems like it would be easier than making you haul clothes around—"

"Oh, I do it all the time." Her heart began to pound. One trip to the men's department with her and he was going to realize she knew nothing about personal shopping.

"Can we go after the workday?"

"Ah—" Nora felt her brain try to shut down and she forced it back into action. A thin layer of perspiration broke out on her forehead. *I need to go home,* she wanted to scream. *I need to track down my sister and kill her.* "Actually, my schedule is pretty tight."

"The party is Saturday. That pretty much leaves tomorrow night."

Tess, I really hate you. She couldn't think of one good reason to tell Erik he couldn't come with her—not without making it sound as if she didn't want him along. To be honest, under other circumstances she might just enjoy having him there—him and those eyes—but not when she was pretending to be something she was not. Still, what choice did she have?

"O-kay, then why don't I meet you at—" *Where? She and Tess hadn't gotten this far in their discussion.* In desperation, she named the only store that came to mind. "Um, how about Bloomingdales at the Westfield San Francisco Center? At six-thirty? That'll give us a couple of hours ..."

Five minutes later she was out the door and back in Tess's car. By the time she had driven two blocks, her heart was pounding so hard she was almost hyperventilating and had to pull over to the curb and breathe. She leaned her head against the steering wheel.

This wasn't just a bad dream—it was nightmare. *Erik Morgan.* She worked with Erik Morgan. She'd been in meetings with Erik Morgan. Damn, every now and then she actually looked at Erik Morgan as a—man. An attractive man. Okay, an attractive, gorgeous, single man ... *in his briefs.*

Omigod. How could she ever face him in the hospital again now that she'd pictured him in his underwear?

No question about it, she was in definite trouble.

5

—————

Erik kicked back into his leather chair and paged through the latest issue of *Outside Magazine.* Though he tried to concentrate on an article about backcountry skiing in Montana, he realized after a few minutes that he was reading the same paragraph over and over—and not retaining any of it.

He flipped to a story on mountain climbing in Tibet and found he did no better with that. His mind just wasn't on skiing or climbing—it was on Tess Carlisle.

He tossed the magazine onto the footstool and thought about the pretty, dark-haired woman who had just interviewed him. Even though she'd been dressed stylishly —as far as he could tell anyway—she hadn't been what he'd expected at all. She seemed too real, too unaffected, to be the personal shopper type.

She was probably fairly new to the business; she seemed a little hesitant and her definition of casual chic wasn't very clear. Though, to be fair, his own definition was pretty murky, too. And she'd wobbled on her high heels a couple of times. He'd almost told her to take the damn things off and put up her feet, but figured it might make her more ill at ease than she already was.

Still, she'd handled Camille pretty well. And anybody who could take on his mother and survive was all right in his book. More than all right, actually.

His phone buzzed and he glanced at the caller ID before answering. His mother. *What a surprise.* "Hey, Mom," he said. "Don't you want to call my sister—you know, Jenny—the child you never get to talk to because she lives across the country?"

She ignored him. "How did it go with Tess?"

"Great. Nice woman. Seems to know her stuff." He let his head drop against the leather cushion.

"She's cute, isn't she?"

Matchmaker Mom hot on the trail. "Ah, yeah."

"And she'll have an outfit pulled together for you to wear on Saturday?"

"She said I was hopeless."

"She did?"

He let out a laugh at her obvious panic. "No. We're going shopping tomorrow night."

There was a long pause before his mother asked in a voice tinged with shock, "You're going along?"

"That surprises you?"

"Well, you did just give me a speech about how I wasn't supposed to introduce you to daughters of friends, friends of friends, acquaintances of friends, so naturally—"

"We're going shopping—not on a date."

"Whatever you want to call it dear, I'm just glad you're going."

Erik rolled his eyes. "*It's a shopping trip.* And just so you don't start thinking I'm about to get involved here, I'm not. There's no way. You might as well know—I'm talking to USSA about coaching the ski team."

"Erik!"

"Easy. Now, keep this to yourself. We just started talking and if it happens, I don't want my partners to hear it through the grapevine before I tell them."

Silence hung on the line. Finally his mother spoke. "You'd give up your practice? And that new rehab clinic you've been working on?"

Yeah, those were the kickers. He'd been pushing the hospital to open a sports medicine rehab clinic for years. And now, when they'd finally agreed to do the damn thing, USSA had come knocking at his door. Why, when it rained, did it always pour? "Coaching the A team has always been a dream of mine," he said.

"But—"

"Yeah, yeah, I know. Don't worry. I'm thinking about all the ramifications. Listen, Mom, I've got an early surgery tomorrow morning. I've got to get some sleep. Go do your knee exercises."

He shut off the phone and picked up the magazine again but didn't open it. He'd been coaching juniors at Squaw Valley for a few years, which kept him pretty well connected with USSA. When he'd heard the rumors that they wanted to take the A team in *a different direction*, he hadn't been surprised at all. The wording was a diplomatic way of cutting loose one of the coaches, an arrogant jerk who was hard to communicate with and had alienated most of the skiers.

He'd started to toy with the idea of putting his name in for the job. But before he'd made a decision, the alpine director had called him, wanting to talk. Their conversation had renewed a dream that had been at the back of his mind for a long time—to coach the U.S. ski team to the Olympics.

Problem was, if he chased down that dream, it meant a four-year commitment—and major life changes. He'd probably be traveling most of the year, would have to leave his partnership and take a big pay cut. None of which was out of the question.

Not really anyway.

He shut off the lamp on the table next to his chair and sat in the darkness, thinking ... remembering how wide Tess's eyes had opened and how pink her cheeks had burned when he asked if she was going to look through the clothes in his closet. His mom was right—she was cute. Maybe if he found her as intriguing tomorrow as she'd seemed tonight, he'd ask her out for a drink when they finished shopping.

———

Nora pulled open the door to Margo's Bistro and hurried toward the annex room with its green-cushioned rattan furniture and large potted plants. Smiling at the others already there—Margo, Selena, and Rosie—she dropped into a chair, pulled off Tess's stilettos and began talking. "You aren't even going to believe what's happened to me now. My sister—"

"That should tell you everything you need to know," Margo said to the other two women. She shook her head, her silky blond hair slipping from side to side with the movement. "Your regular chai latte?" she asked as she headed out to the counter.

"Make it a double," Nora said. "It's been a rough night already." She leaned back into the soft cushions and felt herself start to relax beneath the gentle glow of the candles flickering in the wall sconces.

"Nice outfit," Selena said. "Kind of funky, fashionable. And new streaked hair, too? Did you have a makeover?" She combed her fingers through her own short, chocolate curls. "Plain brown wasn't good enough anymore?" she said with a teasing sniff.

Leave it to the free-spirited artist in the group to appreciate the change. Nora grimaced. "I am my sister." At the puzzled expressions on the two women's faces, she held up a hand. "I'll tell all as soon as Margo gets back. Some of it she already knows ... but why repeat myself on the rest?"

Moments later, Margo set a hot cup on the table in front of Nora and took the opposite seat. "So how did tonight go? Did you fill the girls in?"

"I wanted to wait until you were here." Nora quickly recounted the past day's events, finishing up with the grand finale about her new client's real identity.

"You're kidding me!" Margo said. "Erik Morgan, the Olympic skier who got on the Wheaties box?"

"And you work with him at the hospital?" Rosie asked. "You'd better get out of this before you get in too deep. This is how careers get ruined."

Nora nodded. Rosie's background in politics gave her a unique perspective—she knew all about how dangerous lies and rumors were.

"I'd love to get out," Nora said. "All I have to do is choose one lousy outfit and I'm done. Then, never again, no matter what. Even if it's the only way to get Tess on her feet."

They all murmured agreement. Nora sipped her chai and sat back, listening as the conversation jumped from one topic to another. When Selena mentioned how much better her seventh-grade son was doing, Nora sat forward. Small for his age, Drew had become moody and withdrawn as he struggled with the usual middle school issues.

"I owe this turnaround to the dog," Selena said. "Or, I should say, the incredibly exuberant eating machine."

"Still growing, is he?" Margo asked.

"Bigger every minute. But Drew is so happy—and so much dirtier than he's ever been, I might add." She shook her head. "But he's come out of himself, he's happy, so you won't hear me complaining about any of it."

"Maybe a dog would help Danny," Nora said. "Something's going on with him. He's obsessed with getting a dad. He drags me through the grocery store to see stock boys in baseball caps. Yesterday he zeroed in on Mr. Rogers." She sighed. "I know boys need a dad—all kids need a dad. What makes it worse is that he's never had one."

"You *could* consider dating again." Rosie put her elbows on the table and leaned forward.

Nora exhaled. "Yeah. I thought of that. And, if my goal was just finding a dad for Danny instead of falling in love, maybe I could. But I don't think I'll ever love someone again. Lightning never strikes twice."

"Never say never," Margo said.

"Easy for you to say. You just got engaged to the man of your dreams," Nora retorted.

"All I'm saying is that closing your mind to possibilities closes your heart. And why would you want to do that?"

Nora stared at her. "Because, at the risk of sounding trite, love hurts."

"So does not loving. So does being alone. When my husband left me, it hurt, yes, but to play it safe for the rest of my life ..." Margo shook her head. "It would be like half-living."

Nora felt a familiar ache in her chest. She was so tired of being alone. Sometimes she really did want to try again ... and Margo made it seem so possible.

"Okay, enough of this maudlin conversation," Selena said dryly. "We're supposed to have fun on Thursday nights."

"And we're going to! I have an idea." Margo jumped up and left the room, returning a few moments later with a pencil and sheet of paper. She scrawled *Perfect Dad* across the top of the page. "Let's list the qualities of the perfect dad. Once Nora sees what she's missing, she might just be open to dating again."

Nora stared at her friend. "Have you lost your mind?"

"I may not want to get married, but this I can play," Selena said. "The perfect father, in my opinion, is tall, dark and handsome—"

Margo laughed. "Are we off track already? *Likes kids. Patient.*" She wrote down the words. "*Kind. And tender.*"

"To both kids and mother," Selena added.

"Athletic," Rosie said. "Oh, and has a good income."

"Willing to change diapers," Margo said, writing. "And read bedtime stories. Nora, anything to add?"

Stand up against the world for his kids, Nora thought. *And tell them he loves them no matter what they do.* "I'm not playing. What's wrong with all of you tonight?" She took a swallow of chai.

"Oh, come on." Rosie touched her on the arm. "We're just having fun."

"Hey, here's what we'll do. On the left, we'll write down the single men we know and see how they stack up against the list of desired attributes." Selena grabbed the pencil and paper. "The title is now Perfect Dad *Possibilities,*" she said as she wrote. "And, of course, the first candidate can only be Erik Morgan."

"Oh, please." Nora reached for the paper but Selena quickly slid it away.

"My tax accountant is single. Put him down—Pete Jackson," Rosie said.

The women threw out a few more names before Nora decided she'd truly had enough and snatched the paper out from under Selena's pencil. "Party's over," she said in a light voice. "We're not doing this anymore." She shoved the sheet in her purse to get it away from her friends. Once she got home tonight she'd tear it into a thousand tiny pieces. "Next subject."

"Nora, we didn't do this to torture you," Margo said. "You need to start thinking about letting go. Even if it's only for Danny's sake."

"Letting go of what?"

Margo's lips turned up in that soft understanding smile of hers. "Of your anger. Your guilt. Your regrets. Of the past. It's not a betrayal, you know, to go out with someone else."

Fear kicked into Nora's gut. The same feeling she got every time she had a conversation like this.

Selena caught her eye, then set her cup on the table and cleared her throat. "Did I tell you guys about the new idea I have for a live art exhibition?"

Nora took a drink of her chai and felt herself relax as the conversation veered in a whole new direction.

6

———————

Nora kissed her sleeping son on the forehead and ran a hand over his feathery brown hair. His breath came soft and slow, and she tucked his Spider Man comforter around him, remembering the day she brought him home from the hospital ... alone, with no husband at her side. Danny had come into the world two months after Kevin had left it.

She watched her son a moment longer, then quietly left the room. She was glad he was asleep because she needed some time to think.

Stripping out of Tess's clothes, she pulled on a T-shirt and some baggy sweatpants, letting out a sigh as the soft fabrics touched her skin. Then she went downstairs, poured herself a glass of pinot noir, and plopped into her favorite overstuffed chair. Her gaze slid across the room.

Last year, when Tess didn't have any real clients, she'd turned her attention to updating the decor in blues and tans, said she was going for *shabby chic*. It wasn't all that shabby, though, more like *casual beach chic*.

Shit. Casual chic. Camille Lamont. Ugh, she'd forgotten about the garden club speech.

Well, she couldn't do it—she just couldn't give a talk to Camille Lamont's garden club. It was bad enough that she had to shop for Erik Morgan, especially since she was, inexplicably feeling an attraction to the man. Probably experiencing a regressive adolescent syndrome or something.

But make a speech to his mother's garden club? No way. It was more than she'd ever signed on to do. So if Tess didn't want to miss out on this opportunity, it was time for her to come home—or come clean with her client.

She took a swallow of wine, felt its warmth as it slid down her throat, relaxing her. Then she called Tess. One ring, two, three, four, five ... Just when she expected voicemail to kick in, Tess answered, giggling. The sound of music and lively conversation mingled in a happy buzz in the background.

"Hi, Nora! Hold on a second, honey. Yes, thank you, I'll have another glass of champagne," Tess said to someone in the background. "So, how'd it go?" she said into the phone. "Liza says *hi* by the way."

Champagne? Nora fought her rising annoyance. Tess and Liza were at a party on a cruise ship while Nora was tap dancing as fast as she could. Just once, she wanted someone to bring her champagne. Maybe with a strawberry in the bottom of the glass, too.

"Nora?"

She let out a sharp laugh. "Sorry. *How did it go?* Depends on what part of the evening you're talking about. I did pretty well, if I do say so myself. But there were moments that it was definitely a Murphy's Law kind of night."

"Whatever can go wrong, will go wrong?" Tess asked in alarm. "What happened?"

"You know your new client, Erik Lamont? Lamont is his mother's last name. His name is actually Erik Morgan. Sound familiar?" She sipped her wine.

"No ..."

"The skier, the orthopedic surgeon—"

"Wait. You mean that cute one? He's my new client?" Tess screeched.

Nora sat up straight. "When have you seen him? He's not that cute."

"Oh, please. I saw him on TV during the Olympics, like ten or fifteen years ago. He's cute squared and if you can't see that, then it's no wonder ... never mind."

"Yeah, I know." Nora almost sighed. She dropped back into the chair again. "His eyes are so blue they almost pierce you."

"Camille's son is Erik Morgan. Damn sister, did you luck out—"

"No, I didn't luck out, you idiot. You lucked out—or would have it you were here. I, on the other hand, work with him at the hospital. Now I have to make sure he doesn't figure out I'm me and not you." Nora took another swallow of wine to calm herself before their convoluted conversation put her completely over the edge.

"Well, if you ask me, working with Erik Morgan is not a Murphy's Law phenomenon. More like *all good things come to those who wait*." Her voice grew a little distant. "Oh, thanks. Could I get one with a strawberry in the glass?"

Nora gritted her teeth. "I didn't know I was waiting for anything."

"Sure you are. True love to come again. A knight in shining armor. A hero to complete you—"

"God, what is with everyone these days?"

"What'd you say? Can you talk a little louder? It's kind of noisy here," Tess said.

Nora raised her voice. "Nothing. Anyway, so I was meeting with Erik when his mother showed up—"

"Camille?" Tess sputtered.

"That would be her."

Tess gasped. "Omigod, Murphy's Law! Did she realize you weren't me?"

Nora smiled, happy that Tess was finally beginning to understand everything she'd had to deal with tonight. "I don't think so. But—"

"Thank God. That had the makings of a disaster. My God, my heart is trying to pound its way out of my chest." Tess's words poured out of her. "I can't believe she showed up—"

"Tess, she—"

"I mean if she ever thought I was trying to pull a fast one ... like, that I was shopping to *get* her son instead of shopping *for* her son. It could be ruinous, you know—"

"Tess, let me finish. She invited me—you—to speak to her garden club about what you do. Thought you might get some new clients at the meeting."

Tess let out a shriek. "Oh, Nora! This is the break I've been waiting for."

"Then you'd better get off that ship and onto a plane because she wants you there Tuesday."

"Tuesday? Like in four days?"

"Right." Nora realized she was getting a certain amount of enjoyment out of this conversation. Payback for all the champagne Tess was drinking and Nora wasn't.

"How can I do that? I'm on a cruise. Why didn't you schedule it for when I'm back?"

"I tried. But the speaker canceled next week—that's when there's a need. It's the reason she asked you—me—in the first place. Anyway, I didn't want to piss off your big client, so I told her I had something scheduled and would see if it could be changed."

"Oh good. So you're okay with doing it again?"

"Doing what again?" Nora asked cautiously.

"Being me next week."

Nora put a hand to her forehead. "Tess. No. I'm not giving a speech as you. You want the garden club to hear a speech from The Shopping Goddess, you get off that boat and get home."

"It's a ship. And we're in the middle of nowhere," Tess said as though she were giving a geography lesson. "You know, glaciers, fjords, wilderness ... *emphasis on wilderness.* Who knows where the nearest airport is. I'll remind you we're lucky we even can get a connection right now."

"You're not fooling me. There are airports in Alaska—"

"Not out here on the water."

Nora set down her wineglass and began to massage the back of her neck with one hand. She tried to stay patient, to keep her voice calm. "Tess, I nearly had a nervous breakdown being you tonight. I was lying almost every time I opened my mouth. Imagine what I'll be like when I'm with Camille Lamont, *who knows you,* who will notice little things like ... I don't seem exactly like I used to be, or that I seem to have forgotten all sorts of details about her that I should know. She already mentioned tonight how quiet I was."

"Oh, just laugh a lot. That's what I do." In the

background, Nora could hear the clink of crystal glasses touching one another.

"You laugh a lot?" How could her sister be so cavalier about this?

"Yeah, it makes every conversation so much more friendlier—"

"Friendly."

"Whatever. Like, for instance, I'll say something like, *Isn't it a lovely day?* laugh, laugh, light and airy. Or maybe Camille will try on an outfit I got her and I'll say, *That looks absolutely fabulous on you*, and then she'll laugh because she's so flattered and then I'll laugh, ha-ha-ha, like a wind chime, you know, tinkle tinkle."

Nora moved her hand to massage her forehead. "Tinkle tinkle?"

"Light, easy, friendly laughter."

"Tess, there is no *tinkle tinkle* going on around here. Every muscle in my body is tense and getting tenser. Not only am I not ready to laugh, but I'm ready to cry. So get off that boat and get home. Come take back your job before I blow it."

"I ... don't think I can. Anyway, think of what I've spent to go on this cruise—"

"And think of what you'll lose if you miss the chance to meet these clients." Irritation laced her words.

"Mommy? Why are you talking so loud?"

Nora turned at the sound of her son's voice. He stood next to her in his Superman pajamas. "Danny—what are you doing up? Tess, let me call you back."

She shut off the phone and opened her arms to let her son crawl into her lap. His warm little body curled into her arms, and tenderness swept through her. "What's the matter, honey?"

"Are you fighting with Auntie Tess?"

"No. Sometimes we just talk loud."

"Oh." He gazed up at her. "Guess what. I saw the perfect daddy tonight."

Nora's heart sank. "You did? On TV again?"

"Yeah. His name is Ronald. He works at McDonald's."

Despite herself, Nora began to laugh. "Honey, I'm not sure Ronald and I would be a good match."

"But he'd be lots of fun. He likes kids." He looked at her with wide eyes, *his father's eyes*. "You wouldn't have to cook dinner anymore. And we could go to the playland whenever we want."

Nora nodded thoughtfully. Tears tried to force themselves into her eyes as an ache worked its way across her chest and into her throat. She blinked hard. "Those are some really good reasons, but I think Ronald isn't available. Guys like him are always taken already—"

"I never saw a Mrs. Ronald."

Nora drew a shaky breath. "That's because she's in the kitchen making all those fries."

"Are you sure?"

"Yeah." She gave her son a squeeze and kissed the top of his head. "I'm sure your daddy is watching you from heaven and loving you right now. And I know he would be here if he could."

"But he died."

She nodded.

"Mama?"

"Hmm?"

"Do you think I'll ever have a daddy that's here?"

Her heart shattered then, and the tears she'd been holding back escaped. "Someday, yeah, I think so." She stood, still holding her son wrapped in her arms so he couldn't see that she was crying. "Come on, honey, it's late. You've got to go to sleep. Morning comes early."

She carried him upstairs, laid him in his bed, and drew the quilt to his shoulders. In the corner, a Micky Mouse nightlight took the edge off the darkness, keeping all manner of fearsome monsters away. *All except those in her head.*

She kissed Danny again and whispered, "I love you." Resting a hand on his back, she waited until his breathing had evened into the soft rhythmic sound of slumber before exiting the room. Back downstairs, she finished off her glass of wine before calling her sister back.

"Is Danny okay?" Tess asked the moment she picked up.

"He's fine. It's that daddy thing again." Nora sighed. "Maybe I should take him to a children's counselor."

"Nora, I've been thinking ... I'll talk to the ship's director and find out if there's any way I can get off the cruise." Tess paused. "If I can't, I'll call Camille and tell her I can't do the talk because I'm sick. Since she already commented that you were quiet tonight, I can say I was coming down with something and now I'm really under the weather. I'm sure she'll let me come another time."

Nora looked at the framed picture hanging on the opposite wall, a cozy cottage at the end of a country lane, the trees ablaze in autumn colors of orange and red. She wanted to escape there right now, just run away from all of this. "I don't know if that helps you," she said. "This really sounded like a one-time deal because the speaker canceled."

"I know, but if I can't get off the ship—"

"You need to find a way to make it happen."

"I'll try. I really will."

"Good. Then before this call gets dropped, I need to ask

you some questions. Erik said the event is *casual chic*. What exactly is that? I mean, I have some idea but you'd better make it clear."

"Oh, it's the same as, you know, country club."

"Country club? A little clearer, please." She willed herself to escape into the picture on the wall.

"Resort casual—"

"Tess."

"Come on, Nora, you have to know some of this. It's pretty much what you'd wear to a private country club for dinner. Dress slacks, sport shirt, even a dress shirt. If it's cool, add a sweater. Sport jacket if he wants to wear one. Nice leather shoes and belt—got the idea?"

"Uh, yeah. Maybe he owns some of this stuff already."

"He probably does. Didn't you check?"

She didn't answer.

"Nora, once you knew what he needed the clothes for, didn't you look to see what he already had?"

"No. I just wanted to get out of there. *You have no idea what it was like picturing him in his briefs and then looking him in the face.*"

"*What?*"

"*Never mind.*"

Tess let out a long-suffering sigh. "Okay. Then you'll have to buy everything you think he needs and take back whatever he doesn't want."

"He's shopping with me."

"Erik Morgan's going clothes shopping with you?"

"Uh-huh." Nora went into the kitchen to put another splash of wine in her glass.

"Well, well, well. This changes *everything*."

"What's that supposed to mean?"

"Nothing. Just that you can talk to him about what he already has while you're shopping."

Anxiety wrapped its arms around Nora's shoulders. "I don't know. What if he says he has shoes already, and I can't even tell if they go with what we're buying him or not?"

"You'll do fine. It's not that hard."

"Easy for you to say. You're not the one who has to look into those eyes of his."

7

———

Erik set his elbows on the dark cherry conference table and watched the hospital administrator use red and blue markers on a whiteboard to list and reiterate each of the key points he wanted to make. Good thing his topic was interesting, because his monotone could put caffeine-filled two-year-olds to sleep.

"As we've discussed," the man was saying, "the addition of a sports medicine rehab clinic will be a big benefit to the hospital. Obviously, we'll have the advantage of increased surgeries, but also a whole new clientele. That being, the outpatients currently getting care at other clinics around the city. Plus, we'll get onboard with the aging boomer trend—a growth area if there ever was one."

Damn, this guy was dull. How did people like him get put in charge of things? Erik glanced at his partners to gauge their reactions. Tim O'Connell was sitting back in his chair, his face totally unreadable. Andy Chapman, as usual, was leaning forward and ready to cut to the chase. "We've been through all this before. What's different?"

The administrator wrote *partnership* on the whiteboard.

"The board decided that if we're going to do this, our clinic has to be steps above every other one in the city. So what we want from you is a working partnership. We'd like to see you three move your offices out of the professional building and into the space that we're renovating for the new center."

He opened his arms wide. "You'll still be in a private orthopedic practice with one another, but you'll be located right here next to the best sports medicine rehab center in the city. Let's face it, you three have the experience that gets attention—team surgeons for the Giants, the Raiders ... team physicians for Stanford football." He paused. "The U.S. Ski and Snowboard Teams."

Erik nodded. If that guy only knew what Erik was working on right now, he might not be so excited about making this deal with them.

"The way we see it, we'll feature you three in our advertising for the clinic—your reputations and expertise will bring in patients, making this an ideal partnership. As you know, our goal is to attract elite athletes. Their use of this facility will, in turn, attract others to it."

Andy raised his brows at Erik and gave him a half grin. "Are we still looking at the same timeline?" he asked the administrator.

"Yes. Up and running in six months—"

"And equipment? Have you considered the equipment we talked about last time?" Andy never wasted words.

The administrator handed each of them a sheet of paper containing an extensive list. "I think you'll be pleased with what's been approved. All the usual fixtures, plus a state-of-the-art gym with high level PT equipment, whirlpools, underwater treadmills, weight-lifting equipment of the same caliber professional teams use ... and, because we know you're ultra-concerned with preventing postoperative infection, the hospital will set up a brand-new operating suite dedicated solely to clean orthopedic surgeries."

"That all sounds well and good, but you guys did a piss-poor job with the women's center you opened last year," Tim said, speaking for the first time in the meeting. "Why would we think you'd do a better job with this?"

The administrator winced. "We learned our lesson there. So the board is proposing ..." He paused for effect. "That you three take this over—"

"Complete control?" Andy asked.

"Yes. We're early enough in the planning process that we want your fingerprints all over this place."

"Complete control?" Andy sounded positively gleeful.

Erik sat back in his chair, stunned. They'd gotten everything they asked for and then some. Complete control of the center was something he'd never thought would happen. It was a dream come true.

"We're going to want X-ray equipment and on-site technicians," Tim said, getting into it. "And for staff, I'd like to see physical therapists, sports psychologists, athletic trainers, physiologists, and nutritionists." He ticked the list off on his fingers.

"Don't forget occupational and massage therapists," Andy added.

Erik could only stare. This was suddenly moving really fast and getting way too big. It might be what the other guys wanted, what he once thought he wanted, but now ... he had the USSA iron in the fire, and needed time to follow up on it before making any extensive, long-range commitments.

If he and his partners got involved in this new rehab center to the level the hospital was expecting, him quitting partway into it would really create a hole, maybe damage the entire concept by turning it into a repeat of the understaffed women's center fiasco. His years as a skier and his expertise in knee reconstruction brought a lot of patients into their practice. If he left, that draw would be gone. Plus, there was no way his two partners could do this without bringing in another surgeon—and that would take time to put together, too.

"So, Erik, what do you think?"

He startled. Tim was looking at him curiously.

Hell, it sounded great—if he knew he was staying here. But the pull from the ski team was strong. He didn't just miss the excitement, he missed the sense of community and camaraderie he'd experienced as a member of the team fifteen years ago.

"Yeah ..." he said hesitantly. "It sounds pretty good."

"You'll be in charge of hiring." The administrator's voice was almost cajoling. "Be able to bring aboard exactly the staff you want."

"You okay?" Tim prodded Erik on the shoulder, then turned slightly so he was facing away from the administrator and lowered his voice. "This is what we've been wanting for all along."

"I know. Everything we wanted," he said with forced enthusiasm.

Andy leaned toward him. "I've been thinking about what you said the other day. You're right, a PT is the way to go to run the center. What do you think about bringing one on board right away to be part of planning, ordering equipment, all the general decisions?"

"Good idea." He glanced at his watch. He was supposed to meet Tess for shopping in another hour. And he still had a pile of paperwork on his desk that he needed to finish.

The administrator was talking again. "The board

strongly believes the success of this center depends on having the support of a high-level orthopedic group. If it isn't you three, then ..." He gave a shrug.

It was impossible to miss his message. If they turned the opportunity down, it would be offered to another group—and they all knew there would be many takers for a sweet deal like this.

"No, no. We're in," Andy said. "Right, guys?"

"Absolutely," Tim said.

Erik felt caught. He shoved a hand through his hair. "Yeah, we're in." *Shit, this was getting worse by the minute.*

"One last thing ... the architect who will be working this up for us happens to be in the building right now for another meeting." He set his marker on the table. "I asked him to join us. Can you spare a little more time?"

Time nodded as Andy said, "Good by me."

Erik checked his watch again. Any longer in this meeting and he'd never be able to finish his paperwork and still be on time to meet Tess.

"Whatever it is, cancel it," Andy said.

Right. Far be it for him to say that meeting with his *personal shopper* was more important than business. What had he been thinking when he agreed to go along with her anyway? Other than how intriguing she was, and how her personality seemed almost in conflict with her career choice, and how she had the biggest hazel green eyes ...

He shook his head to clear away the image. "Can we break for a couple of minutes? I need to make a call, then I'll have all the time we need."

Five minutes later he was headed down the corridor, phone in hand, trying to figure out how to reach Tess. He'd left her business card at home, his mother wasn't answering her phone, and an online search didn't bring up a website for either The Shopping Goddess or Tess Carlisle.

Oh, wait. *Nora.* Her sister worked here. She had to know how to reach Tess. He stopped midstride and turned back in the direction of the physical therapy department.

———

Nora had just finished her last patient of the day and was about to head to her desk to deal with a pile of charts when she spotted Erik Morgan walking into the treatment area. Panic shot through her. She bent her head and slid around the corner into one of the storage rooms, where she began to organize a shelf of supplies that was perfectly well-organized already.

Whatever the man wanted right now could be handled by someone else. She didn't need him to see her as Nora right before he saw her as Tess. The resemblance between the two of them might become a bit too obvious.

After a few minutes, she peeked her head out and was relieved to see he was gone. AS she headed toward the front desk, one of her colleagues called out, "Nora, Dr. Morgan is looking for you."

Her throat constricted. "He is?" she squeaked. "Why?"

"I don't know. Said he'd be back in a couple minutes."

That meant she had only a couple of minutes to escape. "I can't really wait around—I've got plans tonight." So much for finishing those charts ... she'd have to come in early tomorrow.

She grabbed her purse and pushed through the doors to the hallway, head down, silently begging St. Jude to come to her assistance again. *Please, please get me out of here without seeing Erik Morgan. I really do promise never to do this—*

"Nora?"

Her brain locked down, and she raised her head to find Erik not three feet away. Unable to speak, she just stared, exactly the way she had stupidly stared at him on his front porch last night. She purposely avoided meeting his eyes.

"Hi," he said.

She stood there, mute.

"I'm Erik Morgan."

Of course, she knew that. She just need to get her brain to work and her mouth to engage before he concluded that Tess had a moron for a sister. "Oh, sure, sure, I know that. I know you. We've met before ... about some patient ... something. Sorry, I'm just a little distracted and, so, I heard you were trying to find me, but I was just ... leaving for the day—" *Shut Up.* "Do you have a question about one of the patients?"

He shook his head and looked a little sheepish. "No. It's about your sister." His eyes narrowed. "You two really look a lot alike. Are you sure one of you isn't living a double life of some sort?" A smile lit up his face.

She reached up to tuck a few loose strands of hair back into her ponytail and forced out a laugh that came out sounding like a bark. "Double life?" Her voice was too high and loud, and she hoped he didn't notice. She cleared her throat. "I think I'd pick a more exciting career than physical therapist or personal shopper if I was going to lead a double life."

"You even sound alike," he said, as though he wasn't entirely convinced there really were two sisters.

Once again she lost her ability to speak, which was just as well because not only did she have a tendency toward nervous babbling, but right now she was sounding too much like her sister. Which only made sense since, to this guy anyway, she was her sister. *Oh, shit.*

"Anyway. I'm supposed to be meeting with Tess tonight to ..." His voice dropped lower. "To go shopping."

"That sounds like something Tess would be doing."

"Anyway, I have to cancel. An important meeting's come up, and I left her card at home."

Relief surged through her. Omigod, her grandma was right, that St. Jude guy really delivered. "I'm sure she won't mind."

"I don't have her number to let her know I can't come. Can you—"

"Oh sure, I'll tell her." Nora held herself back from doing a happy dance. "We live together so I'll see her when I get home."

"Thanks. Can you ask her to call me about getting together tomorrow morning?"

"Tomorrow morning?" she squawked. "To shop?"

"No, to show me the stuff she's bought. I need it for a party tomorrow night."

Oh, right, she forgot about that part. "Of course, no problem." Giddiness bubbled through her. *Freedom!* She didn't have to go shopping with Erik Morgan. She could figure out what to get and bring it to his house and this whole thing would be over before she knew it.

"I'll have Tess call if she's got any questions," she said glibly and started down the corridor again, a spring in her step.

"Tell her I have another project I'd like her to handle. We can talk about that tomorrow, too," he called after her.

She stopped and pivoted back. "Another job?" she croaked out. "I'm sure she'll be just thrilled."

8

____

The Bloomingdale's men's department was overwhelming. Especially when you hadn't paid attention to men's fashions for five years. Nora turned a circle. Racks of clothing stretched in every direction as far as she could see. Well, okay, maybe not as far as she could see, but far enough. Good thing Danny was sleeping at a friend's house because this shopping trip would probably last until the store closed.

She'd worn one of Tess's outfits so she looked professional just in case she ran into anyone, like Camille, which would be just her luck. She'd worn Tess's shoes, too, which she was already regretting because, although they were identical twins, her sister's feet were a full size smaller. Her toes were throbbing already and she hadn't even been in the store ten minutes yet.

Hopefully, Bloomingdales would have everything she needed. She didn't have the inclination, or time, or comfortable enough shoes to be running around in this gigantic mall shopping at a bunch of different stores. Call her lazy—or smart, more like it—but, no way was she going to be stuck returning things at stores spread over nine floors.

Okay, so, pants. She'd start with pants. She took a step, then stopped in indecision. There were trillions of pants, with every possible label, designer or otherwise. Straight fit, slim fit, slim stretch, slim straight, classic fit, flat front, pleated front, khaki, cotton, gabardine, twill ... Her brain began to knot just thinking about the choices.

"Why couldn't the guy just need jeans?" she muttered. "Life could be so simple." She glanced at the jeans section and frowned: skinny fit, tapered fit, athletic cut, classic fit, relaxed fit, bootcut, dark wash, light wash, distressed—arghh.

She spotted a middle-aged, balding male clerk organizing a display and hurried toward him. "Excuse me. I need some pants for my—" She couldn't bring herself to say *client*. Asking for help dressing a client sort of defeated the purpose of being a personal shopper, didn't it? Personal shoppers were supposed to be fashion experts, and Nora had no doubt that if she admitted she was shopping for a client, this shopping trip would backfire on Tess, somehow, someday when they least expected it. Sadly, that was just the way things seemed to be rolling lately.

"Some pants," she repeated. "—for—my boyfriend. I was wondering if you could give me some direction."

The clerk raised his eyebrows; his name tag said *William.* "Of course. What specifically are you looking for?" he said in the kindest possible voice.

She held back from snarking, *If I knew what I was looking for, I wouldn't be asking you, now would I?* "The invitation says *casual chic.*"

He blinked. "There are so many different designations these days. I would venture that something casual ... do you have a sense of what that might be?" He bent toward her and whispered, "This is only my second day."

Oh, great, so now she had to teach *him* about fashion. This escapade might very well be heading for a bust. "I think it's what you wear to the country club for lunch or dinner."

William nodded but made no move to show her anything.

"Nice pants, collared shirt, pullover sweater, blazer, you know, that style." She tried to keep desperation out of her voice. On second thought, maybe she didn't want his help after all. "I think I'll just browse—"

"How about something from over here?" He went to a nearby rack and held up a pair of smart tan-colored slacks. "A very natty dresser bought a pair of these yesterday."

"Natty, huh? That does sound country-clubish." She felt the fabric. Nice. And they looked well-made, too. But the real test was the price. She checked the tag. *More than nice.* "These might work. The party is tomorrow, so just to be safe I want to bring home a few things for him to try. Let's find another pair of pants and then look at shirts."

And then, because she didn't want William to get annoyed that she was planning to return most of what she was about to buy, she said, "He hates to shop, so he may end up keeping pretty much everything I get. Believe me, his wardrobe could use the refresh."

"It might be easier if he came into the store."

"Probably, but there isn't time," she said. "He's really busy with his job."

William flipped through the pants on a couple of display racks. "What does he do?"

Her heart skipped a beat, and for a moment she thought it might stop entirely. Hadn't this guy gotten any customer service training about respecting customer boundaries? Regardless, she couldn't tell the truth. She could still hear Tess harping about how the *client's privacy must always be protected.*

Still, she could make it sort of close to the truth. "Oh ... he's a writer," she said. "He has so many deadlines, he puts off shopping and now we have a big event to attend with his publisher and, well, here I am, trying to get him dressed."

"I always wanted to be a writer," William said brightly. "What does he write?"

Nora waved a hand as though the answer were inconsequential. "Books, magazine articles."

"Really?" Now William was even more impressed. "Can I ask who he is?"

"Oh ... he hates it when I talk about him. Let's just find the rest of what he needs and I'll be on my way." She was sure playing fast and loose with the lies these days. For someone who abhorred dishonesty, she was sliding down a slippery slope.

Over the next hour, she and William picked out several shirts that they agreed fit the *casual chic* designation, a blazer, and another pair of pants. By the time she'd charged her purchases and William had bagged everything, she was exhausted from verbally tap dancing to keep any discussion about her writer boyfriend to a minimum.

She couldn't wait to escape to the shoe department— without William—and began backing away from the counter, bags in both hands. "Thank you so much for your—"

"Tess! Hey, Tess!" A familiar male voice rolled across the department, sending a chill skidding through her. *No, no, no.*

It could not possibly be—

She turned.

No.

Erik Morgan.

What in God's name was he doing here? She forced her lips to curve upward in a broad smile. "Well, hello. I thought you couldn't make it."

As he came close, she raised her eyes to meet his. Big mistake. Her heart stammered and she quickly dropped her gaze.

"The meeting broke up sooner than expected. Figured I'd take a chance and see if you were still here."

Irrational laughter bubbled up inside her and she tamped it down. This was unbelievable; Tess was on a cruise ship sipping champagne with strawberries, and Nora was living a nightmare. If only she'd only headed for the shoe department five minutes, Erik would never have found her.

He took the bags she was holding. "Looks like mission accomplished."

William cleared his throat. "You must be ..." he was saying.

Nora felt everything slide into slow motion. She turned toward William. *You're a clerk,* she wanted to say but not a word came out of her mouth. *You don't get to talk to—*

"Her boyfriend," William finished.

She couldn't breathe. Erik's eyes locked on her in question.

She forced herself to speak. "Uh, actually—"

"This is so handy," William was blabbering. "She was going to take all this apparel home to you. But you could try everything on right now and save time ... and of course, the headache of coming back to make returns or exchanges. The dressing rooms are right over here. I've always wanted to be a writer, too."

Her heart was pounding in her ears and realized it was probably blood trying to explode out of her head. Before she could respond, she slipped her arm through his and began to pull him toward the aisle. "Thanks so much for your help, William. We've still got to get shoes, so we'll just try on some of these things a little later."

When they were a department away, Erik stopped and faced her. "What was that about?"

"Oh, you know how clerks can be. It's his second day and he kept trying to help out. I didn't want to be rude, so I told him ... I was shopping for my boyfriend. *The writer.*" She laughed as light and easy as she could. "I don't always like to admit I'm a personal shopper because ..." *Why not?* What was that old saying about don't start a sentence until you know what the ending is? Or was it, don't ask a question you don't already know the answer to?

"Because?"

"Oh. Right. I don't always tell because, somehow, clerks start steering me toward more expensive items. And my goal, besides outfitting you exquisitely, is to save you money." More lies. And stupid ones, too.

"Thanks ... I think. But money isn't really that much of an object."

No kidding. "That's good because we need to get you some shoes to go with your new clothes."

"Which I should be trying on, don't you think?"

Of course. It made perfect sense. Then she wouldn't have to return anything tomorrow. But once they went back to the men's department so Erik could try on the clothes, they'd have to see William again. And God knew what he would say. "I suppose you could just pop into the closest dressing room," she said, gesturing.

"In the lingerie department? Much as I might enjoy it, they'll probably call security if I go in there."

He started back toward the men's department and Nora followed, almost dragging her feet. Maybe William would be taking a break. As they neared the dressing rooms, she spotted him straightening a rack. Or maybe he wouldn't notice them—

He looked up and smiled.

Fat chance. Another backfire. Yes, things were definitely rolling the wrong way these days.

"Can I get you a dressing room?" he asked.

"Yes, thank you," she said.

"Right this way," he said and Erik followed him into the dressing room area. As the two men rounded the corner, she heard William ask, "What types of books do you write?"

To which Erik replied, "Romance."

She dropped her head and shook it slowly from side to side, mortified at how badly she was messing this up. A few minutes later, Erik stepped out wearing the tan slacks with the pewter shirt—and looking incredible. As he waited for her appraisal, he unbuttoned his cuffs and began to roll up the sleeves. She caught her breath. *Great forearms.* Slow heat slid through her. She could almost be seduced by the sight of good forearms and rolled-up sleeves.

Looking up, she discovered he was watching her watch him. Her cheeks flushed. Blue eyes, great forearms. She was a goner. "If everything fits you this well, we're going to have trouble deciding what to keep," she managed to get out.

"Then I'll keep it all." He grinned and returned to the dressing room.

Before another hour passed, they'd chosen his clothes

for the party, including a new belt and pair of shoes. As they headed out of the store carrying several bags, Nora felt the pressure of the past two days lift. Erik had everything he needed for his mother's party, the account had been saved, and no one had any idea that Nora wasn't actually Tess. Now she could go home, put her feet up and unwind, knowing that all was right with the world of personal shopping.

And she'd hold this over her sister's head for the rest of her life.

"Want to get a drink to celebrate?" Erik asked.

She turned her head slowly. "Excuse me?" He didn't really just asked her to prolong this agony, did he?

"Want to get a drink to celebrate our success? I'm buying. Come on, it's Friday night."

No. Absolutely not. *I want to quit pretending to be someone I'm not. I want to go home and get out of these shoes before my toes are permanently misshapen.*

Surely Tess wouldn't go out for a drink with a client, would she? Nora mentally sighed. Of course, Tess would— especially if the client was Erik Morgan.

Except Erik wasn't an ordinary client, not a wealthy middle-aged woman who hated shopping and wanted help staying in style. Erik was too cute, way too nice, and he looked too good in casual chic. Frankly, she didn't think she could maintain this facade with a drink under the belt and him sitting by her side.

So, her decision was clear—*no way.*

"How about the Redwood Room at the Clift Hotel? We don't even have to drive," Erik said.

How could she say *no* now that he'd actually named a place? Tess was going to owe her but good.

———

Fifteen minutes later, they were ensconced in leather club chairs drinking imported beer and chatting amicably. Soft piano music filled the room. When their conversation hit a lull, Nora let her eyes roam over the room, admiring the dark wood paneled walls, the stunning crystal lighting at the ceiling, the comfortable decor. *Casual elegance* she supposed it would be named. As opposed to *casual chic*.

"So did you and Nora have a lot of fun switching places?"

She jerked her gaze back to Erik. "What?"

"When you were kids," he said. "Did you switch places a lot? I just saw Nora a few hours ago and if I didn't know better, I'd say you were the same person."

Nora let out a laugh, too high and too loud. "We've always confused people. Sometimes even our parents couldn't tell us apart." *Not true, but since she was going to hell anyway, what was one more lie?* "And yeah, we switched places more than a few times. Once, we—" She caught herself just before she said the wrong name. "—Nora paid me to go out with a guy she didn't like who had asked her out."

"How'd that go?"

"When he tried to kiss me, I told him that I—meaning Nora—was going to become a nun and that it didn't make sense for us to get involved." She laughed, remembering. "Then it got all over school about Nora becoming a nun, and she was furious with me because after that *no one* asked her out."

He laughed with her. "Well played," he said and reached his glass over to touch hers.

Nora felt a flash of physical awareness. Oh, this was not a good thing, at all.

"Did you do all the usual twin things people always talk about? Liking taking each other's tests?" He leaned toward her.

A series of memories raced through her mind. "Not too often. I wasn't the most dedicated student. I used to skip school, go off and have fun. I never really took it seriously until I met my—" *Husband.* Her brain skidded to a stop. Shit, she was telling him *her* story—not Tess's.

"Your?"

"My counselor. High school counselor who made me see how important school was." Nervous heat pricked all over her body.

"So you were the wild one and Nora was the serious one, even then, huh? She seems pretty straitlaced, like she doesn't really cut loose."

"She has fun," Nora said defensively.

"Don't get me wrong. There's a place for those buttoned-up people in the world, too."

Buttoned-up people? First Tess told her she used to be an orange, and now Erik Morgan was saying she was buttoned-up? She took a swallow of beer. *I used to be wild once,* she wanted to say. *Wild is still inside me.*

"Well, you'd be surprised at some of the stuff Nora's done," she said instead.

He raised a brow. "Come on. At the hospital they call her *No Nonsense Nora.*"

9

———

No Nonsense Nora? A weird pain shot through her chest and her cheeks heated. "Really? That's what they call ... her?"

"They're not making fun of her. It's just sort of factual. She's a really nice person ... just all business, all the time." He leaned toward her and grinned. "You should take her place some time, just for fun. If you went into the hospital as Nora, you'd sure get people talking."

"Oh, really?" *I don't even think you're cute anymore,* she said in her mind.

She played with her glass and tried to decide if it was too soon for her to say she had to get going.

"So how'd you become a personal shopper?"

I was dragged into it by my opposite-of-no-nonsense sister, the fun one. "I just fell into it. I've always liked working with people—"

"And shopping?" he teased.

"That, too. But it was Nora who made it possible. Without her supporting me while I got this business going, I wouldn't have been able to do it." She paused, pleased that she'd gotten in a good word for herself. "See? There are good reasons to be ... responsible."

"I'm not slamming your sister. She's great at what she does. I think she's one of the best PTs around," he said.

"You do?" Suddenly Erik Morgan looked not just cute, but incredibly handsome.

"Not only is she good at it, she loves doing it," Nora added. "Although even with that, No Nonsense Nora is getting bored working at the hospital."

Surprise flitted across his face.

"What? Isn't she allowed to get bored?" she asked.

"No, of course not. She's so poker-faced no one would ever guess."

Poker-faced? This evening was getting more fun by the minute. She sipped her beer and decided to change the subject. "I heard the hospital's going to open a sports medicine rehab center."

"You know about that?"

She gulped. "Nora told me about it. I'm just bringing it up because I think she'd like to get into—" *Careful now, don't sound too knowledgeable.* "Knowing her as well as I do, I think she'd love go get into other kinds of physical therapy. Like sports-related stuff."

"Seriously? Wow, I'd never have guessed. I don't see her into athletics."

Nora wanted to scream. "What do you see her into?" she said in a deadly calm voice.

"Knitting."

"Knitting!"

He laughed. "Just kidding. Your sister's a nice person, but she's not as outgoing as you are, so it's hard to know her. That's okay, everyone doesn't have to be the same. I mean, she's really good at what she does and everyone knows it."

Effective, but dull. Just what every woman wanted to be. She made a show of looking at her watch. "It's getting late. I should really get going." She grabbed her purse as Erik finished off his beer.

"I'll walk you to your car," he said.

The cool night air felt good after being in the bar. Nora took a deep breath. She was relieved to be almost done with this job, almost done working with Erik Morgan. And then she realized that after tonight, she'd just be Nora again. And the comfortable feeling she had with Erik, this easy camaraderie would be gone. Wistfulness slid through her.

"It's been great working with you," she said. "If you ever need help in the future, just give me—"

"There is one other project I wanted to talk with you about," he said.

Oh, no. Not that thing he mentioned this afternoon. She'd hoped he had forgotten about it. Even the easy camaraderie between them wasn't worth the stress she'd been living with these past few days. He'd have to wait until Tess was back. "I'm sort of booked up right now—remember, I squeezed you in."

"I know." He leaned against her car.

Good thing she'd brought Tess's red BMW instead of her own aging Chrysler minivan.

"But this may be more fun than your other jobs," he said.

She hesitated. "What do you need?" *Whatever it is, the answer is no.*

Erik looked at her, those eyes of his glimmering with fun. "Would you like to come to my mother's party?"

"With you?" Suddenly she felt like the class nerd who'd been asked out by the star football player.

He grinned. "Yeah."

Oh, wasn't this just grand? As Nora she couldn't even get a date—that is, if she'd even been looking for one. But as a version of Tess, she got asked out by the catch of the century. By a guy who actually thought she, Nora, was a loser. Or something quite close to that. So, even if she came clean to him, she could never have this guy for real. *He liked Tess.*

"I'll level with you," he said. "My mother has a habit of trying to fix me up with single women and I suspect she's going to be in prime form at the party. I figure if I bring a date, it'll thwart her plans. What do you think?"

Yes. No! If she went, she'd have to fool his mother again. And the odds she could continue being successful at that would get lower every time she saw dear old mom. "I—I'm pretty sure I have other plans." She fought the urge to tell him exactly who she was—No Nonsense Nora who needed to take up knitting.

Try saying that three times fast.

She unlocked the car door and slid into the driver's seat, wanting to escape before he somehow convinced her to say yes.

"Why don't you check your schedule and get back to me?" he said. "I think we'd have fun."

———

Erik headed toward his car, surprised at his disappointment that Tess had more or less turned him down. Getting a *no* was a relatively unfamiliar occurrence in his life these days. He knew he shouldn't take it personally—after all, he hadn't asked her for a date, just a business appointment—and if she had a conflict, well, that was business. But there was no denying that it stung.

He pulled his keys out of his pocket, clicked open the car door and slid inside, promptly dropping his keys on the floor in the darkness. As he bent to fish around for them, he smacked his forehead into the steering wheel. "Dammit," he muttered and sat back into his seat, irritably rubbing his head.

A faint dusting of fog was rolling in, pale silver beneath the white glow of the streetlamps. Kind of early in the year for fog.

He wished he'd kissed Tess tonight.

He let his head fall against the headrest and hoped she decided to join him tomorrow. He liked being with her—even if she was a personal shopper. She so didn't match his mental image of what a personal shopper should be like, it almost blew him away. Sure, she wore those high-fashion clothes. But they didn't seem to fit her personality. And she wasn't the smooth conversationalist he'd thought a personal shopper would be, either. In fact, she pretty much blurted out exactly what was on her mind, which was refreshing. She didn't have that plastic coating that so many women seemed to have. At least the ones he'd met lately.

The oddest thing about it was, he couldn't figure out why his mother would have chosen to work with a personal shopper like Tess. Mom was a perfectionist—from her hair to her clothes to her house. Much as Tess tried to put on that air, he could tell it wasn't who she was.

Which was another thing he liked. Because, while he valued-perfection in certain things—like skiing and surgery —he saw no point in getting carried away about other things, like clothes.

He flipped on the dome light and bent once more to look for his keys, finally spying them almost beneath the gas pedal. Scooping them up, he started the engine and pulled out of his parking space.

Interesting that Tess had asked about the rehab center. If what she said was true about Nora's aspirations, it might be a good fit—for her and for them. He'd mention it to the other guys and see what they thought. Maybe he'd just found the person they needed to run the place.

Maybe he should stop at Tess's and talk to her about it a little more.

He gave his head a quick shake. He shouldn't be thinking about chasing down a woman before he figured out what he was doing with his life. Not only would it be shortsighted, but it also wouldn't be fair to either of them. Hopefully, he'd be flying out to meet with USSA soon, so he'd know if he had a major life decision to make.

The sooner he knew, the better. Because, whether Tess Carlisle was busy tomorrow night or not, he'd already decided this wasn't going to be the last time he saw her.

———

Nora stretched out on the sofa, watching the news without seeing a thing. *No Nonsense and buttoned-up?* She wasn't that bad, was she? Part of the reason was because she had a child—a person had to be responsible with a kid, didn't they?

She dialed Tess's cell, listening while it kicked into voice mail: "Hi, you've reached Tess, The Shopping Goddess. Whatever your fashion wish, you can count on me to make it come true. Leave a message and I'll call you back."

"Well, Goddess," Nora said, staring at the ceiling. "I just want to know if you think of me as no-nonsense and buttoned-up. The kind of person who never has any fun and should take up knitting. Call me back."

No doubt Tess was at another party right now, tinkle tinkle. Because somehow, over the years, Tess had managed to continue sparkling like silver, while Nora had tarnished to dull. Tess was still the fun one, while Nora was busy being the responsible one. Tess got asked out on dates by guys like Erik Morgan, while Nora sat home on Saturday night ... *knitting*.

Her phone rang and she snatched it up. Thank God her sister was on the ball tonight. "Hello?"

"Nora! How did the shopping go?"

"Margo?" Her heart fell. As much as she loved Margo, she didn't want to chat with her right now. What she wanted was answers from Tess.

"You're on speaker. Rosie's with me," Margo said. "Sorry to call so late, but we got to wondering how your shopping expedition with hunka man went."

"Fine. Mission accomplished—he's got something to wear," Nora said flatly.

"And?"

"Nothing."

"Oh, spill it. Something went wrong. I can hear it in your voice."

Nora debated whether to tell all, finally deciding that it might be nice to know how Margo viewed her, as well. "We went out for a drink afterward—"

"Out for a drink!" Margo repeated gleefully.

"Somehow we started talking about my sister ... Nora. He said that Nora was buttoned-up and no-nonsense." She eyed the dirty fingerprints around the light switch near the door and wondered how she'd never noticed them before. "Is that what I'm like?"

"No! Not all the time."

"Not all the time?"

"Hardly ever," she added quickly.

"Screw him," Rosie said "We like you just the way you are."

"Oh, wait a minute here. So what you're saying is, I *am* buttoned-up and no-nonsense?" She felt like hyperventilating.

"That's kind of extreme and a poor choice of words. You're less buttoned-up and more starched shirt—"

"Starched shirt? That's even worse—"

"Another poor choice of words," Rosie interjected. "You're not a starched—"

The call waiting beep sounded and Nora glanced at the phone number. *Tess.* "Hey, Margo? Rosie? I have to go. Tess is on the other line and I've been waiting to hear from her. I'll call you later." She switched over to Tess. "Hi!"

"What's the matter now?" her sister asked.

"You heard my message. Is that what I'm like?"

"Buttoned-up and no-nonsense?" Tess sounded puzzled.

"Yeah. Is that how you see me?"

"You mean specifically like that?"

My God, was her sister hedging? "Yeah. Specifically or close to it."

"Why are you asking this?"

"Why won't you answer the question?" Nora's irritation rose.

"I asked you first."

Nora pushed herself to sitting and swung her feet to the floor. "No, you didn't. I left a voice mail first. So you have to answer first."

Tess made a squeaky noise. "What was the question again?"

"You're stalling. You *do* think I'm buttoned-up and no-nonsense, don't you?" After several long moments without an answer, she said, "Tess? Are you there?"

The silence she got in reply told her that another call had just dropped in the Alaskan wilderness—either that, or Tess had gone into avoidance. She threw herself back against the couch in frustration and pushed speed dial for her sister, half expecting Tess not to pick up. When she did, Nora asked, "Did you just hang up on purpose so you didn't have to answer me?"

"No! Now what was the question?"

"Am I buttoned-up and no-nonsense?" Nora asked.

"Not exactly."

"What exactly, then?"

"First tell me who said it," Tess said.

Nora pursed her lips, reluctant to name her accuser. "Erik Morgan said it. Tonight."

"Why would he say such a thing? I thought you were acting like me. Tinkle tinkle and all that. I don't need my clients to think I'm dull—not in this business."

A slow burn started inside Nora. "I *was* tinkle tinkle," she said slowly. "He wasn't saying me as you was dull. He was saying me as me was dull. Get it?"

"Oh. So you and Erik were talking about ... you ... I mean, Nora?"

Nora straightened the magazines on the coffee table. "Yeah. We went out for drinks—"

"You went out for drinks with Erik Morgan?"

"No, dear sister, *you* went out for drinks with Erik Morgan. To celebrate your shopping success. The job is complete and you haven't lost your big client." Nora wandered into the kitchen to find something to eat. Chocolate preferably. Pounds of it.

"Really?" Tess's voice rose in excitement. "That's amazing. Thank you so much. I can't believe you two went out for drinks—"

"Oh, it gets better. After he told me how Nora is so no-nonsense—and obviously, I, Tess, am a lot more fun—he invited me to go to his mother's party tomorrow night at the yacht club."

"I have a date with Erik Morgan?" Tess began to chortle. "Hey, Liza!" she called to their cousin. "I have a date with Erik Morgan!"

"No. *I* have a date with Erik Morgan. You're on a cruise ship, remember?" After the cupboards revealed not so much as an ounce of chocolate, she pulled a string cheese from the fridge and tore it open. "Well, actually, I don't."

"Don't tell me you turned him down."

Nora didn't reply. She was trying to figure out exactly why she had turned down a date with Erik Morgan—handsome, smart, athletic, great forearms—even if it was a *professional date.*

"Nora? Don't tell me that," Tess said.

"Okay, I won't." She took a bite of string cheese, not nearly as satisfying as chocolate but at least it was food.

"*You turned him down?*"

"That would be correct."

Tess blew out her breath. "Please, please Nora, who I know would meet the next great love of her life if only she would let it happen, please explain to me why you turned him down."

"He was saying I was no-nonsense and buttoned-up. Only he was *with* me and saying it *about* me ... Do you know what that feels like? And I know I didn't used to be like that ... and I wasn't being like that right then—"

"Because you weren't being you! I can't believe you turned him down! Nora, I told you before. We both used to be oranges ... and then you turned into an apple."

"So you're saying that what he said is true?"

Tess hesitated. "Maybe a little."

"A little?"

"Okay, a lot," Tess said quietly.

"A lot? I'm a lot dull?" An ache started deep in her chest and her shoulders slumped. She'd worked so hard these past years to keep it together for her and Danny ... sometimes it had felt like she was hanging on by her fingernails.

"I'm sorry. You weren't always this way. Only since Kevin died. It's like you withdrew and never fully came back."

"I can't believe this. You have no idea how much pain I felt." *Still feel.*

"I do. You're my sister. Your pain was mine, too. If you hurt, I hurt ..." Her voice broke. "All I wanted was to be able to fix it for you ... and I couldn't. And when you finally started to come back from that place where all you felt was the agony of losing Kevin, you came back different."

"How could I not? How could anyone go through that and not be changed?" The ache in her chest wrapped itself around her heart, squeezing. She pressed a hand to her breastbone and tried to swallow down the knot in her throat.

"I know. But, Nora, you used to be tinkle tinkle all on your own. No one ever had to tell you how to do it." There were tears in Tess's voice. "And when you came back, you were functioning, doing your job, taking care of Danny ... But it was like you had closed a door ... protecting yourself

... you weren't going to ever take a chance again. On anything or anyone. Boring and lonely was better than risking being hurt again."

Nora tried to draw a breath. She clenched her hands together in her lap and focused on the tightness of her grasp, as though the pressure of her fingers against one another would dull the pain in her heart. The room blurred behind the sudden tears in her eyes. "You don't ... have a clue."

"I didn't live it like you did. But I lived it right beside you."

"It's not the same." Nora's voice shook. "It's not the same. *You don't know.*" She could hear Tess breathing and knew she was crying, too.

"I know I don't know. I know. I just want to see you happy again. I mean, what are the odds that my new client is the single guy who works down the hall from you in the hospital? And he wants you to go to a party? It's like that thing Grandma says—sometimes the thing you want most is right around the corner. That you shouldn't look so far and wide you miss out on the bachelor next door."

"I'm not even looking far and wide, let alone next door."

"I know. That's not what I mean. You don't have to go out with Erik Morgan—that's not what I'm saying."

"What are you saying?" What did everyone seem to be saying these days?

"I don't know. I just want my sister, the orange, back. I miss who you were. I love you, you know."

"Yeah, I know." Nora knew she had to get off the phone; she couldn't deal with this conversation anymore. "I think I hear Danny awake," she lied.

"Don't be mad at me."

"I'm not. I love you, too." She shut off the phone and set it carefully on the table before giving in to the sobs that had been building inside her—deep, wracking sobs that seemed to lay bare her soul. She wanted to come back, too. She wanted to love and be loved. But she was so afraid. What if she got hurt? What if she hurt someone else?

No Nonsense Nora. Even Kevin would have laughed at that one. She wiped the back of her hand across her eyes. They didn't come much better than him.

She looked at the television, where *Sleepless in Seattle* was playing on cable for about the fiftieth time this year already. And the words that seemed to run through her brain on a regular basis forced their way out of her mouth. "I'm so tired of being lonely."

She stared at the phone for a long minute, then retrieved the text message Tess had sent at the beginning of this charade, the one containing Erik's phone number. Taking several deep breaths for courage, she tapped in the number and started talking as soon as he answered. "Erik, hi, this is ... Tess Carlisle. My, ah, phone is dead so I'm using my sister's—Nora's—phone." She could hardly hear over the pounding of her pulse in her ears.

"Hi." He sounded shocked to hear from her.

She plowed ahead. "I, ah, checked my schedule and actually I'm free Saturday so if you still want me to, ah, well, what I'm saying is that I would love to go to your mother's party," she said in a long rush. *Lunatic,* she chastised herself. *Slow down.*

"Great!" He sounded shocked. "I'll pick you up at seven." He laughed. "And in case you're wondering what to wear ... it's *casual chic.*"

10

———

NORA PULLED ON TAN LINEN CROPPED PANTS WITH A white three-quarter length sleeve blouse and checked out her reflection in the mirror. Blagghh. Too tight in the butt—she looked fat.

She peeled the outfit off and threw it on Tess's bed, which was strewn with clothing she had already discarded as she tried on one outfit after another in an effort to figure out what to wear to the party. Her stomach churned with nervous excitement, she couldn't eat, she was beginning to feel weak from starvation—and Erik would be arriving very soon.

Standing in front of the open closet in her underwear, she brought one hand level with her eyes and watched it tremble slightly. That confirmed it—she was a total wreck.

The last time she'd been on a date was more than ten years ago ... when she and Kevin were going out. She sat on the edge of the bed and remembered the past, thought about her husband for a long minute, then pushed herself to her feet. Enough. She couldn't do this to herself, not tonight. Who knew if this thing with Erik was a date anyway? She wasn't entirely sure what to call it, which seemed appropriate because, regardless of what it was, she didn't know how to act, or what to say.

She pulled on a blue knit top and looked at herself in the mirror ... and thought about Erik.

What if he didn't like her? What if he did? What were they supposed to do when the date ended?

Kiss?

Maybe she should throw up.

This was just too much to deal with. And she was way too removed from these sorts of activities. It wasn't that she thought it would be awful to kiss Erik. In fact, quite the opposite.

But, oh, God, she wasn't even sure she knew how to date anymore, let alone kiss. All of this would be so much easier if he didn't have those eyes and those forearms and, okay fine, if she didn't feel an attraction to him.

It was always easy to go on a date with someone you didn't like. Well, maybe not *easy*. But at least you weren't so nervous. Then again, you might be more nervous because you didn't really want to go and were afraid the guy might try to kiss you and you knew you would have to either stop it before it started or kiss him back halfheartedly or even really kiss him back just to be nice which then made the predicament even worse—

Stop! Her brain was overheating. She sucked in a deep breath and exhaled slowly. Maybe Erik was thinking of tonight as strictly business and there was absolutely nothing for her to worry about.

She checked her reflection again and cringed. *No way.* Peeling off the blue top, she tossed it on the bed.

Although ... she and Erik had never discussed any type of fee for tonight. So maybe he did think it was a date.

She pulled a sundress out of Tess's closet, slipped it on, then turned to critically appraise herself in the full-length mirror. Way too casual even for casual chic. She stripped it off and added it to the growing pile of clothes. Too bad she didn't have a lady's maid to hang all this stuff up again.

Clearly, the problem was *she had nothing to wear.* She should have run out and bought something new this afternoon. Maybe there was still time. Omigod, she was losing her mind, all over a date.

Or a business agreement.

Whatever it was.

She perched on the edge of the bed in her underwear again and forced herself to calm down. It was only a date. Probably just a business date. She and Erik had fun talking together, laughing together. This was obviously just an extension of last night's shopping trip. It wasn't like the all-important meet-the-family date.

Except ... the whole family *would* be there.

So what? That meant nothing. This was a business arrangement—not a date. Final answer. Put a lid on it.

She smiled, relieved to have settled her mind.

But what if it started out businessy and turned datey in the middle? And either way, what happened at the end of the night? Did he walk her to the door? Shake her hand? Kiss her? Maybe she could have him drop her at the corner and she could just run home ... screaming.

The question did nothing to settle her stomach, which was now hungry and nauseous at the same time. She ran down to the kitchen to grab some cheese and crackers and force her racing thoughts away.

Forget what was going to happen at the end of the night. Erik would be here any minute. If she didn't figure out what to wear soon, he was going to find her in her underwear.

Mortified, she raced for the stairs. Good thing she sent Danny and the sitter to the park half an hour ago; she didn't need Erik calling her *Tess* and her son pointing out he had the name wrong.

———

Erik pulled up in front of Tess's house and killed the engine. A little boy and a young teenage girl sat on the front steps eating Popsicles, the frozen treats melting in the seventy-five degree heat and dripping onto the ground at their feet. He wondered for a moment why the neighbor kids were hanging out on Tess's porch, then he remembered being a kid and hanging out on whatever porch was available.

He shoved open his car door and started up the walk. "Hi," he said.

The little boy grinned at him—lips, teeth, and chin stained blue. "Are you here for my mom?"

Erik stopped. *Mom?* "Do you live here?" He looked directly at the girl. If this was Tess's daughter, she would have been pretty young when she gave birth.

Or maybe Nora. These could be Nora's kids.

"I'm just the babysitter, Ashley." She hooked a thumb at the little boy. "He lives here. This is Danny. His mom is getting ready. I'll tell her you're here." She dashed into the house.

Wow. Tess had a kid. And she hadn't mentioned it. Though, he hadn't really thought to ask, either ...

Danny stood and stuck out his blue-stained hand. "Nice to meet you."

Erik shook his hand, feeling the sticky Popsicle juice migrate from the boy's fingers to his own.

"Do you have a wife?" Danny asked.

Ashley pushed open the screen door just in time to rejoin the conversation. "If he had a wife, he wouldn't be taking your mom out, Danny." She stood there in the open doorway. "She said to tell you she's running a little late and you can just go in the living room if you want."

"Or you can stay out here with us." Danny looked up at him with big brown eyes.

"I think I'll stay out here with you."

Danny grinned. "Do you have a dog?"

"I do. Her name is Willa," Erik said.

"I wish I had a dog."

Ashley stepped onto the porch and let the screen door bang shut behind her.

"Do you have a bike?" Danny asked. "I have a bike. Want to see it? It's a two-wheeler."

Ashley snorted. "With training wheels."

"My mom's gonna take 'em off." He started down the driveway toward the garage. "Come on."

Erik followed him, with Ashley right behind. "So, Danny, you like riding?"

The little boy nodded and disappeared through the open garage door, returning a minute later proudly pushing his bike, a shiny new red number.

Erik ran a hand over the top tube and rang the little bell on the handlebars. "I used to have a red bike, too, when I was about nine. Had a lot of fun with that bike." Lots of fun. The first winter he had it, he and a friend took the wheels off and attached the front and back forks to two halves of a broken ski. Since it was his idea, he got to be the first one to take it down the sledding hill—after they'd iced a section of the hill with buckets of water. His wipeout had been spectacular. So had his broken arm.

"You're ready to take off the training wheels, huh?" he asked.

Danny nodded. "My mom said she would do it a million years ago. Zach doesn't have training wheels anymore. And I don't want them, either."

"Who's Zach?"

"My friend. Next door." He knelt next to the bike and tried to twist off the nut that held the training wheels in place. "Can you take this off for me?"

Erik frowned. "I don't know, buddy. Your mom probably wants to do that."

"She always says she's going to, but she's too busy," Ashley said.

"I need to ride with Zach."

"You know you can't just jump on and ride when those training wheels are off. You've got to learn to get your balance first," Erik pointed out.

The kid ignored him, just tried to twist the nut off again. Erik turned to Ashley. "You're sure she was planning to pull them off?"

"Uh, yeah. She's said it, like, every day for the last two weeks. I babysit here a lot."

"You think she'd care if I took them off?"

Ashley shrugged. "One less thing for her to do."

Erik considered her answer for a moment. Hell, Tess would probably thank him for helping out like this. "Okay, let me see what I can do." He went into the garage in search of tools, grabbed a wrench off the pegboard on the wall, and headed back to the driveway.

He knelt next to the bike. Ashley bent over to watch while Danny began to hop from foot to foot in adrenaline-fueled anticipation. A couple of minutes later, the training wheels were off. Erik wiped his hands against one another to remove the dust, then took hold of the handlebars and gestured at his new friend. "Okay, kid, hop on. Let's go for a spin."

Danny ran into the garage and came out wearing a helmet, elbow pads, and wrist guards.

"You wear all that stuff riding your bike?" Erik held back a laugh.

"Mom says I have to."

Seemed a bit over the top. For about four seconds he wondered whether Tess really intended to take the training wheels off or not. Then Danny climbed onto the bike, and he put the whole thought out of his mind.

"Take those wrist guards off," Erik said. "Those are for Rollerblading. You won't be able to hold on right. Here." He pulled the guards off and tossed them to the ground. "Okay, now, let's ride." He high-fived the kid, then started to gently run down the driveway while holding on to the bike seat.

"Pedal, Danny. Harder. Steer! Steer the bike!" They headed down the sidewalk, the front wheel veering from left to right and back again as Danny struggled to find his balance. Erik jogged a little faster.

"Don't let go!" Danny cried.

"I'm not. You just steer. Pedal. Keep pedaling. *Pedal, Danny.*" He ran faster and let go of the seat for a second as he jogged alongside the bike. "You're doing it, Danny!"

The bike wobbled, Erik grabbed the seat again, and Danny hit the brakes at the end of the block. Erik's breathing was coming a little hard, it crossed his mind that casual chic probably wasn't the best choice for this activity. "Okay, let's go see if your mom is ready."

Danny turned the bike around, and they headed down the sidewalk toward home. Erik spotted Tess on the porch, a hand on one hip, the other shading her eyes as she watched them. In a pink sleeveless dress and sandals, a soft breeze blowing the fabric around her legs, she looked like she belonged in a painting of a glorious summer afternoon. Erik's breath caught for a moment and all he could do was look at her. He could freeze-frame this shot forever.

"Hey, Mom!" Danny yelled.

"Keep pedaling, Danny, pedal." Erik picked up the pace so the bike was moving along at a brisk clip. Then he let go and watched proudly as Danny rode untethered past a couple of houses before veering onto the grass.

"Steer, Danny, steer!" Erik took off running in pursuit.

"Danny!" Tess screamed.

The kid's feet were off the pedals now, out straight to either side for balance, the bike barreling right for a hedge between two yards. Danny crashed into the bushes and tipped sideways, landing sprawled across his bike.

Tess got to Danny just as Erik did. She picked her son up and started running her hands over his arms and legs. "What hurts? Does anything hurt? Are you okay?"

Danny pulled out of her grasp and grinned at Erik. "Did you see me, Mom? I rode by myself."

"Yes, I saw you," she said sternly. "What were you doing? Look at that scratch on your leg. You could have been killed."

"Mom, you're a worrywart and a spoilsport." He grabbed Erik's hand. "Can we go again?"

"Who took the training wheels off?" Tess asked softly. There was a definite frozen quality to her voice and Erik felt suddenly like he was about to be sent to the principal's office.

"Mom, did you know he's not married?"

Tess rolled her eyes. "Yes. I did. What does that have to do with taking training wheels off?"

"Well, Ronald was married."

A faint blush crept up Tess's cheeks and she rolled her eyes. "In case you're wondering, he's talking about Ronald McDonald."

"I wasn't wondering," he lied.

"So?" Danny asked his mom. "What do you think?"

"We'll talk about that later," she said. "Now how did the training wheels get off your bike?"

Erik raised an eyebrow at Ashley. He should have known better than to believe a teenager. "I took them off," he said. "I ... thought you were planning to do it and just didn't have the time."

"Daniel—" Tess frowned at her son.

"You said you'd take them off."

"When you were ready. And clearly you aren't ready."

"Yes, I am," he said defiantly.

"Where are your wrist guards?"

Danny scowled. "I can't hold on right with those."

Based on Tess's responses so far, Erik knew Danny was heading into really big trouble now.

"So you just didn't wear them?"

The kid shrugged.

Unbelievable. Danny wasn't going to rat him out. "That would be my fault, too," he said. "I told him not to wear them. But he's right, he can't hold on properly with them on —they're designed for Rollerblading ... not biking."

Tess glared at him and, somehow, the evening of fun he had pictured them having seemed very far away. "Sorry," he said.

"Let's go wash up that cut." She marched Danny back inside.

"I guess I'll put the training wheels back on." Erik started down the driveway with the bike.

Ashley sauntered along beside him. "His mom's kind of overprotective."

"It might have been nice if you'd mentioned that before."

"Yeah, well, Danny's right. She *is* a worrywart and a spoilsport."

11

———

Nora sat stiffly in the passenger seat of Erik's car and tried to calm her jackhammering heart. And she couldn't believe Erik had taken her son's training wheels off without checking with her first. And she couldn't believe Danny and Ashley had come home early from the park. And she couldn't believe Erik hadn't called her Tess in front of the kids—thank God for small favors.

No wonder her heart was pounding a million beats a minute. Besides her child almost getting hurt, she had just dodged one of the biggest bullets of her life—that being, her own child unmasking her.

At least these new events had temporarily buried her concerns about whether Erik was going to kiss her at the end of the night.

"I'm sorry," he said.

The sincerity in his voice melted her anger and she began to relax.

"It didn't seem out of line when both of them said you'd been promising to take off the training wheels for weeks."

"I had. But I didn't really mean it. You don't have

children so you don't realize what can happen to them." She knew she sounded overly cautious and, for the first time ever, felt a little embarrassed about it.

"Considering that I've been throwing myself down mountains on two thin pieces of wood since I was five, and survived—"

"It's different when it's your own child."

Erik just looked at her, and she had a hard time telling if he was understanding her point of view or not.

"I guess," he said. "You know, I didn't even know you had a son."

Her brain kicked into overdrive. *She was Tess—not Nora.* Tess had no children. Good God, she'd just given it all away. Her heart started to thud again. She should never have agreed to come out with him.

"Oh," she said weakly. She frantically scrambled to come up with another lie to add to the pyre that would soon destroy her life. "I guess I didn't have any reason to mention it before. It's not the thing I typically mention to clients because you know, I'm typically talking—" *Stop talking.* "—about shopping."

Although Erik nodded, he had the strangest expression on his face. He couldn't have figured out the entire charade, could he?

"So ... are you divorced?" he asked.

Divorced. Hmm. *Should she be divorced?* What was the answer here? He couldn't possibly know her story—Nora's story, that was. Unless someone at the hospital blabbed it to him. But, that was probably pretty unlikely. So, should she be divorced? Or widowed? Or—what?

She drew a breath. Okay, she'd just go with the truth— her truth, not Tess's. A fine bead of sweat prickled across her shoulders. "My husband was killed shortly before Danny was born."

"Oh, God, I'm sorry."

She had to be more careful. After actually succeeding at getting the shopping done and saving the account, she'd almost blown the whole thing in the space of a couple of minutes—all because she was going on a date to prove she hadn't become dull. "My friends say it's made me too cautious with Danny ... and maybe it has."

"Even if it's true, it's understandable." He glanced at her sideways. "But, I have to know. Did you go on a date with Ronald McDonald?"

Nora laughed, a big rolling laugh that shook loose all the tension that had piled up inside her.

"Not that I don't think he wouldn't be a great catch," Erik continued.

She laughed again, touched by the warmth in Erik's voice. He really was a nice guy. "No, I did not go out with Ronald. But Danny thought he'd be the perfect man for me."

"You wouldn't have to make dinner anymore."

"I think that was his point," she said.

Erik pulled up to the yacht club, with its impressive white colonial revival facade and Corinthian columns. A valet in a black tux opened Nora's door and helped her out of the car.

"Let's forget about training wheels for the rest of the night," Erik said. "I'll show you a better time than Ronald ever could. Come on, the grand ballroom's upstairs." He reached out to take her hand.

Wait until she told Tess all this—her sister would positively die.

They stepped into the high-ceilinged grand ballroom,

and Nora caught her breath, completely captivated. The redwood-paneled room had gleaming hardwood floors and a stunning stone fireplace. A large crowd of people had already arrived for the party, and their voices and laughter mingled into a happy, uplifting sound.

They weren't inside more than a minute before a waiter tapped Erik on the shoulder and directed him across the room to where his mother was holding court.

Nora gulped. Here came the moment of truth.

Or lies, depending on your point of view.

———

Camille's eyes swept over Erik and she smiled broadly. "Oh, Tess, he's perfectly dressed. Thank you. I'm so glad you could come." She clasped one of Nora's hands with her own, and her gaze roamed over the crowd. "Erik honey, Mary Jean is here ... so is her daughter. I'm sure they'd both like to meet Tess. Once they see what a nice job she's done with you, I suspect they may want to take advantage of her services as well."

Nora mentally cringed. Oh great, more people to lie to.

"Be sure to tell Mary Jean that I've got a hot date," Erik said.

Camille's lips quirked a little. "I suppose I'll have to. Your sister is here somewhere, too. I told her you were bringing Tess so be sure to do the introductions. Oh! And don't forget to register for the door prizes. Right over by the bar."

"Isn't it kind of poor form for family members to enter?" he asked.

"Of course not. It's my party, I make the rules. Go on, you two, and have some champagne. Enjoy yourselves." She waved them away and turned her attention to a couple who were waiting.

Erik looked around. "I have no idea where my sister is. I guess we could get the door prize thing out of the way." As soon as they were out further away from Camille, he leaned toward Nora and said, "My mother's the epitome of *you can take the girl out of the small town but you can't take the small town out of the girl.*" He shook his head. "Door prizes."

A waiter appeared with a tray filled with flutes of champagne, each with a strawberry in the bottom. Erik snagged two glasses and handed one to Nora.

Well, wasn't this the cat's meow? Tess wasn't the only one having a grand time tonight. Nora took a swallow and relished the feeling of bubbles wiggling their way down her throat. This was exactly what she needed. A little champagne would calm her nerves and she'd be just fine tonight, no matter how much lying she had to do.

As they were filling out the door prize entry forms, Erik pointed to a woman standing near the large windows overlooking the bay. "There's my sister, Jenny. Come on. I'll introduce you."

Nora dropped her entry into the fancy decorated box on the table, took a fortifying swallow of champagne, and sent up a silent prayer that his sister wouldn't ask for fashion advice. Jenny saw Erik coming across the room and a grin lit up her face. "I thought you'd never get here!" She launched herself into his arms.

"You should talk. When did you finally get in?"

"Oh, don't remind me," she said as they pulled apart. "I knew we should have flown yesterday. The flight got so delayed, I thought we were going to miss our connection and the party." She smiled at Nora. "You must be Tess."

Nora smiled back and extended a hand.

"My mom told me all about you," Jenny said. "Maybe you can give me some style tips."

Nora's smile froze. Could she call this stuff or what? She took another sip of champagne and nodded.

"Nope, she's not working tonight," Erik said. "You want tips, call her next week and make an appointment."

She could have kissed him. And then she realized what he'd just said. *She's not working tonight.* Did that mean this was a real date?

Was she on a date? With Erik Morgan?

Suddenly she couldn't even look at him—what if she turned red? Unable to think of a thing to say, she looked out the windows to the bay, sparkling beneath the setting sun, the water dusted gold and pink. Piers stretched out from the yacht club, like fingers, with boats of every shape and size docked along them.

"This is really gorgeous. Does your mom have a boat?" she asked.

"Yeah. Her husband's a big sailor," Erik said. "Races this big fifty-six footer. Built for speed but with a cruising interior. Best of both worlds he always says."

"Speaking of which, I need to find out if he's racing tomorrow," Jenny said. "I'll be right back." She danced off.

"Do you ever race with him?" Nora asked.

"Sometimes. I always spent my free time skiing. Never really learned to sail that well—it's pretty different. Sailing you have a whole crew, skiing you do alone."

"Are they so different really? Flying down snow instead of flying across water?"

He narrowed his eyes, thinking. "In a way, I guess you're right. Except the boat needs wind. And when the wind dies, you can go nuts from the sound of the empty sails flapping and the boat just rocking on the water."

"Since I've never been sailing, I'm having a little trouble sympathizing," Nora said wryly.

"Be nice to me and I'll get you out sometime."

Be nice to me. No problem. There was just that little issue about him thinking Nora was a bore and Tess was a barrel of fun. So, while Tess might get to go sailing sometime, it was unlikely Nora would ever get the chance. She took a gulp of champagne. "Okay, it's a deal."

By the time she finished her second glass of champagne, she wished she hadn't been too nervous to eat all day because the bubbles were going straight to her head. And by the time she finished her third glass, she vowed not to have another—especially once she discovered she was seated for dinner at the head table with the family. Already, when she turned her head, her brain came along later. She could only imagine how mortifying it would be if her brain didn't come along at all, and here she was at the head table.

She watched as waiters attended to each table, pouring wine for dinner, and knew that if she had even one sip it would be the end of her. Dinner arrived after a few minutes, every table served at the same time. Each plate looked artistically designed—filet mignon and crab, with green and yellow vegetables piled on top, long crunchy salad sticks poking out, and swirls of sauce over everything. Talk about presentation. She took a bite; it tasted as incredible as it looked. Hopefully it would absorb some of the champagne in her stomach.

As everyone was eating, Camille's editor went to the podium, thanked everyone for coming, and spoke warmly about the twenty-five years she and Camille had been working together. Other people came forward to toast her or roast her or just tell funny or touching stories. Finally, when the main course was finished and the waiters were passing out dessert, Camille went to the mic.

"It's has truly been a journey," she said. "Thank you all for being part of it. I hope the road ahead has many more exciting plot twists and turns. Now, without further ado—because it's my favorite part—let's award the door prizes."

Someone brought the entry box forward, and Camille began to pull names and give away signed copies of her latest book, fancy pads of writing paper, elegant pens and—

What? Who? Everyone was clapping and smiling. Nora gave her head a little shake to clear the champagne bubbles from her ears. "What?" she asked stupidly.

"Tess, you won! Get up there!" Jenny motioned at her excitedly.

Nora's mouth dropped open and she slammed it shut. "Won what?" she managed to say without slurring.

"You're in the next book," Erik said. "It's your fifteen minutes of fame."

People were clapping and looking at her. She flushed—God only knew whether it was from alcohol or embarrassment. Heat rolled over her. *Help me,* she said in her head and quickly added *St. Jude* to the end of the sentence. Then she pushed her chair back and stood.

So far, so good. Thank goodness she'd worn flat sandals and not Tess's stilettos. She concentrated on making sure she didn't sway as she made her way to where Camille Lamont waited to give her a hug.

"I'm delighted that Tess won this prize," Camille said. "She's my personal shopper and fantastic at what she does. I can't wait to work her character into the story." She took Nora by the arm and pulled her toward the podium. "Tess, how about giving us an idea ... something off the top of your head I could put into the book."

Nora looked out over the audience. An idea? How about not drinking too much champagne on an empty stomach? "Uh, maybe the heroine could have a twin sister," she said giddily as she accepted the award certificate. "Maybe she could change places with her sister and find out what people really think about her." *What the hell was she doing?* "Or, you know—" She gestured weakly with one hand. "—maybe not." She stepped back from the microphone and slunk back to her chair.

"I'm going to run to the ladies room," she whispered to Erik before escaping down the hall. She splashed cold water on her cheeks, careful not to smear her makeup, then dabbed her face dry with a paper towel. Though she already felt more alert, she probably should have some coffee with dessert. She stepped into the corridor and started back to the grand ballroom, relieved to be feeling a bit more coherent. Thank God, she'd eaten every bite of her dinner.

Someone grabbed her by the arm and pulled her toward a dark corner. As she turned her head, her brain still sluggishly following along, she heard a man say, "Hello, Nora."

12

———————

SHE FORCED HER EYES TO FOCUS AND FOUND HERSELF face to face with Tess's ex-fiancé—all dark good looks and a small amount of gray matter. Her heart rate slowed and she sobered even more. "Keegan! Shhh. What are you doing here?" She knew the answer before he even spoke. "You're setting up the band."

He worked a toothpick between his teeth. "You got it. So what's going on? Why are you pretending to be Tess?"

She shushed him again. "It's a long story. I'm just helping her out, so keep your mouth shut."

"Huh." He eyed her thoughtfully for too long. "Switching places, huh? What's my silence worth to you? And Tess?"

"What?"

"You heard me."

Nora laughed. "Keegan, you'd make a lousy Mafioso."

"How come Tess won't return my calls?"

A *very* small amount of gray matter. "Maybe because you dumped her."

"Yeah, well, I need to talk to her. That cruise we were going to take on our honeymoon? I paid for it."

Uh-oh. "I don't know anything about all that stuff." She tried to move past him but he blocked her way.

"You tell Tess to either return my calls so I can get refunded for the cruise—"

"You want the money back?" The room seemed to spin. She was going to really kill her sister this time.

"Damn right. And she's got all the paperwork."

He wanted his money back. And Tess and Liza were, at this moment, enjoying that cruise ... or actually a different cruise ... she'd traded in the tickets for an earlier departure.

Nora put a hand against the wall for support. "Well, Keegan, see, I don't think she has the money because, you know, she's still trying to get this business going." She paused in an effort to pull her thoughts together. "Which is why I'm helping her out tonight."

"She just has to give me the paperwork—she doesn't need to come up with any money. Then I can get a refund."

Nora thought about champagne and parties and light, easy, happy laughter, tinkle tinkle. "She's been so busy lately ..."

"I'll tell you what." Keegan's voice took on an edge. "You tell your sister to give me my tickets or I'll tell Mrs. Big Client Lamont that her personal shopper is not who she says she is."

Nora dropped her fake smile.

Keegan sneered. "And, I'll also tell her that you two have a history of scamming people."

"What? That's ridiculous!"

He shrugged. "And maybe," he added, "I'll tell the hospital what you're doing in your spare time."

"The hospital isn't going to care if I'm a personal

shopper in my spare time." Except, if she ever did apply for a job with the new sports medicine rehab center ... getting caught lying to Erik Morgan would probably mean the end of that dream. The thought left her disquieted.

"We'll have to see, won't we?" Keegan looked down the hallway and she followed his gaze. Erik was coming toward them.

"I was wondering where you went," he said.

"Erik, this is an old friend—"

"I was engaged to her sister—"

"Nora," Nora said, locking eyes with Keegan.

He didn't say anything for a second. "Nora," he finally said around the toothpick.

"Keegan's with the band," Nora said evenly. "A roadie."

The two men shook hands. "Good to meet you," Erik said. He touched Nora on the arm. "Hey, want to go outside? I can only take so much of this."

That made two of them. "I'd love to. Good seeing you, Keegan, I'll tell ... my sister to give you a call."

"Do that." He sauntered back toward the party.

Unbelievable. Why was it whenever she agreed to something with her sister it turned into a fiasco? She needed to talk to Tess—*now*.

She opened her purse and pulled out her phone. "I, um, can you excuse me just one minute?" she asked. "I have a missed call and just want to make sure everything is okay at home." She hurried downstairs and stepped outside, wandered down out onto one the wooden docks as she waited for Tess to pick up. A breeze ruffled her hair and she could hear the rigging on the boats softly clattering as they rocked gently in their slips. Under other circumstances she would consider this an incredibly romantic night. But not anymore. Not since she'd run into Keegan.

Just when she was sure the call was about to go into voicemail, Tess answered: "Nora!"

"All right, smarty party girl," Nora replied. "We are now in deep, deep, deep, deep trouble. Deep with a capital T."

"Have you been drinking?"

"No, why?"

Tess laughed. "You can't spell. You never could hold your liquor."

"Oh, fine, I had a couple glasses of champagne. But that, dear sister, is the least of our worries. Does the name *Keegan* ring any bells?" She stopped at the end of the pier and looked into the darkness.

"Gee, I don't know. You mean like Keegan, the jerk who decided he didn't want to marry me? Like Keegan, the shit who decided he needed to go out with some babe twelve years younger than him? Like Keegan—"

"That would be him."

"What about him?" Tess asked in a bored voice.

"He's here at the party, setting up for the band. And he wants to know why you won't return his calls."

"*What party?* And excuse me? He wants to know why *I* won't return his calls? Tell him what's good for the goose is good for the gander. Kindness is as kindness does, and all that crap."

Nora controlled the urge to yell at her sister. "Tess. Has he left you any messages about getting the paperwork back for the cruise tickets *he* bought?"

"Yeah. So what?"

"Well, he wants the paperwork so he can get a refund."

"Too bad, so sad. You tell him that I, and Liza—who is not just a cousin, but a true friend who stood by me when my fiancé didn't—we are taking a little mental rehab cruise through the Alaskan Passage. Tinkle. Tinkle."

"It's not going to be that easy," Nora said. "Because Keegan recognized me. *He knew I wasn't you.* He said if you don't give him back the tickets, he's going to tell everyone the truth about what we're doing. And if that happens, there will be no more tinkle tinkle. You'll be—"

"Screwed. And no longer working on the Camille Lamont account." Tess's voice pitched up. "Nora, you can't let it happen!"

"*I can't let it happen?* You've already set the stage for it to happen. This isn't just about you. If Keegan talks, I could lose the chance to get the job of my dreams, too."

"He wouldn't dare."

"He seemed awfully set when he talked to me. Tess, this is the kind of stupid mess I got into ten or fifteen years ago when I was a kid. Not now. I'm responsible now. I've built a life ...and I'm trying to build you one, too."

A couple of people looked in her direction and she realized she'd been talking way too loud. She lowered her voice. "So may I suggest you give old Keegie a call and, at least, put him off a bit? And may I also suggest that you get the hell off that boat and get home, for a multitude of reasons, but particularly because you now have a pressing need to find the money to pay Keegan for the tickets you just used."

She spotted Erik coming down the dock. "Here comes Erik. I have to go before he realizes something isn't right about Keegan and me and you and personal shopping." She shut off her phone and dropped it into her purse.

"Everything okay?" he asked when he was closer. She nodded. "You know kids. Danny's so excited about you helping him today. He's going on and on. Wanted to ask about riding his bike tomorrow. Of course, without training wheels."

"I know we agreed to put the training wheels issue aside tonight, but the kid is ready. You should let him."

She frowned. "He might get hurt."

"He might also get self-confidence."

She considered his words. "*But he might get hurt.*"

"And he probably won't. Like I said before, I started skiing when I was his age."

"That's the problem. When you're young you don't realize how quickly it all can end. You don't have any idea the pain that comes with risk." For a moment, those words sounded odd coming out of her—or rather, odd coming out of the person she used to be.

He took a step back. "I don't know ... what is life without risk? Are you really living if everything is smooth all the time?"

"You like bumpy?"

He shoved a hand through his hair. "Sometimes life bumps are good. Moguls on a ski run are tough, but when you do them, you learn to control your skis, to concentrate, maneuver through tough terrain and come out standing. In the end, you have this exhilaration from having conquered the mountain." He grinned. "Or at the very least, surviving."

This conversation was cutting too close to home. She looked up at the moon so she could avoid looking at Erik. "You think pain is worth experiencing, just so you can celebrate surviving?"

"I wouldn't exactly put it like that. More like, when you survive you always come out stronger. That strength is what lets you challenge life again. And challenges are what make us feel alive."

She thought of Kevin. "Sometimes it's not that easy."

"You mean a death."

She nodded.

"How did he die?"

She tamped down the ache that always seemed to well up when she talked about Kevin dying. "Car accident one night. Teenage kid driving a stolen car, ran a red light …"

"Oh God, I'm sorry."

"Yeah. He kind of saved my life. And then he lost his. He was a cop. I used to skip out of high school, and he'd pick me up and haul me back there."

The breeze messed her hair into her face and she brushed the loose strands back. "In the squad car, he'd give me lectures about the importance of education. Something must have sunk in, because after high school ended, I got my GED and then went to college. After graduation, I tracked him down to thank him."

"He gave you something to hold on to."

"Yeah." She thought back to those years and felt the pain of missing him again. "He was only six years older than me … we started dating, got married. He wanted to get on the other side of the law and become a lawyer. I wanted to become a physical therapist—"

"Like Nora?"

She froze. Damn all that champagne. She was going to blow this thing one way or another.

13

SHE CLEARED HER THROAT. "AH, YEAH, LIKE NORA. But, then I got pregnant. He never made it to law school ... never met his son." Her voice dropped to a whisper and she looked out over the bay, dark in the moonlight. "He always sacrificed for me. And then he died too soon ... before I could give back to him."

Erik didn't say anything for so long, she finally turned toward him. He was looking at her, just looking, his gaze so intense it almost scared her.

"I think you're probably underestimating the value of what you did give him," he said. "Most people just want happiness, acceptance—" He broke off for a moment. "It isn't about jobs, and money, and trips and owning things. I know, easy for me to say when I have all that. But it's not ..." He glanced away, and Nora knew suddenly that Erik Morgan was not content, had a longing, a hole in his soul he was searching to fill.

"My dad," he said, "died when I was eleven. He used to recite this poem to my sister and me at bedtime ... about a child running to his father when he got home after work and showing him all the bruises and cuts he'd gotten that day. And, as the father makes them better, he laments the fact that, someday, the greatest hurts his child will have will be those of the heart. Sometimes I can still hear him as he sat on the edge of the bed in the dark." He paused for several long beats. "And then he got sick. And died within six months."

"So you know."

He nodded. "Not exactly what you feel, but, yeah, I've done that mogul run."

"Sometimes, the reminders come out of the blue and hit me ... and I have to back away from everything," she said softly.

"And then what happens?"

"I come back out. I have to. I have a child, a job ..." *I want to have a life again.*

He looked at her curiously, watched her as though assessing something. Finally he nodded. "About Danny and the training wheels ..."

She let out a quiet laugh and felt her sadness seep away with the sound. Her eyes met his and she saw understanding there ... and she thought to herself that, for such a wild hotshot skier, this man had a gentle soul. At that moment, she wished he would put his arms around her and hold her close.

And then her phone rang and she wanted to crawl under the dock. Caller ID showed that it was Tess. *Now what?* "Hold that thought," she said. "The babysitter is calling again."

She hurried down the dock and swiped the phone. "What now?" she said in lieu of hello.

"*What party?*" Tess asked. "You never answered me before—where are you?"

"That's what you're calling for? I'm busy."

"Don't tell me you actually went to Camille's party."

"Okay, then I won't," Nora said, enjoying herself.

Tess squealed. "You went? I thought you told him *no.*"

"Yes, well, I decided to put a little risk back in my life. Because this charade of ours wasn't quite risky enough."

"I can't believe it. *So you're busy, huh?* Making out with Erik in a corner somewhere?"

"Right. That's so not going to happen." Nora checked to make sure Erik was still at the end of the dock.

"Erik Morgan can kiss me anytime he wants," Tess said.

"Well, when you get back he may have to. Because then you'll be you and I'll be me and *you'll* be going out with him."

"God, Nora, this is getting way too complicated."

"I'm glad you're finally reaching that conclusion." She waved at Erik. "I have to go. Erik's going to get suspicious if I'm on the phone all the time. I keep telling him the babysitter's calling."

"Don't hang up on me! We need to figure this Keegan thing out."

"I already have—it involves you getting off that ship and coming home. I'll call you later." Nora shut off the phone and hurried toward Erik. "I'm really sorry. Danny isn't feeling well."

"Do you want to get going?"

She shook her head. "Probably just tired. Overexcited from riding his bike ..."

"I've been standing here thinking about him, too. How about teaching him to ski?"

She froze. "Isn't that sort of a big leap from training wheels? I could never send him down a mountain with a stranger—"

"You mean a ski instructor?" He bent toward her, and the nearness of him and the smell of his aftershave made her catch her breath. "What if it's not a stranger? How about I take the two of you skiing? Some hills are open until Memorial Day. Hell, most years you can ski at Mammoth Mountain until July."

Apprehension skidded through her and she shook her head. "He's so young—"

"Yeah, exactly. It's a great age to learn. When I lost my dad, skiing gave me something of my own to hang on to."

Nora thought about Danny's obsession with finding a dad. Could something like skiing help him past that? As an outlet? Did five-year-olds really need outlets? Wasn't life just one big fun outlet already at age five? "You also got really hurt." She looked pointedly at Erik's knees.

"Skiing gave me a lot more than it took away. What do you say?"

She couldn't bring herself to reply.

"Tell you what. You think it over and I'll ask again in a few days." He took her hand. "Come on, I'll show you my stepfather's boat, *Mojo*."

They crossed the lawn and headed down another dock, his hand still wrapped around hers. She loved the warmth of it, the way it made her feel secure and wanted. *Mojo*. Erik Morgan sure had it in spades.

They halted next to a big sailboat with a long white hull, tall mast, and large cockpit where several people were sipping drinks and chatting. Erik stepped onto the teak deck and reached out to help her aboard. A trim, gray-haired man stood to meet them, and Erik introduced her to his stepfather, Jack Lamont. He had an open, friendly face and she liked him immediately.

"Good to meet you, Tess. I understand you're responsible for Erik's newfound fashion sense."

She nodded. "This is really an impressive boat," she said, hoping to change the subject.

Erik let out a laugh. "Don't worry, he's not into clothes, either. I wouldn't doubt if my mom has you shopping for him soon." He waved a hand toward the companionway, a stairway leading below deck. "I'm going to give Tess the nickel tour," he said as he headed down.

She followed him below, awed by the luxurious, varnished wood interior, the L-shaped settee and teak chairs around a large table, the soft lighting that gave the space a romantic glow. "This is a racing boat?" she asked.

"Yeah. But it's a really comfortable boat to cruise in, too."

They stepped into the galley, which was beautifully designed with a sink and stove. She rubbed her hand on the counter. This boat must have cost a fortune.

"Only the best," he said as if reading her mind. He pulled a couple of clear plastic glasses from a stack on the counter. "Want a drink?"

"I think a Diet Coke is what I need."

"Coming right up." He scooped ice into the glasses.

Nora shook her head. "Somewhere between seeing Keegan and taking all those phone calls, I lost my champagne high."

"I can see why." He popped open a Diet Coke and poured it into the cups. "I don't know your sister very well, but that guy didn't seem anything like her type."

She felt a niggling irritation. Here they were discussing No Nonsense Nora again. "Oh, really?" she said nonchalantly. "What's her type?"

"You know, a more staid kind of guy. An accountant or an engineer ... not a roadie."

Staid? She wanted to tell him that *she* was the one who used to cut school. *She* was the one who used to sneak out of the house at night to meet her boyfriend. *She* was the one who used to get the party started, so to speak.

That's when she realized all her thoughts contained the words *used to.* Tess was right—she had changed. "So, if Nora's type is an accountant, then what's my type?"

He turned, a glass in each hand, and looked at her. Looked at her so long she had to break eye contact just so she could breathe.

But when she glanced back she was caught instantly in his eyes again. Heat tiptoed up her core. He took a step toward her, and then another and another, backed her right up against the companionway wall until she couldn't move away from him, until their bodies were touching and their eyes were still locked. And then, arms out to the side, still holding a glass in each hand, he dipped his head and covered her mouth with his own.

He kissed her.

Her heart clutched with such intensity that she trembled. She hadn't been kissed in five years. His lips moved over hers, his tongue teasing, playing with her mouth. Her body tightened and she brought her hands up against his chest, could feel the beating of his heart beneath her palm. She wanted to bury herself in the warmth of him, the smell of him. She took hold of his shirt with her hands and pulled him closer, gave herself up to the kiss. Her body went into a slow melt, every nerve relaxing as she leaned into him, happily drowning in the moment.

When they finally pulled apart, she stared up at him, stunned by his actions—and shocked at her response. Guilt tweaked at her conscience, resurrecting her sadness and fear over losing Kevin. She could actually feel an ache in her heart. What was she thinking? This couldn't happen; there were so many reasons why she and Erik couldn't get involved, not the least of which was that she was Nora, not Tess.

At the sound of voices at the top of the companionway, Erik stepped back and held out a glass. "Diet Coke."

She shook her head. This night was definitely not something she should be doing. Besides, Tess would have a nightmare to take care of when she came back. *Not that she didn't deserve it.* "I'm sorry, Erik. Now that I think of it, I probably should get going. I'm pretty worried about Danny and it's getting late."

14

———

Nora's phone rang twice more on the ride home, and she ignored it. She was tempted to see if it was Tess calling to say she'd found a way to get off the cruise ship, but there was no way could she answer the phone in front of Erik and risk him overhearing the conversation.

If only she hadn't been so stupid to think going to this party would make her fun again. So much had gone wrong —from drinking too much on an empty stomach, to seeing Keegan ... to kissing Erik.

As soon as they pulled up to her house, she popped her door open. Erik did the same.

"You don't have to walk me up," she said. "It's been great working with you. If you ever need Shopping Goddess services again, be sure to give me a call." She jumped from the car and raced up the walk before he could reply. *That certainly eliminated her concerns about what would happen at the end of the date.*

Once inside the house she leaned against the wall and pushed her hair back with both hands. What was wrong with her? The minute she met someone with potential, someone she wanted to get close to, someone who appeared to want to get close to her, she ran. She and Erik had a connection. There'd been something special between them all night, especially when they kissed.

That had made her want to run all the more.

She shouldn't get involved with Erik anyway. The rational side of her knew that. She was pretending to be someone she wasn't, which had the potential to become a disaster. So, regardless of what was up with her heart, she'd been smart to discourage him. She'd done the best thing for Tess's business, the best thing for her own future.

So why didn't she feel so good about it?

She watched the sitter get safely home cross the street, then punched in speed dial for Tess. A deep male voice answered the phone. She was so taken aback she couldn't speak for a moment. "Ah ... ah, I'm calling Tess Carlisle ..."

"Tess is somewhat ... *indisposed* at the moment," the man said lazily.

Her sister's laughter fluttered in the background.

"You tell Tess that she has five seconds to get herself *un-indisposed* or Keegan and Nora are going to have a chat." She had no patience for romantic dalliances at the moment.

Five seconds later, Tess was on the line. "It was just a joke, Nora. Settle down."

"It's not funny. You've been calling me all night and now you're *indisposed?*" Nora paced from the living room to the dining room and back.

"You weren't returning my calls, so I found something else to do."

"Don't get indignant with me. I didn't get us into this disaster that seems to be quadrupling by the day," Nora said. "So why did you call? Please say you're coming home." She started up the stairs, too wound up to sit down.

"No. But Liza and I came up with another solution. I'm going to call Keegan from here and pretend I'm at home. He won't have any idea I'm on the ship ... and I'll stall him until the cruise is done."

Nora's optimism evaporated. "Somehow, I don't think Liza had anything to do with that idea. What about the garden club speech on Tuesday? I thought you were going to come back for that."

"I tried. We're on open water now—and we'll be on it then. There's no way off the ship unless it's an emergency." She paused. "So ... the thing is ... if you don't do the speech for me, I'll miss out on the opportunity, and think what that will mean."

You'll live with me for the rest of my life. Irritation flared within Nora. "How come I feel completely trapped?" she said.

Tess didn't answer.

Nora waited until her anger faded to resignation. She'd managed to do the initial client assessment with little help from Tess; she could do this, too. She blew out a breath. "Okay. Fine. Whatever. You'd just better prepare me this time so I have plenty of things to say."

"I will, I will! Thank you, Nora. I owe you big-time."

"Yeah, yeah. Just don't blame me if Camille Lamont figures it all out and you lose the account anyway."

"She won't. Half the time she's so caught up in the plot of her latest book, she's, like, walking around with her head in the clouds."

Nora peeked into Danny's room to check on her son. He was sound asleep, sprawled across the bed, uncovered. "I thought writers were supposed to be really observant. Like they notice things about people, understand their feelings, read their emotions ..."

"They do? I never saw her doing that. Do you think she already knows you're not me?" Tess asked in a panicked voice.

"I doubt it." Nora pulled up the Spider-Man quilt to cover Danny. "So, now, back to Keegan," she whispered so as not to wake him.

"Don't worry. I'll take care of Keegan. By the time this is done, he'll be putty in my hands."

———

Erik pulled into the left lane and tapped his fingers on the steering wheel. What had happened tonight? Based on Tess's sudden need to leave the party and her businesslike goodbye, he must have done something wrong.

Maybe he'd moved too fast. He hadn't been planning to kiss her and once he'd started, hadn't planned to make it so ... pleasurable. But she'd kissed him back. Had pulled him closer.

He shook his head; he'd brought Tess to the party to ensure his mother didn't try to foist single women on him. Instead, he'd foisted himself on Tess. She'd come along as a favor to him and, somehow, he'd started treating her like a date. There were just so many things that drew him to her— her internal strength, her love for her son, her quiet confidence, her smile, the way she laughed.

He'd thought she was attracted to him too—until she backed away at warp speed. Still, the way she'd kissed him back said far more about the connection between them than did her quick retreat. Something didn't add up.

He knew he should just let it go—let her go—especially since there was the decent chance he'd be coaching in the future, which meant he'd be gone ten months of the year. Why complicate his life?

At the next stoplight, he turned left and headed back toward the yacht club. He wasn't ready to go home yet—and he wasn't ready to give up on Tess. There was more to her than met the eye, and his mother was the only person he knew who might be able to give him some insight.

Back at the party, he grabbed a beer and joined his mother and sister at a table near the dance floor. Though the crowd had thinned a bit, there were still plenty of dancers.

"You took her home already?" Jenny raised her voice to be heard over the band.

"The babysitter called—her son wasn't feeling well."

"Her son?" his mother asked.

"Yeah. Danny."

His mother's brow furrowed. "Her son?" she repeated.

"Yeah," Erik said louder.

"I didn't know she—"

"She's cute. Are you going to see her again?" Jenny leaned forward onto her elbows and grinned.

He laughed. "We had fun. She's nice."

"Oh! He avoids the question! You'll be seeing her again —I can tell." Jenny clapped her hands.

"Maybe. She's sort of hard to read."

His mother nodded slowly, looked about to speak, then paused before coming out with, "Sometimes Tess can be a little ..." She searched for a word. "... reserved. She's probably just nervous about involving someone new in her —son's—life."

Maybe that's what it was. Maybe she was worried about Danny getting attached to him if it didn't work out. "So she's like that with you?" he asked.

"Yes. Yes, she is. Quieter, more reserved."

"I think it's partly because her husband died five years ago."

His mother's eyes widened. "What did you say?"

"Why don't you tell the band to turn it down?" He raised his voice. "Her husband died. Didn't she tell you that?"

She didn't answer for a second. "She told me—"

"Maybe *that's* why she's so reserved," Jenny offered.

"I asked her to speak at the garden club meeting," his mother said randomly.

"Oh, really?" Jenny winked at Erik. "When is that going to be?"

Leave it to his sister to read something into this.

"Tuesday night. Seven o'clock." His mother absently stirred her drink with a red cocktail straw. "She's still has to get back to me, though."

"Maybe you'd better follow up," Jenny said. 'Tell her how *important* it is that she be there to speak to the ladies." She grinned at Erik, and he rolled his eyes.

Although on second thought, maybe it wasn't such a bad idea. He could drop in at the event and stay way in the back. It would be a chance to see her again, to find out if that mysterious allure he found so enchanting was just a figment of his imagination—or an innate part of her being.

He exchanged a look with his sister. "I think Jen's right, Mom."

"Oh, don't I know it," his mother said with a knowing smile.

15

Nora sat on a sunny bench in Golden Gate Park and watched Danny on the playground while she waited for Margo and Peter to arrive. The two boys had been begging to come to the park and ride the carousel for weeks. And today was promising to be the perfect day for it. She inhaled the scents of spring, leaves bursting open, and flowers coming into bloom—life renewing itself.

From behind her came a whoop, and she turned to spy Peter racing across the lawn toward them, his blond hair glinting in the sun. She stood and went out to meet Margo, strolling more sedately behind him.

"No Ellie today?" Nora asked, looking around for Margo's daughter.

"She's at a friend's. It's just me and Peter," Margo said. "So tell me. I'm dying to hear. How'd the date go?"

Nora lifted one shoulder in a shrug. "I don't know." Her eyes followed the two boys, already running down the path toward the carousel.

"That doesn't sound good. What happened?"

As they followed the boys, Nora recounted the

evening's events—from drinking too much champagne and her encounter with Keegan, to the kiss and her sudden decision to go home. She debated whether to say more, then blurted, "Maybe I need a therapist. There I was, really enjoying this guy and then, suddenly, I was thinking *I can't do this*, and I just wanted to go home. I mean, yeah, there's the whole problem of me pretending to be Tess, but this has nothing to do with that. It's more me and—"

"Fear," Margo said.

"Of course. Tell me something I don't know."

"You've come to the right place. I think I'm going to have to start charging for all the advice l give out," Margo said.

"I'll buy you an ice cream. So really, what do you think is wrong with me? Everyone says I should try again. I think I should try again. I meet a great guy who seems like he might like me." She threw up both hands. "And I run. Am I just out of practice?"

"Hurry up!" Danny yelled from up ahead, and she waved at him.

"You like him a lot?" Margo asked.

"Yeah, I do."

"That's what it is, then. The more you like him, the harder it'll be for you to get involved."

"Margo, honey," Nora said. "You're losing your touch. That doesn't make any sense."

"Think about it. The more you like him, the greater the risk that you could get hurt if it goes bad, so it makes getting involved scarier." She took hold of Nora's arm and made her stop, as if the mere act of walking was too distracting. "If he were some guy you didn't like, you wouldn't care if he rejected you, so no real risk of pain there. But liking Erik means you have to open yourself up to the possibility of a broken heart if he decides down the line he doesn't like you."

Nora blinked. "You're saying this is about me actually being afraid of pain that may never even happen?"

Margo nodded. "You're just trying to protect your heart."

"Mom!" both boys yelled in unison. "Keep moving!"

They starting walking again, faster. "Letting yourself care about someone else opens up the potential—no matter how remote—that he could leave you, walk out—"

"Die," Nora said quietly.

"Right. That's where your fear's coming in. What if you care about this guy and you have to live through the pain you felt with Kevin all over again?"

"So if I don't let my heart go out there—if I pull back—I can't get hurt."

They caught up with the boys at the concession stand, and Margo reached a hand out to tousle Peter's blond hair. "One ride apiece. Does that sound about right, boys?" she asked, teasing.

"Mom!" Peter shouted as Danny groaned loudly.

Nora dug a twenty from her pocket. "I think I'm going to buy a long period of peace. Let's see, how many rides can we get ... Margo, you want that ice cream bar now?"

"Drumstick."

Nora exchanged the money for a handful of carousel tickets and two drumsticks. The boys dashed onto the carousel, weaving their way among the colorful, prancing horses as they argued over which was the most perfect stallion. They clambered astride their mounts, the carousel began to turn, and Nora and Margo moved to a spot in the shade to watch.

"I hate to say it, but you might be right," Nora said

around a mouthful of ice cream. "I don't think I could bear having my heart broken again, no matter how wonderful Erik seems to be. I'm just not sure I can do it again. There's a big part of me that says it's easier not to get involved than to take that risk."

"Then you spend the rest of your life alone. And you've already said you're tired of being lonely."

Nora waved at the boys as the carousel turned past. "Yeah. But what if I get hurt?"

"And what do the nights feel like?"

"I miss Kevin. I want someone."

"I know." Margo put an arm around Nora's shoulders and gave her a squeeze. "That's why you have to think about taking the risk with Erik. You can't run forever."

"Some people never fall in love again."

"And that's a good thing? I don't think so. It's human nature to want someone to love, to want someone to share with, to want someone to just *have.* Don't bury that part of you. Not when you've actually met someone you connect with."

Margo was right. Deep inside, Nora knew it. But when she got scared, like last night with Erik, it just seemed easier to be alone. Until she was alone again. And then she hated it.

"Even if I wasn't scared, there's the whole problem of Erik thinking I'm Tess. I'm lying to him. In a big way."

Margo licked the ice cream dripping down the side of her cone. "If you decide to go for it, you have to tell him the truth."

Nora drew a breath and exhaled. "I can't even consider it until after the garden club speech."

"I thought Tess was coming back for that."

"Can't get off the ship."

Margo's face scrunched up in disbelief. "So she wants you to do it?"

"Basically."

"Hey, Mom! Look at this—no feet!"

As the carousel rounded past them, Danny stuck his legs out from each side of his horse. Both women waved.

"Are you going to do it?" Margo asked.

"If I want Tess to keep her client—and I do—if I want Tess to someday move out of my house—and I do—I don't think I have a choice. I just have to call Camille and let her know that I'll be there."

"You want me to go with you?" Margo asked.

"What? For moral support?"

"Yeah. I could be your assistant. Hand out business cards." Margo made a little bow.

"You'd do that?"

"That's what friends are for."

Nora opened her arms and gave her friend a hug. "Thanks. I'd love to have a face I trust in the audience."

"It's done, then. Seven o'clock Tuesday night."

————

Nora pushed through the doors into the garden club meeting room and wondered, for about the fiftieth time in three days, how she had gotten herself into this nightmare. It had to be payback from all the times she'd dragged Tess into messes when they were kids.

At least Keegan was out of the picture for the time being. Neither of them had heard from him since Tess gave him a call, so whatever she said must have been enough to settle him down. How long he would stay settled was anyone's guess.

Tess had tried to help her prepare for the speech as best as she could in between dropped calls. Finally, exasperated, she told Nora to go to the websites for *Vogue*, *Women's Wear Daily*, and *Elle*. "Maybe you should just go to the library and page through a bunch of the actual magazines," she said. "That way you'll be able to see the ads, too. Some of the ads are as amazing as the photo spreads. And make sure you check out the Collections Issues. Those'll give you a good idea of the season's upcoming fashions."

Nora had hung up feeling more than a little overwhelmed. After doing multiple Internet searches to gather basic information about personal shopping, she convinced Margo to go to the library with her the next night and look at high fashion magazines. By the time they'd finished their fashion research, they were in agreement that, while some of it was beautiful, some of it was the ugliest, most impractical clothing they'd ever seen. Maybe high fashion was like *The Emperor's New Clothes*. No one wanted to admit that some of it was hideous.

Well, she would. She'd shout it from the rooftops.

Just not tonight.

Tonight, she would say what she needed to say to get this presentation behind her and, if she was lucky, get out of building in time to catch the tail end of Danny's soccer game. It boggled her mind that she was about to give a speech about fashion. Even worse, she was skipping her son's game to do it. A feeling akin to panic hit her in the chest and she took a breath to calm herself.

She could do this. And when she was done, she would never do anything like it again.

She stood in the back with Margo and let her gaze travel over the hundred or so women in the room. "There's a lot more people here than I thought there'd be," she whispered.

"Ten women or ten thousand," Margo said reassuringly, "doesn't make a difference." She shifted the stack of business cards from one hand to the other, revealing her own nervousness, despite her strong words.

"Easy for you to say. You're not the *fashion expert*."

They'd purposely arrived with only fifteen minutes to spare in order to minimize interaction time, particularly with Camille Lamont, the one person who could blow this charade out of the water if she ever got truly observant.

Nora spotted Camille across the room and went over to say hello. The woman was wearing a three-plaid outfit like one that had been featured in a recent issue of *Vogue*. Nora suppressed a shudder. It was such a train wreck. "What an exquisite ensemble," she said.

"I should hope you think so." Camille patted her on the arm. "You helped me pick it out."

Nora laughed, tinkle tinkle. *Get me the hell out of here.* "Are we almost ready to start?"

"Yes, I was beginning to get a bit nervous. It's not like you to cut the time so close." Camille introduced her to the current club president, who promptly swept her away to the front of the room.

"As we discussed on the phone," the woman said, "you'll talk for twenty minutes, take questions, and then we'll socialize for the rest of the meeting. You can mingle among the group at that time and give personalized answers to individual questions."

Mingle? Personalized answers? Her shoulders tightened as her stress level rose. She'd rather concentrate on handing out business cards and encouraging people to call in a week or so—when the real Tess was back. She forced her mouth into a smile and nodded. "Sounds great."

Camille went to the microphone. "Welcome everyone.

This month, we're taking a quick detour from making beautiful gardens to making the rest of our lives beautiful. To that end, I asked Tess Carlisle to join us. Tess is a personal shopper—in fact, she's my personal shopper—and she really knows colors, styles, fashions, and how to pull together a look that is distinctly your own ..."

Nora regarded her own outfit, taken directly from Tess's closet. She did look great, even if this bra of Tess's felt like it was pushing her right up and out of her white V-necked blouse, and her feet were so badly squashed in Tess's shoes her toes were falling asleep. She tried to wiggle her toes to get the blood circulating again. The thought burst into her head that lack of circulation could lead to gangrene. Omigod, that was something Tess would say. She was turning into her sister.

Gradually her brain registered that everyone was clapping. Nora's eyes darted left and right, then came to rest on Camille, who was smiling and motioning her forward. How had she missed her own introduction? Nora smiled as though she had been paying complete attention and stepped to the podium, almost dropping the notecards she'd made late last night.

"Thank you for having me," she said into the microphone. She spotted Margo hovering at the back of the room near the door, and her self-confidence rose. "Tonight I'm going to discuss the concept of: *you are what you wear.* Everything you put on, from the top of your head to the tips of your toes is making a statement about you—and not just a fashion statement. Clothes talk. So the question is, what are yours saying?"

The women's faces showed their interest. Nora glanced at Margo and was pleased to see she was rubbing her nose, a signal they had set up in advance to let Nora know everything was going well. As long as Margo didn't scratch her head, which meant *abandon ship*, everything would be all right. Nora began to relax. She slid easily into the rest of her prepared speech and finished up at just about the twenty-minute point. "Are there any questions?" she asked enthusiastically. She held her breath, hoping she'd covered anything anyone would ever want to know. Her toes throbbed in her pointed shoes.

After a beat with no response, a tentative hand went up in the back. "What's the most interesting thing you've had to buy for someone?"

Oh shit. Why hadn't she paid better attention when her sister was regaling her with her client tales? "Oh, well—I guess maybe the time I had to ... there are so many different situations," she blabbered, frantically trying to think of *any* story Tess told her. Something had to come to mind ... anything. "I once had to ... buy anniversary gifts for a husband and wife to give each other—and neither knew the other was using my help. That was pretty interesting." That was an out-and-out fabrication—and a stupid one at that. She had better remember to tell Tess this story just in case anyone ever asked about it.

The ladies tittered, and Nora gave herself a mental pat on the back. She might make it through this thing in one piece after all. "Any other questions?"

A plump, middle-aged woman stood. "What statement is my outfit making about me?"

Nora blinked. *Maybe that you blindly follow fashion without ever bothering to see if it suits you.* "Um, well, it very much shows ... that you have an eye for sophistication and a zest for embracing whatever comes your way." *What was she saying?* "It's a ... style that says you know who you are and aren't afraid to show it."

The ladies applauded. Another woman waved her hand and stood. "What statement do I make?"

Margo was gently scratching her head. Nora tried not to panic; there was no way she could make up something about every woman's outfit in the room. She looked at the questioner and thought, *you wouldn't catch me dead in those clothes.* "Your style is definitely one to ... live in." Her brain stopped and she tried to give it a jump-start. *Something else. Say something else.* "I think it shows that you're comfortable with who you are and live life with a ... casual chicness."

16

CASUAL CHICNESS? ERIK CROSSED HIS ARMS OVER HIS chest and leaned against the doorjamb. That phrase sure was popping up a lot lately. Just for fun, he was tempted to raise his hand and ask her to define the term, but decided she might not find the question amusing.

Tess had invaded his thoughts a lot since Saturday—too much, in fact. And that wasn't a good thing. He had patients to see, work to do, a clinic to plan, a coaching job to chase down ... Instead, he kept getting distracted by daydreams of kissing her and holding her and stripping her clothes off—

Not a good train of thought. He dragged his attention back to the podium and admired Tess's ability to come up with something flattering to say no matter how ridiculously these women were dressed.

Another hand waved. "I've heard corsets are coming back. What do you think of that?"

"So much for liberated women," he muttered.

The cute blond woman a few feet to his right glanced his way, then began to vigorously scratch her head like she had lice. He slid out the door and went out into the hall to wait for the program to end.

———

Nora choked off a laugh. *Corsets? What modern woman would even consider wearing a corset?* "To each their own. I personally won't be wearing one, but there are those who will follow the fashion."

Camille came to the podium and leaned toward the microphone. "Let's break here and have some refreshments. Tess will be mingling, so there'll still be time to ask any other questions."

Nora smiled at the audience. "I have business cards if anyone would like one. I'll leave a stack up here on the front table—and my assistant has some as well."

Margo waved a hand in the air, then began to pass out cards.

As the women applauded, Nora stepped from the podium, stopping briefly to talk to Camille and the garden club president. "I'm going to run to the ladies' room," she said. "Be right back."

As she passed Margo, she whispered, "Let's go."

Once out of the meeting room, she headed for the front door, not even bothering to see if Margo was following. She couldn't take any more questions. She was one answer away from making Tess sound like she didn't know what she was talking about. Better to escape and have Tess make an apology later if anyone noticed she was missing. But odds were good that, with more than a hundred women milling around in there, no one would notice her absence.

Besides, she had to get out of these shoes before her toes required physical therapy. She peeked at her watch. If she hurried, she'd be able to catch the second half of Danny's game.

"Hey, wait up!" Margo jogged up beside her.

"Sorry." Nora pulled her shoes off and wiggled her toes. Who cared if her feet were filthy by the time she got to the car? At least they wouldn't hurt. "My feet are killing me," she said.

"Erik Morgan's here," Margo replied.

Nora's heart skipped a beat. "What? Where?"

"Didn't you see him standing in the doorway off to my left?"

"No. He couldn't have been there the whole time, I would have noticed. He's not a garden club member, is he?"

Margo snorted. "Unlikely. My guess is he came to see you. Go back inside."

"No way." Nora opened the front passenger door of Tess's car. "If the guy wanted to see me, he would call. He wouldn't go to a garden club meeting."

"He probably doesn't know what to think. That's why he's here tonight."

Nora hesitated. "I promised Danny I'd be at his game."

"You also said you weren't going to keep running away."

"I said I'd think about it—and I'm still thinking." She gave Margo a hug. "Thanks for coming. Being able to see you in the audience made this so much easier." She climbed into the passenger's seat and shut the door, feeling a twinge of guilt as Margo walked away shaking her head.

Was Margo right? Should she go back inside? The thought of seeing Erik again gave her butterflies—good ones. But, oh, what would she say? It was all too much to contemplate when she already had a plan for tonight.

She gave her head a shake. Better to stick to the plan— get out of these clothes and get over to Danny's game.

Thank God she was parked between an SUV and a minivan so she had some privacy to change into something more comfortable.

She tossed Tess's heels onto the floor and reached behind her back to unclasp her bra. How did Tess stand these push-up underwires? She'd only worn this one because of the cut of her blouse. And frankly, it wasn't worth the discomfort. Tess would probably be one of those women who got a corset if they really did come back in style. She leaned over the seat to grab her jeans and casual shirt from the back, then began to peel off her clothes.

———

Erik followed Tess out into the parking lot. She sure hadn't stuck around long to answer questions. The woman with the lice had chased her down and the two crossed the lot together, Tess flipping off her shoes and walking most of the way barefoot. Yeah, he knew there was more to this woman than met the eye.

He waited a moment for the blond to leave, then started toward Tess's car. Itchy woman passed him going the other way. "Lovely night for romance, isn't it?" she asked with a grin.

He ignored her. Apparently she was as off-balance as she was infested. As he neared Tess's car, he saw her feet appear on the dashboard, then disappear again. What the hell? Was she okay? He tapped on the side window just as she pulled her bra out of the sleeve of her shirt.

She jerked her head around to look at him through the closed window and her mouth formed a shocked circle. He winced.

Changing clothes.

He knew this. Women changed clothes in cars all the time. They could change clothes without taking other clothes off. They were born with some sort of skill that way. He gave a self-conscious wave and stepped back from the car. "Great way to make an impression," he muttered to himself. "Surprise her when she's taking off her underwear."

A minute later, Tess was out of the car, casually dressed, slightly breathless, her dark hair mussed around her face—probably from pulling shirts over her head. *And from taking off her bra.* He thought about her breasts, braless under that T-shirt, and willed his eyes not to look. His mind swerved hack to where it had been earlier, stripping her clothes off, and it was all he could do not to pull her into his arms and kiss her.

"So ... you belong to the garden club?" she asked.

He couldn't tell if she was joking or irritated. "No, just thought I'd stop by. Sorry about the ... interruption," he said with an apologetic smile.

"Don't worry about it. Did you, um, need something?"

She seemed rushed. That fact, combined with the Herculean effort he was making to keep his eyes from straying to her breasts and his mind from undressing her, was scrambling his brain. "Ah, ah, yeah. I was just wondering if you'd eaten yet. Do you want to get something? To eat, I mean?"

"I haven't, but—" She made a vague gesture with one hand. "I can't. I'm trying to get to Danny's soccer game before it ends."

He shoved his hands in the back pockets of his khakis and tried to think of something to say. For an Olympic skier who'd given countless impromptu interviews, he was sure failing tonight. Problem was, he wasn't into rejection—who was, actually?—and sensed she was about to hand him an even bigger rejection than she'd delivered Saturday.

Suddenly she smiled and said, "Um, maybe another night," and raised her hazel eyes to his.

His mood soared. Maybe this wouldn't be a blow-off after all. He grinned back. "Yeah. Okay. I'll call you."

As she headed around the front of the car toward the driver's door, his brain finally engaged. "I have an idea," he said, "how about you and Danny going skiing with me this weekend?"

She looked at him, her expression totally unreadable, and he knew she was thinking about Danny getting hurt. She opened her mouth.

"Danny would like it," he said before she got a word out.

She nodded. "I know he would. Where would we go?"

He knew she was making a big effort to control her over-protectiveness and give her son some freedom. "We could run up to Squaw Valley. It's only four hours away ... spend the weekend."

She caught her lip between her teeth, and he remembered what it had been like to kiss those lips.

"I can't really afford—"

"My treat," he said. "Let me take the two of you."

She took so long to answer, he was stunned when she suddenly said, "Okay. Yes. Thank you."

He blinked. "Okay." *Okay. She'd said okay.* "Great. I'll pull together the details and give you a call."

They grinned at each other across the car. Then Tess said, "Well, I'd better get to the game before it ends." And as she drove away, he walked across the parking lot kicking at the loose stones on the blacktop like a kid.

17

————

ERIK GRABBED A CUP OF COFFEE IN THE HOSPITAL cafeteria and headed to his favorite corner table to think over the phone conversation he'd just finished with USSA. Things were moving forward nicely; he was flying out next week to talk with them in more detail.

He'd rather have gone out this week, would like to put some closure on the whole thing one way or another, but he had surgeries and other appointments scheduled that couldn't easily be changed on such short notice.

As he crossed the cafeteria, he realized someone was already at *his* table doing paperwork. The woman moved her head and for a moment he was taken aback. *Tess.* His heart rate sped up, even though his mind logically told him this was Nora, not Tess.

He stopped. Here was the sister of the woman who seemed to be taking over his thoughts. Couldn't hurt to say hello. He strolled over to where Nora was sitting and bent down to ask, "Need any advice with a patient's treatment?

————

Startled, Nora jerked her head up to see Erik Morgan holding a cup of steaming coffee.

"Mind if I join you?" he asked.

Her thoughts froze and her mouth moved, but no words came out. Unbelievable. She'd just spent the better half of an hour debating whether she and Danny should really go away for a ski weekend with this man. And now, here he was. Adorable as ever.

Margo would say her mental debate was nothing more than preparation for running away again. But it really was more complicated than that. Because, if she didn't run, she would have to keep lying about who she was—and, surely, that couldn't be good for any relationship.

"Sure," she finally croaked out. "Have a seat."

She couldn't keep going like this. Before they knew it, Tess would be home and the problems would be compounded. If she'd never agreed to switch places, none of this would have happened. Then again, if she'd never agreed to switch places, she would never have gone out with Erik.

Because he thought Nora was boring.

Well, okay, maybe not boring. But certainly not worthy of his attentions.

God only knew what his response would be when he learned the woman he thought was Tess was really Nora, and this had all been just fun, tinkle tinkle.

Which brought her to the fundamental question—did she want to go out with Erik again?

He slid into the opposite chair. "Thanks for letting Tess know I couldn't make it shopping last week."

She nodded. Was his appearance here a sign? Did it mean she should tell him the truth? Did it mean she should definitely go skiing with him, start a relationship? Maybe it was a sign that she should leap to her feet, scream, *Fire!* and race out of the building.

"No problem," she managed to say. Omigod, all she could come up with was *no problem?* No wonder Erik thought Nora was dull. "But she said you caught up with her after all." That sounded a little better.

She looked at him, met his eyes, started to sink into their blue depths, and thought, *yeah, I would like to see him again.* An inkling of panic ripped through her, and she shoved the feeling away as hard and fast as she could.

"We're going skiing this weekend," he said.

"She mentioned that. I think she's really looking forward to it."

"She is? That's great." He sipped his coffee. "She seemed apprehensive when I first brought it up."

Nora pressed her lips together. "She gets protective because, well, she lost her husband, so she …"

"Worries about losing her son, too. I know. But the runs we'd be on with Danny would be pretty gentle."

Silence fell between them, stretched out so long it felt awkward. Nora searched for something to say. "We used to ski when we were younger. Haven't gone in a long time, though …"

He leaned toward her, and she caught a whiff of his aftershave and was sucked back into the memory of kissing him on the boat at his mother's party. She wrenched her thoughts back to the present.

"Why don't you come with us, too," he was saying. "I rented a two-bedroom condo, so there's plenty of room. Sleeps six."

She started shaking her head. "Oh, I don't know—" She took a drink of her cold coffee and almost choked. "Actually

I already have plans this weekend." *To go skiing with you.* "But thanks, really, for asking."

"Okay, but if you change your mind, just tell Tess. Even if it's the last minute." He set his elbows on the table and narrowed his eyes. "I'm going to have to see you and Tess side by side so I can try to tell the difference. Right now, you've really got me stumped."

She let out a light laugh. *Not going to happen.*

"Hey, before I forget," he said. "Tess asked about the sports medicine rehab center the hospital's opening. Said you might be interested in a job."

She sat back in her chair, stunned, a shy smile slipping onto her face. She thought this conversation had gotten lost the other night in all the discussion about Nora being dull. She couldn't believe he even remembered, let alone was following up on it. "Yes, actually, I would be."

"The director position was posted Monday. We want to get someone on board right away to help with purchasing and design decisions. You should apply." He smiled and she melted.

"For the directorship?" *He thought she could run the place?*

"You'd be good at it. A couple of us were already discussing possible candidates and your name came up more than once."

"It did?" Her voice pitched so high she almost squeaked. *Oh, how professional ... and self-confident.* She took another drink of her ice-cold coffee just to have something to do.

"I don't know how soon interviews will be scheduled, but it never hurts to get a jump on it." He pushed his chair back and stood. "Say hi to Tess for me. And if you change your mind about coming along this weekend, there's plenty of room."

As he walked away, Nora stared at his back—his broad, strong back—and couldn't help being touched by his thoughtfulness. Ever since Saturday, thoughts off him had been popping into her mind when she least expected it; suddenly she could see him smiling at her, hear his laughter, *feel his kiss.*

And then she would remember Kevin. And what they had together. And how easy it had been after knowing him all those years. She knew his face, his touch, how to touch him, what he loved, his hopes, his dreams ... his soul. *As he knew her.*

She wanted that easy understanding with someone again, that comfort that came with time spent together. That place she'd already found with Kevin.

Tears pricked at the back of her eyes. She knew she would never find any of that again unless she went out there and tried, unless she forced herself past the fear of getting hurt, past the fear of feeling loss again.

But this thing with Erik, this attraction ... she hadn't even realized it was happening. And now she cared for him more than she knew was safe. Not only was her heart out there, but she was hiding the truth from him. He didn't know who she really was, and there was no telling how he would react when he found out he'd been lied to.

She felt a queasy flutter of fear.

———

Nora had hardly stepped into the house before the sitter was out the door, babbling something about needing to get to a special band sign-up meeting. She kicked off her shoes and went over to sit beside Danny on the living room floor, a tall Lego tower rising up from the rug in front of him.

"How's my favorite boy?" She pulled him close and kissed his head.

"Good. Watch out for my tower, Mom."

"Anything exciting happen at school today?"

"A guy came to our class." He sorted through the Legos strewn across the floor until he found a rectangular blue piece.

"A guy. What kind of guy?"

"A fireman. We talked about stop, drop and roll."

"In case of a fire, huh? That's good." She nodded.

"I'm gonna be a fireman when I grow up." He concentrated on putting more Legos on his foot-tall stack.

Amazing how every kid wanted to be a fireman at some point in their lives. "That'll be exciting." After watching him add to the tower a while longer, Nora stood. "Okay, well, I think I'll go rustle us up some dinner."

"He was really nice."

Oh, no.

"He said he doesn't have a wife. But he wants one someday."

"He does, huh?"

Danny looked up at her, his face hopeful. "Maybe you could go to the fire station and say *hi*. I told him I would tell you that."

She sat cross-legged beside him again. "Honey, I would give the world for you to have a dad." *I would give the world to love a man who would be your dad.* "But things like this can't be forced. You just can't go out and find someone to be your dad. One of these days, I'm going to meet someone ..." Anger welled up inside her, then quickly dissipated into sadness as tears sprang to her eyes. "Someday I'll meet someone and we'll feel this connection, and before you know it we'll be in love and getting married and you'll have a dad." She lifted him into her lap and kissed the top of his head.

"Just like that," Danny said.

"Yeah. Just like that."

"Okay."

She drew a long, slow breath. "Ashley's coming over tonight to watch you for a while. It's coffee group night."

"Okay." He grinned at her and added some pieces to his tower. "Can we have ice cream later?"

"You bet. I got some cones, too—they're in the cupboard." She pushed herself to her feet and went into the kitchen and stared into the refrigerator without seeing anything.

———

Nora pulled open the door to the bistro and stepped inside, exhaling softly as she felt herself begin to relax. Between the décor, the menu, and the playlist, Margo had managed to create a comfortable, harried-free ambience, one that enveloped patrons with warmth. It was the perfect atmosphere for their group meetings. And after the week she'd had, she really needed the support of friends.

Margo came toward her, mug in hand. "You're early."

"There's no soup." Nora waved a hand at the chalkboard where specials-of-the-day were usually listed.

"We sold out of everything. So ... you want soup tonight?" Margo looked at her quizzically.

"No, no. I ... don't know what I want."

"How about your usual chai latte for starters?"

As soon as the drink was made, Margo linked her arm

through Nora's and headed toward the back. "Come on, let's go into the annex. We've got a little time before everyone else shows up."

Nora dropped into a comfy rattan chair and sipped her chai while Margo lit several candles around the room.

"Okay, what's going on," Margo said as she took the seat opposite. "Erik Morgan?"

"No. Yes." Nora tried to focus her thoughts. "Sort of. He's just one piece of the puzzle that my life has become. Danny and I are going away skiing with him this weekend—and he thinks I'm my sister. Keegan wants his money back from Tess—and she's off on a cruise and won't come back, but he doesn't know it. Danny wants a dad—and I think any man would do. Erik told me—Nora—to apply for the job as director of the new sports medicine rehab center. And—" Her voice dropped. "He does something to me—" She touched her chest above her heart. "—here. And, it's scaring me."

18

———

"You're afraid? So ... what's the problem?" Margo asked.

Despite herself, Nora laughed. "Yeah, what am I so worried about?"

Margo sat quietly for a minute. She took a long drink from her mug.

"What?" Nora asked. "I can almost see your mind working in there."

"I'm thinking about what we talked about on Sunday. About fear ... and your heart."

"I've thought about it, too."

"I know you want Tess to get it together and move out. And I know you want this new job. And I know Keegan could blow it all if Tess doesn't pay back his money." Margo lifted her mug and took another sip. "But, really, I think that's all secondary."

"Secondary? It's turned my life into chaos. If something doesn't give pretty soon, I'm going to have to start taking antacids. Or Valium. Or hemlock. And if that doesn't work, I'm going to need a long vacation—which I can't afford because I'm supporting my sister who can't afford to move out."

Margo nodded knowingly. "Secondary. The biggest issue I see in your life is that you're falling for Erik."

"Don't you think that other stuff is more import—"

"No. That's all just life. Yours may be a bit more complicated than most right now, but ... you know, life comes, it goes. These problems, too, shall pass." She sipped her coffee. "But, Nora, this thing with Erik is ..." Her voice took on a passionate edge. "*It's what living is about.*" Margo glanced away. "When my marriage broke up, I was devastated. And when I met Robert, well, everything was all wrong for me to get involved with him. He was trying to find a job, the bistro was struggling, then Peter was diagnosed with diabetes ..." She looked at Nora. "That was all *just life.*"

"In other words, deal with it."

"I might not put it quite so bluntly, but, yeah. I'm trying to figure out a way to say this that makes sense. Life is all the shit that happens. But living is ... stepping deeper into life, taking risks, allowing yourself to feel, to love, to care beyond the bandages you've wrapped around your heart." She leaned forward. "Because, really, how much can any part of you feel when every part of you is wrapped in bandages?"

"But it protects against the pain."

"And it blocks the pleasure, too. You know how when you hurt yourself, the muscles tighten up around the injury to protect it?"

Nora nodded.

"I really think that's what happens with broken hearts, too. Metaphorically speaking, that is. It's like the muscles tighten up to protect the heart from more pain, and the wound never heals. The only way out is to let those muscles relax. Take the bandages off … and open yourself up again."

"But what about Kevin?" Nora whispered. "I loved him. Really loved him. How many times in one life do you get that kind of love?"

Margo's eyes filled with understanding. "You're looking at it all wrong. You'll never duplicate the love you had with Kevin. *Because no two people are the same.*" She shook her head. "The love you feel for one person can't possibly be the same as the love you feel for another. And that's okay. It doesn't mean one is any better or worse than the other. *They're just different.*" She drew a breath and exhaled. "No one ever said you have to stop loving Kevin. Why would you? He was your husband, the father of your child."

Tears bit at Nora's eyes and she wiped a hand across her lids. "But if I don't stop loving him, then how—"

"Oh, Nora. I said this once before, you don't just need to move on, you need to let go—of your anger, of your guilt, of your regrets … of Kevin. I'm not saying you have to stop loving him. You just need to accept that it's okay to let go, that he won't be angry or hurt that you fell in love with someone else. You need to accept that, though life with him was wonderful, it was in the past." She teared up and her mouth curved up in a sheepish grin. "See, I'm going to cry now. I'm no expert, but I do know this—letting go doesn't mean you didn't love him, won't always love him. But it's the only way you can give yourself a future that involves loving someone else."

Nora looked down, both hands wrapped tight around her mug. "But what if I risk again and it doesn't work, or the next guy dies, or—"

"There are no guarantees with anything, except this. Life is better well-lived. You can float along, never venturing much beyond your security zone, and you'll never have to worry about being hurt—not much anyway. But you'll also never feel the great highs that make life so absolutely grand."

"Nothing ventured, nothing gained."

"Yeah, I guess I could have skipped all that other stuff and just said those four words." Margo looked up at the ceiling for a moment. "From my own experience, all I can say is this ... if you are lucky enough to find someone who makes you laugh and brings you joy, and for whom you do the same ... someone with whom you have things in common, with whom you feel contentment when you're together ..." She choked up. "God, now I really am crying. Then you should grab that person. Because it's a gift. A chance to—"

"Hey, ladies!" Selena danced into the room and plopped onto the sofa next to Margo. She looked from one to the other. "Let's see. Red eyes, sad expressions. You're telling jokes in here, right?"

They both laughed.

"We're talking about Kevin," Nora said. "And Erik." She didn't want to go over the whole thing again, needed some time to digest everything Margo had said.

"You know I'm not big on getting into serious relationships." Selena drummed her fingers on the armrest. "But what's right for me isn't necessarily right for you. Oh, and by the way, I already had a ton of coffee today—can you tell? Anyway, I'll give you my piece of unsolicited advice because ... well, because I happen to be here right now ... and I'm wired." She gave a delighted chuckle. "Life is short. God isn't up there with a stopwatch saying, *Nora has more grieving to do.* And Kevin isn't flying through heaven saying, *She'd better not be making it with another guy.* They both have plenty of other things keeping them busy."

She pushed her fingers through her curly hair. "If you could somehow ask Kevin whether he wanted you to stay alone the rest of your life because of him, I will guarantee—without ever having known the man—that he would say *no.* I promise you, if he was half the man you've said he was, he would want you to fall in love again. *He would want you to be happy.* And he wouldn't want you down here comparing every other guy to him and saying they come up short."

She sat back and took a drink from her espresso cup. "And that's all I have to say on that topic—for at least the next ten seconds."

Margo and Nora exchanged an amused look. "I just have one comment," Nora said, laughing. "Please tell me that's decaf."

———

Nora trudged upstairs, bone weary despite the caffeine she'd had. Her conversation with Margo kept replaying in her mind. She didn't know if she had it in her to try again—at least not yet, not with Erik. What if it didn't work and all she got was more pain?

And what if she didn't try and spent the rest of her life in regret?

She stepped into her bedroom and let her gaze roam. This was the room she had shared with the man she loved. She ran a hand over the blue and tan striped comforter she had picked up on sale years ago and remembered how happy she had been to put it across their bed. Moving slowly, she changed into a comfy pair of gray knit pajamas, then dragged a box from the top shelf in her closet and set it on the bed. She hadn't gone through this stuff in a long time —too many memories.

She lifted the top off the box and sat there for a minute before reaching inside to pull out an old, worn, navy blue polo shirt. It had been Kevin's favorite; he'd refused to throw it away no matter how beat up it got. Used to joke that everyone else bought shirts that were enzyme-washed to make them look old, but he had the real thing.

She pressed the shirt to her face, tried to find the scent of him in it, but after five years it was gone.

"Oh, Kev, everything would be so much easier if you hadn't died." Tears filled her eyes and her voice broke. "It'd be you and me sitting on the front stoop watching our children ride their bikes. You and me who would have known each other for all those years already. I wouldn't be out in the world meeting some new guy and kissing him and messing it all up."

She took Kevin's robe from the box, heavy white terrycloth. She never knew exactly why she'd kept it—he only wore it when her parents came to visit. And then he'd rip it off when they were alone in their room and he would kiss her passionately and threaten to make boisterous love to her with her parents down the hall. They'd laugh like teenagers who were getting away with something. And then they'd make love quietly, every breath soft and tender.

She'd kept a pair of his jeans just because. Because she loved his legs, big and muscular, and his tight butt, and how well he fit those jeans. She used to wrap her arms around him and shove her hands in his back pockets and pull him close. The pain hit and she squeezed her eyes shut, sucked in a breath through clenched teeth and waited for it to ease, as she knew it would.

Then she opened her eyes and took his watch from the

box, a sport watch, the kind with a timer in it and a stopwatch, the battery long since dead. It hadn't been expensive, but it had been his and he'd liked it and she just hadn't been able to give it away.

And there was all that other stuff she'd saved. The last issue of *Sports Illustrated* that had arrived when his subscription ran out, the ancient, dog-eared paperback dictionary he kept on his nightstand so he could look up words he didn't know when he was reading in bed at night, the ticket stubs to the last movie they'd seen together.

She pushed around the little things, then refolded the jeans and the robe and the shirt and shoved them into the box and put the lid back on. Then she went to her jewelry box and took out his wedding ring, and held it in the palm of her hand, just felt the weight of it. She slipped her own gold band onto her finger. It felt cool next to her skin ... and odd. So many years had gone by since she'd worn this ring. So many years and yet, it didn't feel like much time had passed at all.

She sat on the edge of the bed, filled with melancholy and longing and regret. For things she wished she'd said to Kevin or not said, for things she wished she'd done or not done, for things she wished she could take back, do over, try again. She looked at her hand a long time before finally sliding the ring off and putting it away.

What was past, was past. All the wishes in the world wouldn't bring it back. Theirs had been a good marriage, she knew that. And somewhere deep inside, she knew that Kevin, if he could be here now, would probably get angry and say, *What matters is that we were happy.* She could almost hear what he would say next—go *find that again.*

The ache returned, filled her heart, and she lay her head

on the box and let the tears flow. Margo was probably right. It was time to let go.

"Hey, Kev," she said quietly. "I kind of figured something out tonight. It's not just about getting Tess moved out ... and it's not just about Danny getting a new dad ... and it's not just about me being more challenged in my job." She wiped her nose with the back of her hand. "I *can't live* without loving someone, Kevin. I thought I could, but I can't."

She stopped crying and sat up, hands on her knees. "I have to say goodbye, Kev, because I can't fathom living the rest of my life like this. I'll always love you ... but I've got to take a shot at loving someone else."

After a few minutes, she picked up the box and returned it to the closet shelf. The phone rang and she swiped it on. Tess greeted her from the other end. "What's happening? You haven't called me in two days," she said accusingly.

Nora sighed.

"Are you okay?"

"Just missing Kevin."

"Oh, honey—"

"No, it's not so bad. I've come to realize something. I'll always love him. I'll never forget him. But I can love again." Her voice cracked. "It won't be the same—it'll be a different man, a different time. But I don't want it to be the same. That was Kevin. This will be someone else. There's no way it can be the same, but that doesn't mean it can't be just as wonderful."

"Nora—"

She could hear the smile in Tess's voice. "Yeah, I know. It's taken me a long time to get here."

"Nora—"

"Mind you, I'm only going to stick my toe in the water and see how it feels."

"Nora!"

"What?"

"I think Erik Morgan might be one lucky guy."

"Yeah, well, we'll see what happens. I'm going to tell him the truth this weekend. Come hell or high water, he's got to know who I really am," Nora said into the phone to Tess. She zipped her black suitcase shut and hoisted it to the floor beside her bed. "My stomach's already in knots and we haven't even begun the trip."

"Text me as soon as it's a done deal, because I'm going to have to tell Camille," Tess said. "And I'm not savoring doing this via cell phone from Alaska."

Nora snorted. "I'm not exactly savoring telling Erik, either."

"Do you have a plan?"

"Yeah, wait for what seems like an opportune moment."

Tess let out a laugh. "Like when he calls you Tess, and Danny tells him he's got your name wrong?"

Nora sat abruptly on the edge of her bed. "I know. I've been worried about that happening ever since Erik came to pick me up for his mother's party."

"If Danny lets the cat out of the bag, it could be a nice segue to baring your soul."

"Yeah, except I don't think it's the best idea to have this unveiling discussion in front of my son. Danny doesn't know I'm pretending to be you. In his eyes I'll just be a liar. Not exactly the best role model."

"I'll keep my fingers crossed."

"Thanks. Hopefully Danny won't out me before I get a chance to tell Erik. But if it happens, I'll deal. That's the price of dishonesty, I guess." Nora carried her suitcase downstairs and set it next to Danny's smaller one in the living room. The thought of telling Erik that she'd been pretending to be Tess was making her stomach quake and she could feel the beginning of a headache. "Any more word from Keegan?" she asked. "I'm starting to feel like something's going to explode when we least expect it."

"No, no. He's fine. He called me again, and I reiterated that I'm out of town for a client and won't be back for a week—"

"Great, more lies. And what happens in a week when he wants the cruise paperwork or his money, and all you have are souvenirs from Alaska to give him?" Nora peeked out the window to see if Erik had arrived yet.

"Stop worrying. I know how to handle Keegan. You just go on your ski trip and make sure that, when you're done, you haven't lost your bachelor next door."

19

———————

EARLY THE NEXT MORNING, DECKED OUT IN SKI GEAR, Nora drew a breath of fresh air and looked up at Squaw Mountain, snow-covered and dotted with skiers. Temperatures were in the mid 50s, the sky a clear, clean blue.

"We really couldn't have picked a better time to teach Danny how to ski," Erik said.

Nora nodded. Last night she'd vowed she wouldn't let on how apprehensive she was about Danny starting to ski so young. She was determined to dump *Nora the apple* and bring back *Nora the orange.* But already it was feeling easier said than done and the day was still young.

Erik handed her a set of ski poles. "Since you haven't skied in fifteen years you might as well follow along as I teach Danny, because skis have changed—and so has technique."

"I'm a beginner again?"

"Close." Erik patted Danny on top of the head. "You ready, bud?"

Danny nodded, his expression open and full of contagious excitement.

"He's a good kid," Erik said to Nora. "You've done well."

His compliment touched her heart.

Erik stomped his skis up and down on the ground and grinned, his own enthusiasm obvious. "Now, you two, here's how you stand on skis. I want you to make French fries with them."

"Hey, Mom, just like Ronald's wife."

Erik caught her eye. "I'm starting to think there was more to this thing with Ronald McDonald than you're letting on."

She laughed. "Oh, yeah. A lot more. I was using him for apple pies and hot fudge sundaes."

He grinned and turned back to Danny. "Okay, line your skis up even with each other—flat on the ground. Like this," he said, demonstrating. "Two crispy French fries in a row. Then flex—that means bend—at your ankles, your knees and your waist."

Danny followed his directions, bending so low his face was almost touching the snow. A smile quirked on Erik's lips. "Not quite that much, kid—just a little," he said, his voice never wavering from its patient tone.

For not having children, he certainly had the ability to relate to them.

Erik checked Danny's stance and hers, then nodded. "Now, hands in front. Like you're holding a tray of—oh, let's see—hamburgers, and look ahead with your eyes." They imitated his arm position.

Erik pointed a pole at Danny. "The kid's a natural."

"Don't even think about teaching him to race—I don't

want him to break his neck." She mentally groaned. That sounded like an overreaction even to her.

"We're not covering ski racing until this afternoon's lesson. Right now, we're just going to glide down this little hill. Follow me."

"Wait a minute," Nora said. "Shouldn't he be on a leash or something? I've seen people with those—they seem like a good idea. You ski behind him and hold on to the leash so if he falls, you can stop him from rolling down the hill."

"Leashes pull kids too upright and make them off balance. I want him comfortable on his skis, not tipping backward."

"But what if he falls?"

"I'm not gonna fall," Danny said.

"Even if he does, it isn't far to the ground."

"And the snow's soft, Mom."

Erik didn't wait for any more discussion. "Okay, class, follow me." He slid down the small incline they were at the top of.

Becoming an orange again would be a lot easier if Erik would take things more slowly. She tried to hold herself back from saying anything more and failed. "Shouldn't Danny try gliding along flat ground for a while first?"

"Sweetheart, if this part of the mountain were any more level, it would be called a flatland. Come on, you two."

She flushed, feeling a little silly.

Danny followed without hesitation, so Nora did, too.

Erik nodded approval. "Won't be long and you'll be ready for the big time."

Nora let her gaze sweep over the mountain's difficult runs. *Over her dead body.*

Erik caught her glance and let out a laugh. "Not all the

way up there. We're only doing the green runs. For beginners."

After they repeated the exercise a few more times, Erik stopped in front of Danny and said, "You ready to go up the mountain a little?"

Danny's head bobbed enthusiastically, and Nora could tell that Erik had crossed the line from man to hero.

"This is plenty steep down here for a five-year-old." She mentally cringed at how completely she was failing to hide her protectiveness.

"Mom, this is boring."

"Ditto," Erik said.

"It's my job to make sure you don't break your neck."

"You're a worrywart and a spoilsport."

"Quit saying that," she said. Those words had become a sort of mantra for him lately—and a regular reminder of how cautious she'd become.

Danny wriggled his body. "I wanna ski."

Erik placed a hand flat on Danny's head. "Your mom just wants to make sure you don't get hurt, Danny. That's what moms do. My mom still worries about me and look how old I am." He flashed Nora an understanding smile, and she felt a rush of warmth. "We're going to take everything slow, so she knows it's not dangerous, okay?"

Danny threw his head back in melodramatic exasperation. "I bet your mom doesn't worry about you falling like mine does."

"She's more worried that I'm *not* falling," Erik said.

"Huh?"

"Has to do with love. You'll understand when you're older." He turned to Nora. "As for skiing, we're not going to do anything even remotely dangerous for him. I want

Danny to *like* skiing at the end of the day—not walk away and never do it again. So, let's go try a beginner run."

Fifteen minutes later they had ridden the chairlift and gotten off without any mishaps.

"That wasn't so bad, was it?" he asked.

"If you like heart palpitations," she said, reliving Danny scootching himself to the edge of the chair and jumping off when they reached the disembarking point. All totally safe, but still stressful for her.

"If you haven't noticed by now, I live for heart palpitations. That's what makes life exciting." They glided to the top of a small beginner run. "What I'm going to do now is make a snow snake down this hill, and you two follow me."

Nora held up a stop sign hand, feeling more than a little foolish about what she was about to ask. "I just have to ... well, what if he loses control and goes too fast?"

"I think I'm with Danny. You're a worrywart and a spoilsport," Erik teased.

Her eyes widened.

"But I still like you," he said. "Let's just take it down this hill and see how he does. It'll be okay. He'll be fine. You'll be fine. *Let go a little.*"

She hesitated, knowing he was being inordinately patient with her. She also knew he was right; kids learned to ski at age five all the time. Danny was growing up—he needed room to take chances. And she needed to let go a little if she was ever going to get past everything she'd been through. She drew a breath. "Okay. Ready when you are."

Erik winked. "Follow the leader." He set off down the hill.

———

Hours later, Nora tucked Danny into bed in the mountainside condominium Erik had rented for the weekend. She pulled the fluffy down comforter to his shoulders and sat on the edge of the bed. "So you liked skiing, huh?"

He yawned. "It was the best," he said sleepily. "I want to be a ski racer when I grow up."

Oh, brother. She gave him an inch and he wanted a mile. "What happened to being a fireman?"

Danny scrunched up his face. "I guess I could be a ski racer in the winter and a fireman in the summer."

"Sounds about perfect."

His eyes drifted shut and his breathing grew slow and even. She bent to kiss his forehead.

"Mom ..."

"Yes?"

"Maybe Erik wants to be a dad." His eyes opened a crack.

She ran a hand through his silky soft hair. "Maybe he does. But, sweetie, that isn't something I'm going to talk to him about. Not unless he brings it up first."

"But, Mom, if he maybe does—"

"What did we talk about just a couple of days ago?"

"I know ... *someday*. But how do you know when *someday* is? Maybe if you fell in love with him, *someday* would come."

Her heart wrenched. She'd loved someone once. And here she was talking to that man's son about loving someone else. Fear tried to make an inroad into her mind and she pushed it away. She'd made her choice ... she was moving forward.

"Good night, honey. I love you." She kissed him on the cheek.

The door opened. "Hey, buddy, you did good today," Erik said from the doorway. Casually dressed in jeans, the sleeves of his shirt rolled up, he leaned against the jamb holding a bottle of beer in one hand. Her heart nearly stopped at how handsome he looked.

She stepped out of the bedroom and closed the door behind her, sneaking a glance at his forearms. If he only knew the effect they had on her.

"There's more beer in the fridge ... unless you'd rather have wine?"

"A beer is fine. I'll get it." Anything to get his arms out of her sight. Nora grabbed a Corona from the refrigerator and joined him on the couch. Willa curled into a ball at their feet.

"You're really a great teacher," she said. "I'm sorry I was so overcautious."

"It's okay. You got much better as the day went on. Besides, it's not like you don't have good reason to be that way." He hesitated, then asked, "Do you miss him a lot?"

"Enough. Sometimes the most unlikely thing will trigger a memory—like buying an anniversary card for a friend or the smell of lilacs blooming. I wonder if it'll ever completely go away."

"I don't think it does. But why would you want to completely forget someone you loved?" He took another swallow of beer. "I still get reminders of my dad. Still miss him. Yeah, the raw edges smooth over, but love doesn't just stop ..."

"Because that person is gone," she finished.

"Yeah. It's more of an acceptance that they're gone, that things will remind you of them and that's okay." She wrapped both hands around her beer bottle. "A lot of people don't get that. They want you to just get over it."

"That's because our society doesn't do grief well. We'd rather pretend the sad stuff isn't happening."

Nora relaxed into the couch, touched by his insight, his understanding. A sense of contentment filled her. Maybe Danny was right. Maybe this was a man to love.

He took a drink of beer and wiped his mouth with the back of his hand. She thought of sliding her fingers up those forearms, across those shoulders, around that neck. Of kissing him again, long and deep. Her heart began to pound.

She lifted the bottle to her mouth and took a swallow of beer. She shouldn't be thinking these thoughts. Couldn't be. Not yet, anyway. What she really should be thinking about was telling him she was Nora. Right. She just needed to open her mouth and say *I've got something to tell you.*

She looked at him and he smiled, and suddenly the thought of having that discussion at this moment felt like an intrusion. She peeked at his forearms again. There would be time enough for the truth later.

———

Erik rubbed the back of his neck and turned his head to stretch the muscles. "I don't know why I'm sore—it's not like we were doing hard skiing today."

"Maybe it's from looking backward watching Danny and me. He had so much fun. Good thing he's exhausted because otherwise I think he'd stay up all night talking about it."

"He's a great kid. Fearless," Erik said. Exactly the kind of kid he'd always wanted to have. One he could take on adventures. Yeah, he liked her kid.

"Fearless is a good thing?" she teased.

"He'll know what it's like to live." He rubbed the back of his neck again. "Maybe I need to take some Advil."

Tess looked at him sideways. "I could probably get that stiffness out of your neck in a few minutes."

He contemplated what it would be like to have her hands on him, working his muscles—*all of them.* He shoved the image away. "So what? Did Nora teach you everything she knows?"

She blinked and opened her mouth to speak, hesitating a moment before saying, "Yeah. She did. Makes me work on her neck and shoulders sometimes when she's had a long day. Go sit in the chair so I can get behind you."

He moved over into the upholstered chair and braced himself for her touch, expecting her fingers to be cold. But nothing prepared him for the jolt of heat that slid through his body when she actually laid her hands on his neck.

She began to knead the muscles, putting pressure at the tight spots, forcing the muscles to relax. As the tension in his shoulders eased, another tension began to build inside him. He closed his eyes and pictured her hands on his chest, his hips, his legs, pictured her holding him, stroking him. He thought of pressing his mouth to hers, of stripping off her shirt and cradling her breasts in his hands, of tracing her curves with his tongue as he unzipped her jeans.

His body tightened. This was the dumbest mind game he'd ever played. He tried to think of something else. "So Danny's ready to go tomorrow, huh?" he asked in a voice so calm Tess would never be able to tell what he was actually feeling inside.

"Hmm," she said absently.

Her fingers massaged his neck and moved down to his shoulders and his brain was stolen again, back to sliding off her jeans and trailing kisses down her belly until he stroked into her with his tongue and made her writhe with need, made her want him as badly as he wanted her. His heart was already pounding, his breath almost coming short, the pressure inside him growing as her hands kept working his neck and shoulders. He wanted her lips where her hands were, wanted her hands where his thoughts were, wanted her mouth to follow—

He tried to freeze his thoughts, to think of snow and skiing—something *cold*. He really should know better. Somehow the combination of fresh air and exercise always made him ... randy. He glanced back at Tess, to see if she had any inclination in the same direction, but she merely smiled serenely down at him.

"Getting better?" she asked.

He gulped. "Not yet." *Not until I have you naked.*

He sat there, still, every nerve in his body aware of the woman behind him, fighting wanting her, until finally he gave in to the need and action took precedence over thought. He reached back to take her arm.

"Am I pressing too hard?" she asked.

"Stop." He drew her around so she was facing him, looking at him with those big hazel eyes. "Or don't stop. One or the other."

She smiled as if she knew his every thought, and that was all the invitation he needed. He pulled her onto his lap and kissed her hard, took her mouth in exactly the way he wanted to devour the rest of her.

20

―――――

Nora trembled at the suddenness of his movement, pulled back to meet his eyes for an intense moment before his lips were on hers again and she opened her mouth to him, tasting him in awe, as if this were their first kiss. He cradled her head in his hands and sensation skidded through her and her whole body tightened from the heat of it. She slid her hands over his shoulders and pulled him closer, and he kissed her deeper, his mouth drawing her with him into a dark, sensual place. Something began to build in her, a need so long suppressed she didn't think she'd be able to pull away from Erik again—and didn't want to. And then his mouth was on her neck, trailing kisses, his tongue teasing that tender spot at the base of her throat, touching her with fire. She whimpered.

"Sweetheart," he whispered. "Stop me now or I'm not stopping."

She met his eyes again, saw her own need mirrored there and shook her head, her decision made. "I don't want you to stop."

He didn't kiss her then, just looked at her and looked at

her as he slid his hands under her sweater, trailing heat with his touch, across the soft skin of her lower back and around to her stomach. He caressed her breasts through the silky fabric of her bra, slipping the clasp with one hand. She sucked in a breath, letting her eyes close as she leaned into his strong, warm hands and brushed her mouth over his. He kissed her back like she was everything he'd ever wanted and couldn't get enough of all rolled into one. And it made her want him more.

Then he grasped the hem of her sweater and pulled it up over her head, sliding her bra off at the same time.

"You're making me crazy," he said. He bent to kiss the curve of her breast, his tongue tracing circles until finally he took her in his mouth and sucked hard, sending heat shooting through her.

"Crazy's not the word for it," she said on a gasp.

He kissed her throat, her cheeks, her forehead, her hair, and she knew, without a doubt, that she wanted this man.

She paused at the thought and knew Erik felt her hesitation because he pulled back to look at her. "You really okay with this?" His lids were heavy on his blue eyes, drunk with passion.

"Yeah, I am." The sense of freedom was incredible, to face her fear and step over it. She grasped the front of Erik's shirt and pulled him toward her, slowly popping open each button and kissing his chest all the way down to his stomach. His breath caught and she smiled, happy she was having such an effect on him. Then she pushed the shirt from his shoulders, and he shrugged it off the rest of the way as she ran her hands over his chest, over his muscled forearms and biceps. She touched a wide scar on his shoulder.

"What's this?" she whispered.

"Rotator cuff surgery."

"When did it happen?"

"Who the hell cares?" He kissed her again, hard and long, making her too dizzy to want to ask anything else. Mouth still on hers, he slid forward in the chair and stood, setting her on her feet. Without breaking the kiss, he led her into the bedroom and locked the door behind them.

She shivered against the heat of his body and he kissed the curve of her neck, her jaw, her eyes, her mouth. "You're incredible," he murmured, and she laughed because it had been so long since she'd gotten a compliment like that.

He unzipped her jeans, slid his hands into the back of her pants to cup her bottom and pull her against him. And she thought she might die from the nearness of him. She could feel his heart beating against hers, could feel the strength of his desire and the tremble of her own need building. He pushed her jeans down, sliding his hands along her legs. She stepped out of them as he pulled his own off.

Then he laid her on the bed and she stretched against him, reveled in the heat of his skin, the feel of his hard body against hers. He kissed her deeply, thoroughly, and slid a hand between her legs, pressed against her, stroked her, tormented her until the blood pounded in her veins and the pressure built and she broke, arching toward him as the world exploded into waves, one rolling over the next and the next, taking her breath with it.

As she floated there in a pleasured haze, he grabbed a condom from the nightstand and put it on. She reached for him and he rolled her beneath him, pressing into her, loving her then until the weight of him on her, inside her, his mouth possessing hers, drove her up and over the brink again.

Later, he held her in the darkness, and she drifted, contented by the feel of his skin against hers, the soft touch of his breath on her neck. In her heart she felt the stirring of emotion and she refused to acknowledge it. *Too soon,* she warned herself. *Don't care too soon.*

He ran a hand down the curve of her back and across her butt. "I think we should do that all night."

She snuggled into him, could feel the heat building between them. "I might be persuaded."

His hand stroked up her thigh, across her belly to cup her breast, while his mouth came down on hers, hot and insistent. The world tilted deliciously, the thrill dizzying, and she let herself slide away with it, gave herself up to the moment, shoving aside the inkling of disquiet over the fact that she had, once again, postponed telling Erik the truth.

"I've got something to tell you," he said when they woke in the middle of the night, his arms around her from behind, his hips cupping her bottom.

"I've got something to tell you, too," she whispered. *My name is Nora.* "You go first."

"Okay. I'm thinking about taking another job." He nibbled at her ear and she felt a rush of warmth.

"You mean with the sports medicine rehab center."

"No. I used to ski on the Olympic team—"

"Really?"

"Yeah, a long time ago." He ran his fingers over her hip.

She gave him a playful nudge. "Of course I know you were on the Olympic team. Who doesn't know it?"

"Probably lots of people. It's been more than fifteen years—"

"You were on the Wheaties box."

"Okay, so maybe people do know. It still was a long time ago. Anyway, I'm talking to the U.S. Ski Association about coaching the men's A team. It's something I've always wanted to do—just never pursued it at that level. I've been coaching nationally ranked juniors part-time for a few years."

"You'd leave orthopedic surgery?" She struggled to make sense of what he was saying.

"That's the big decision."

She looked at him over her shoulder. "Might be a pay cut," she teased.

"Just a bit. Like three-quarters of my income pay cut." He paused. "My years on the team, though, were some of the best of my life. I miss it. Being part of a team like that."

Nora squirmed out of his arms so she could roll on her back and look at him. Despite everything he'd accomplished in his life, Erik Morgan was still searching. She'd suspected it that night on the dock when they were talking. Now she knew it was fact. She pressed a hand against his chest above his heart. "Aren't your partners your team now?"

He exhaled. "In a sense. But at the end of the day, we go our separate ways. They go home to their families ... and I just go home. With the ski team it'll be different."

"How?"

"Ten months of the year we'll be traveling together—training and competing all over the world. You get close ... like family."

She lay still in the darkness, loving the feel of him next to her, and wondered whether there would be room in his life for her once he had this new job. Erik was lonely. *Just like her*. But he thought the answer was to run away.

And she'd finally just realized running away never worked.

She wanted to wrap her arms around him and tell him that. Wanted to make him see that he didn't need to coach skiing to belong to a team—he just needed to stop running. But she knew from experience it was the kind of thing people had to figure out themselves.

"What will you do about Willa?"

He exhaled. "Yeah, I know. That's sort of killing me. My sister loves dogs, so I'm hoping she might take her."

"When do you find out?" she asked. "About the job, I mean."

"I fly out to Utah Tuesday for an interview and to talk through the details. Nothing's certain. The job isn't mine yet—I'm just talking to them."

She nodded, her heart bereft. Even with her limited knowledge of the ski world, she had no doubt that Erik, with his incredible background, would get the coaching job. This was a done deal regardless whether he'd interviewed yet or not. "That's pretty exciting," she said with forced enthusiasm. "So does this mean the Olympics?"

"I'd take them to the next Games."

"You'll be pretty busy for a few years then." A dull ache started beneath her breastbone.

"Yeah. I'd be gone a lot." He ran his thumb over her jaw, and a shiver slid through her. "Even though it may not even happen, I wanted to be up front with you."

She nodded.

"I haven't even told my partners yet. But I wanted you to know that ... even if I get the job, I still want to see you." He brushed her lips with his and she kissed him back.

When? The third Tuesday of the second week in July? Why was it that when she finally decided to let go of the past, the man she decided she wanted was leaving her? She had a flash that she'd done this already, had lived this before. She drew a slow breath. No, this wasn't the same as Kevin dying. It wasn't. This was completely different.

"So what did you want to tell me?" he asked. He played with her hair, ran his hand over her shoulder, nuzzled the soft skin of her throat.

She hesitated. Was there a point anymore in telling him who she was? He was going to be gone very soon—for a very long time. And even though, at this moment he thought he wanted to see her again, she knew how it worked—*out of sight, out of heart.* Soon she would just be a nice memory, an interlude between one life and the next. An ache spread across her chest. Once Erik was deep in his ski world again, Tess Carlisle would likely never cross his mind again.

Knowing that, was it really necessary for him to know she wasn't Tess?

No.

Even though she might be interviewing for the job at the new rehab clinic and he would likely be one of the interviewers?

No. He'd probably be gone before the interviews even got scheduled. Besides, there was no guarantee she'd get an interview anyway.

Her heart shattered. She'd let herself get attached—too much, too soon. No wonder she hadn't dated these past five years—it came with pain.

"So?" he asked.

"Oh, it's nothing as exciting as your news. I just wanted to say how glad I am that you brought Danny and me skiing."

———

By four o'clock Tuesday afternoon, Nora was ready to call it quits. For the week.

She put her elbows on her desk, stuck her chin in her hand and tried to concentrate on the medical chart on her computer screen.

Time had been dragging ever since they'd gotten home from skiing. No matter how much she tried to ignore her thoughts, she couldn't get the weekend out of her mind, couldn't stop thinking that Erik had flown to Utah to talk to the USSA, couldn't forget how much her heart was hurting.

She'd texted Tess Sunday morning to tell her she hadn't told Erik the truth, but it wasn't until Tess called later that night for an explanation that she'd filled her sister in about his plans. Tess had been stunned speechless, which was a rare thing indeed. Nora smiled at the memory of her sister's righteous indignation. Tess was nothing if not loyal.

When she'd finally been able to form words again, she'd burst out with, "After the weekend you two had together—after you had sex with him—he has the nerve to tell you he's taking a job that will keep him busy ten months a year?"

"It's not a sure thing yet," Nora replied.

"Oh, please. Former champion wants to coach and they'll turn him down?" Tess had definitely been riled. "I'm glad you didn't tell him who you really were. With this turn of events, all we'd get for putting the truth out there would be another unnecessary complication in both our lives."

Nora gave her head a shake and tried to force her thoughts away from the weekend and back to the file on her computer screen. Her phone rang and she snatched it up, eager for the distraction.

The caller identified herself as being from the hospital's human resources department. "You put in an application to the new sports medicine rehab center, and I'm calling to schedule an interview."

"Oh yes, great." Nora tried to keep the surprise out of her voice. She hadn't expected anything to happen with the application for weeks.

"The doctors want to fast-track filling the PT director position so whoever gets hired can be involved in planning decisions. Are you available to meet Friday?"

Three days? Panic darted through her. This was too soon. Erik would still be here in three days. And of course he'd be part of the interviewing process; he and his partners were integrally involved in developing this clinic.

Unless ... maybe this initial interview would be with a human resources person only, a preliminary screening kind of interview to narrow the field. She quietly blew out the breath she hadn't even known she was holding. That had to be why they were calling so soon—only the top couple of candidates would make it through to an interview with the docs themselves. Those guys were far too busy to spend hours and hours of time interviewing multitudes of candidates. She relaxed. "Friday's fine. Whatever the time, I'll make sure my schedule is clear."

"How about early afternoon. Say one-thirty?"

"Perfect." She scrawled the details onto a notepad.

"You'll be meeting with several people at once," the woman said. "The hospital administrator and the three orthopedic surgeons who will be involved with the center."

Shit. So much for preliminary screening interviews. "Ah, which surgeons would that be?" she asked, already knowing the answer.

"Dr. Chapman, Dr. O'Connell ..."

And Dr. Morgan, she said to herself as the woman said

his name aloud. *The man she'd slept with two days ago.* The one she was still lying to.

Nora let her head fall forward into her hand.

"Do you have any questions?"

Yes, can you get Dr. Morgan off the committee? "Not at the moment. But if I think of something, I'll give you a call."

As soon as the call ended, Nora dropped her head to her desk. "I knew I should never have agreed to switch places. I knew it. I knew it. I knew all this lying would come back to haunt me," she muttered. "The piper always wants to be paid."

She mentally ran through all the issues. Erik thought she was Tess. Erik had made love with her. Erik could determine whether she got her dream job or not.

How had she gotten herself into this mess? A simple decision to help her sister had escalated into an out of control nightmare. She tried to assess the situation rationally. She and Tess hadn't done anything illegal, all they'd done was switch places.

How angry, really, could Erik get if she told him she had taken Tess's place?

Uhh, probably pretty angry. Because the switch hadn't been just a one-time deal. And, not only was Nora lying, but Tess was, too. To Erik. His mother. His sister. And just about everyone else who came along.

She should have gotten out of this ages ago. It might have been okay if she'd just done the *shopping for Erik* thing. But it had gotten so much bigger. She never should have gone away for the weekend with him. She rubbed a hand over her eyes. So now what did she do? Come clean? Or just keep it up?

21

———

Erik slouched into his seat in the Salt Lake City airport waiting area and flipped through the news on his phone. His flight had been delayed because of mechanical problems, and boredom had set in more than an hour ago.

He'd just spent the better part of the last two days in meetings with USSA officials about coaching. The job was his—if he wanted it. He had done his best to assure them he was nearly certain this was exactly what he wanted—even if, deep down, he wasn't so sure anymore.

He thought about last weekend with Tess and almost pulled up her number to give her a call, just to hear her voice and talk through this new job with her. She'd probably be able to give him a whole different perspective. But he stopped himself. It wasn't as if she had any sort of interest in his future; they'd only just met. This was his decision to make ... alone.

Before today's meeting, he hadn't thought he would have to move to Utah, had been thinking he could keep San Francisco as his home base so he could still keep his hand in orthopedic surgery even while coaching. But USSA officials strongly encouraged he move to the area. Though it wasn't a requirement, more and more ski team coaches were making Park City, Utah their home.

He had to admit, it was probably unrealistic to think he could fit medicine into the schedule he'd have as a coach. He could accept that. The real problem with moving was, would he ever see Tess again?

May and June the team would practice in California, at Mammoth, because it always had snow late in the season. The resort was only a seven-hour drive from San Francisco —maybe he could get Tess to come up once in a while.

Part of August they'd be up at Mt. Hood in Oregon. The rest of that month and all of September they'd be in New Zealand or Chile. Late September and October would be Europe—Austria, Italy. Then back to the U.S. for the World Cup in November, with the rest of the circuit to follow, running through March. After that, they'd have a little time off, attend ten days of meetings in Utah in April and then start all over again.

He was really looking forward to the competition, the emotion, working with the skiers to help them improve, the feel of winning again, even the dejection of losing. But somehow, the schedule didn't sound as appealing as it used to. He shifted into a more comfortable position.

Then there was that *waiting in airports* thing. There would be a lot of that in the coming years. And that *delayed flights* thing. There could be a lot of that, too.

He shoved the negative thoughts away and focused on the positives—working with talented athletes, helping them overcome obstacles and succeed, building chemistry on the team.

He checked his watch. He'd be getting in really late tonight, which was fine. He was in no hurry to talk to his partners about the offer—and what it would mean for their partnership if he took the job. What he needed tonight was the time to really think this through and make sure he made the right decision.

———

Nora pulled the clothes from the washer and shoved them in the dryer. She'd survived more in the last two weeks than she'd ever thought possible—impersonating a personal shopper, convincing Camille that she was Tess, giving a speech to the garden club, making love with Erik ... She should be happy she'd pulled it all off.

And she would be. Except she was too depressed about Erik taking the coaching job and leaving. Not to mention having to interview with him as Nora.

A sock fell to the floor and she bent to pick it up, only then noticing the water trickling from beneath the washer across the floor to the drain. Damn. What now?

She unplugged the machine, got on her hands and knees and tried to peer under it.

Danny rounded the corner and got down on his knees next to her. "Whatcha doing, Mom?"

"The washer's leaking. I'm trying to see where the water's coming from."

"Oh." He sat back on his heels. "Too bad we don't have a dad."

She lifted her head. "Danny! Men aren't the only ones who can fix washers. Women can fix washers, too. I can fix this washing machine."

"You can?" He sounded impressed.

She looked at the machine and the water running from

beneath it. *Yeah, right.* "You bet. But just to be sure, let's go Google it."

Hand-in-hand they went upstairs. Nora scanned a couple of online articles listing potential washing machine problems and probable solutions. It seemed sort of complicated. She glanced at her son who was watching her with something akin to awe.

She couldn't back down now. Might as well take it in steps. First, remove the back from the machine and try to figure out where the leak is. She could do that.

"Come on, Danny. Let's go fix it," she said with more confidence than she felt. She rummaged through the kitchen junk drawer until she found a screwdriver, then marched downstairs with Danny right on her heels. "The first thing we have to do is take the back off," she said.

"How do we get behind it?"

"Well, actually, the first thing we have to do is pull out the washer." She grabbed the front two corners and pulled forward as she rocked the washer from left to right. As soon as the machine was far enough away from the wall, she climbed over the top and dropped down behind it.

"Cool! Can I come back there, too?"

"No. It's dirty and linty back here," she said, but Danny was already squeezing his little body between the washer and dryer.

He sat on the floor beside her. "This is like a fort."

"Yeah." Nora began to unscrew the back of the washer, shoving each screw into the pocket of her jeans as she removed it.

"Hey, Mom, check out this spider!" Danny practically shouted.

Nora lurched away from him.

"It's eating a bug! Look, Mom!"

She eyed the nature show he was studying and suppressed a shudder. "We'll have to vacuum him up later."

"Miss Joy at daycare says spiders are our friends."

"Let them be someone else's friends," Nora muttered. She pulled the back off the washer and realized she couldn't see much of anything by the light of the single bulb hanging from the ceiling. She drew an irritated breath.

"Danny, honey, run up and get me the yellow flashlight in the kitchen drawer, will you please?"

"I wanna stay in my fort."

"When I'm done with it you can use it to watch your new friend, Mr. Spider." *Before I vacuum him up.*

"Okay!" Danny raced upstairs.

She waited behind the washer, eyes on the spider. "You stay over there or it's squish time—got it?"

From upstairs came Danny's yell: "Mom, I can't find it."

"In the junk drawer!" she called back. "It's yellow."

After a few minutes without any sign of Danny, impatience enveloped her. Nothing was ever simple anymore. Everything always had to be so damn complicated. She was tired of it all—the washer, her sister, Erik, her late husband, her job, even her son. She let out an angry huff.

Danny squeezed back behind the washer with her and held out a pack of matches.

"Where's the flashlight?" She was ready to scream.

"I couldn't find it."

"It's right in the junk drawer." It took everything she had not to shout at him.

He held out the matches again.

"It's right in that drawer," Nora repeated, as if insisting the flashlight was there would make it magically appear in Danny's hand.

He bent to look at his spider, still holding the matches toward her.

"Matches won't work, honey." She sighed. "I'll get it."

She closed the pack of matches in her fist, climbed over the washer, and marched upstairs. Why was it that no one could ever find what you sent them to get? She knew for a fact that she would get upstairs and find the yellow flashlight in the drawer exactly where she'd said it was. Probably right in front.

She yanked open the drawer and dug around, spotting the flashlight almost immediately. Par for the course. Kevin could never find anything, either. Maybe it was a male thing.

The clock on the stove glowed white, reminding her that it was already past Danny's bedtime and they were taking apart a washing machine. No *Mother of the Year Award* for her tonight. Shaking her head she returned to the basement and climbed behind the washer again.

"It was right in the drawer," she muttered to her son, who was bent over his spider and poking at it with a Popsicle stick. "Some spiders bite," she warned him.

"We're playing a game."

Whatever. She wasn't in the mood. Flipping on the flashlight, she shot the beam into the cavern of the washer to look for signs of moisture As far as she could tell, water wasn't leaking anywhere. She touched her fingers to the spot where the hoses were attached to the washer, thinking they might not be tight enough. But everything was dry.

Frustration turned to despair. If she had to call a repairman, he would probably cost at least a hundred bucks an hour—and it wasn't like she was rolling in extra cash.

She peered inside the washer again. *Nothing was leaking.* So where was the water coming from?

She slumped against the wall. What more? Seriously, what more? Tears filled her eyes and she didn't even try to hold them back. She was so tired of facing decisions—facing life—alone. *Damn you, Kevin,* she thought as the tears flowed. *Why did you have to die?* Even if he knew nothing about fixing washers, at least they would have had each other to lock arms with, to lean on, to hold each other up when the world got overwhelming.

She swung out a hand and smacked the side of the machine. Old piece of junk, probably too expensive to fix. So now she'd have to buy a new one. *And damn you, too, Erik Morgan,* she thought. *Why did you ever ask me to go to your mother's party?* The tears flowed steadily and she rested her head back against the concrete block wall, spider friends be damned. What a basket case she was, sitting on the floor in the basement behind the washer, sobbing, while her son played with a spider—probably a black widow—next to her.

Danny was right. Where was a man when she needed one? This was a man's job; men fixed washing machines. It was in their genes or something.

God, she was tired of doing it alone.

The irony of the moment was breathtaking. When she'd finally decided to let go, to move forward with someone, he promptly told her—after having sex, of course—that he was going to be extremely busy for the next four years. But just so she didn't think too badly of him, he tossed in one of those throwaway lines men say to make themselves feel better: *I still want to see you.* What was with guys? Why did they have this stupid need to say something about getting together in the future when they had no intention of following through?

And shit, the worst was, she'd never expected it out of

Erik. She thought of last weekend, of making love with him, of the possibility of never making love with him again. And she crumbled.

Danny spotted her tears and sat back on his haunches. "Why are you crying, Mama? Should we call a man to fix it?"

Nora drew a hand across her eyes. "No, honey, we don't need a man," she said. "I'm crying because I'm so happy. I fixed it myself."

22

Late in the afternoon, Erik shoved open the front door of his mother's home and stepped quietly across the large foyer.

"Hey, Mom, how's the knee?" he called as he neared her office. He could hear the light tapping of her fingers on the computer keyboard. "How's the knee?" he repeated from the doorway.

Camille looked up. "Oh hello sweetie. Were you talking to me?"

"Is there anyone else in the house whose knees I would be concerned about?" He walked to her desk.

"Now, Erik—"

"You doing your exercises?"

"Every day." She saved the document on her screen and spun her chair to face him. "And how's my personal shopper doing these days?"

"How should I know?"

His mother laughed. "Erik, I've known you for every one of your thirty-nine years. I know you've been seeing her and I couldn't be happier about it. Why don't you bring her to dinner Sunday night?"

Erik's mouth dropped open. What was it about mothers? Did they have an entire network of spies? And what age did their children have to reach before they were safe from their mother's meddling?

"Oh, all right," she said. "Jack saw you kissing her on the boat. And I write romance, you know. So—"

"Naturally, you created a romantic story to go along with Jack's report."

"Naturally." His mother gave him her *I'm the mother and always right* smile.

"What if I said you were wrong?" Although, after last weekend he had no desire to deny his involvement with Tess.

"It's certainly within your right to say that. Go ahead. I'll sit back and decide whether I believe you."

Erik bent to open the small refrigerator in his mother's office and pull out a can of Doctor Pepper. He held it up. "You want one?"

She shook her head.

He popped the top and took a swallow. "Okay, you're right. I've been seeing her."

"Is it serious?"

He thought of their lovemaking and desire skimmed through him so strong he physically felt it. Under other circumstances, he might think things were getting serious. But not now, not with a possible job change and move looming ahead.

"No. We have fun together, laugh. But it's not serious." He shook his head as if to reinforce his words.

"Laughter's important in the long haul."

"Mom," he said patiently. "We may have fun. But this isn't the long haul." He dropped into the plaid overstuffed chair in the corner. "The long haul is why I stopped over today."

"Oh?"

"You know how I told you I wanted to coach the A team? I just got back from Utah, talking to USSA."

"Erik, you mean you were actually serious about that?" she asked, shocked.

He couldn't believe how taken aback she was. "Mom, how can you be surprised? I told you I was doing this."

"I thought it was just another wild idea of yours—like becoming an Olympic skier."

"I actually did that," he said.

"It was still a wild idea." She waved a hand at him.

"I'll take one of those sodas now. Seven-Up. Put a little vodka in it."

He rolled his eyes. "Mom—"

"But you have a career. And what about the new rehab center? You've been pushing for that for years."

He grabbed a Seven-Up from the refrigerator and handed it to her. Yeah, that was the rub. To have this coaching opportunity come up at the same time as the clinic —and especially now that the hospital was offering them complete control—made the decision all the harder. "It's not the same. Skiing was always my first love."

"Isn't it enough that you coach juniors? And the schedule, Erik. You were gone almost the whole year. What kind of a schedule would you have now?"

"The same."

She popped open the Seven-Up. "What about Willa? You have a responsibility—"

"I'm hoping Jenny will take her."

Her face took on a look of disappointment. "And Tess?

What about her?" Her voice went up a notch. "How can you carry on a relationship when you're gone all the time?"

He'd been trying not to think about Tess as he worked his way through this, didn't think his decision should be influenced by feelings for a woman. He wanted to make this decision logically, not emotionally. "I wouldn't be able to carry on a relationship with her anyway—they want me to move to Utah."

Her eyes widened and her mouth dropped open. It wasn't often he shocked his mother. Kind of gave him a perverse sense of satisfaction ...

"Erik! Out of the blue you come up with this coaching idea and now, suddenly, you're moving to Utah and leaving your girlfriend and your dog?"

"It's not out of the blue. And she's not my girlfriend," he said irritably. He hadn't talked to Tess since the weekend, had left a message on her phone and hadn't heard anything back. So at this moment, he wasn't exactly sure what she was.

"You're moving ... when you've just met a young woman whose company you enjoy?"

"Life is all about timing," he said. "Unfortunately, she and I seem to have *bad timing*." He pushed aside the vague emptiness he'd been feeling whenever he thought about never seeing Tess again.

"Don't be so cavalier. Finding someone you connect with is not an easy thing in this world." She paused—no doubt for effect "Especially when you get to be your age."

"Now that you mention it, I do feel decrepit."

"Erik," his mother said in her ultra-patient voice, "it's a rare thing when you find someone you're comfortable with. You would give that up for one last shot at glory?"

"This isn't about *my* getting another shot at glory. It's

about helping other athletes get their shots at glory. It's about being part of a team."

"There are many different kinds of teams in this world."

Oh, hell, here it came, the lecture. He wondered whether she'd still be lecturing him when he was sixty. He glanced at his watch and started to stand, ready to make an excuse that he had to be somewhere.

"Don't you dare think of leaving yet," his mother said, her voice stern. "You may be grown up, but I'm still your mother."

He dropped obediently back into the chair, waiting.

She gave him a nod. "When you make this decision, you need to fully understand what you're giving up. Not just your job and the income ... but a chance for real happiness."

"I hardly know Tess." He actually felt like he knew her pretty well, but he wasn't going to admit it. "This could fizzle out in six months for all I know, and then I'd have given up the chance to coach." He pushed himself out of the chair and wandered across the room to look at the row of framed book covers on the wall—all of them romance novels written by his mother. "Life doesn't play out like a romance novel, Mom. At the risk of sounding clichéd, life is what you make it."

He could hear her sigh.

"So is love, Erik. *So is love.* If you never let it have the chance to germinate, if you never water it, if you run from it whenever it begins to sprout in your life, then you will never know what it is to be *whole.*"

"You're a romantic." He picked up one of her novels from the side table and flipped it open, pretending to read aloud, "Darling, you mean everything to me—"

"Oh, stop it. I've never written drivel like that," she said with a laugh. "I may be a romantic," she said quietly, "but I also lived through your father's death and thinking I would never love again. I know that love heals, that it creates teams where none existed before. Love can be grand and powerful and fulfilling and humbling. *If you let it in.*" Her expression grew soft. "Love is what you make it, Erik. I would hate for you to grow old, still searching, never having let yourself feel all that, never having realized that all you ever really needed was love."

"Is that from one of your books?"

"You're determined to do this, aren't you?"

He nodded. "I like Tess. But I wouldn't consider giving up an opportunity like this for her. I hardly know her." He shoved his hands in his pockets. "I just came by to let you know about my decision—not discuss my entire future."

His mother pushed herself out of her chair and gave him a hug. "I guess you're old enough to know your own mind by now. So, honey, let me leave you with this. One of the things I've learned writing all these romance novels is that love and commitment are a tug of war between intimacy and identity."

He let out a groan. "Mom, I really don't want to know, but what does that mean?"

"It's kind of simple," she said. "In order to achieve intimacy with someone else, you have to give up a part of your identity. It's a hard balance—some people never get it." She slid her arm through his and began to walk with him toward her office door. "Your identity is wrapped up in who you are. Injured skier whose incredible future was cut short by a knee injury, dedicated coach who gives up his personal time to work with junior skiers, brilliant doctor, perpetually single, hard-to-get. If you ever want to have a truly intimate relationship, then you will have to sacrifice something of that identity. The question is, my dear son, do you ever want a truly intimate relationship? And if so, what are you willing to give up for it?"

She let go of his arm. "Lecture ended. I'll plan on the two of you for dinner Sunday unless you let me know otherwise."

23

———

"Come on Danny, we're going to be late." Nora grabbed her son by the hand and hurried across the asphalt parking lot toward the grade school. She put a hand up to shade her eyes as the blinding rays of the setting sun shot over the top of the building.

Danny hung back, dragging his feet.

"What's wrong?" She tried to be patient, but it was the night before her interview and her stomach was already jumping.

On top of that stress, Erik had left two phone messages for her—on Tess's phone, of course—and she hadn't returned either of them. She couldn't bring herself to talk to him, not with everything that had passed between them last weekend and the job interview tomorrow.

Never mind that if she called him back he would surely notice the phone number didn't match the one he'd called— and she would have to come up with a believable reason why she was using Nora's phone again. Claiming to have a dead phone made her sound like a moron because it was so easy to just plug the phone in and charge it back up.

Her stress level was shooting through the roof. She hadn't told him the truth because she thought he'd be out of the picture, gone to Utah. Except now she had to interview with him, still lying about being Tess, and knowing that every time he saw her as Nora increased the odds he would realize that the Tess he'd met was actually Nora.

"What's wrong?" she repeated, kneeling beside her son.

He shrugged.

"Sweetie, it's Family Fun night. Come on, we're going to have fun. All your friends are probably in there already."

He shrugged again.

"Cookies, punch, games ... *come on.*"

"Who's gonna be my free throw partner?"

Nora's heart flopped. *Not this dad thing again.* "I will. You and me—we're partners." She gave him a hug.

"You're a girl."

"Girls play basketball, too, you know." *Stay calm ... patient.*

"Couldn't Erik come with us?" He kicked at the asphalt.

Why did it seem like everywhere she turned lately it was Erik, Erik, Erik. She held back a scream and replied in a calm voice, "No, Erik can't come with us. He's just a friend. And Danny—look at me." She waited until her son raised his head. "Erik is going to be really busy soon, gone away for a long time ... traveling with a new job."

Danny's expression clouded. "He said we would go skiing again. He needs to watch me ride my bike."

She shook her head. "Maybe, if he has time. But he might not. Danny, he *can't* be your new dad."

"Why not?"

Because he thinks I'm Tess and I'm never going to tell him otherwise. Because he won't have time in his life to fall in love. "He just can't."

"It seemed like you felt a conniption."

"Conniption?"

He nodded, his expression so earnest, she pressed a hand to her chest to still the ache.

"You said someday you would meet someone and feel a conniption."

She smiled. "Connection. I would feel a connection."

"Didn't you feel it?"

"Yeah, I felt it. But sometimes it isn't enough. Sometimes people have reasons for staying apart—like moving." *And like protecting themselves from getting hurt ... and like searching for something to make them feel as if they're part of a team and not realizing they've already found it.*

"Couldn't you just ask him to stay?"

"I don't know him that well, sweetie." She brushed a hand over his head. "Besides, it's his decision to make."

"But—couldn't you just tell him about your conniption? And see what he says?"

"Oh, Danny—"

"Pleease, Mom."

Tell Erik how she felt about him? No. That would also mean she'd have to tell him she'd been deceiving him. At this point, it would only accomplish one thing—Erik would move forward in his dream job, while she would lose any chance of getting hers.

Suddenly she longed to be five years old again, when life was uncomplicated. "I'll think about it." she lied.

"I bet he felt a conniption, too."

She nodded. "He'd probably feel an even bigger conniption once he heard what I have to say."

"Really?" Danny's eyes lit up.

"Oh, I have no doubt."

———

Nora stepped out of the hospital conference room after her interview and held herself back from dancing down the hall. She'd just faced Erik, his partners, and the hospital administrator, and everything had gone really well. She'd been herself, just Nora. And as far as she was concerned, she would never be Tess again. Her sister was due back in two days, which meant the charade was as good as over.

Life would be back to normal in no time.

Seeing Erik hadn't been as painful or difficult as she'd expected. He related to her differently as Nora, more businesslike, which made him feel like a different person. She'd almost been able to compartmentalize their relationship—shove her feelings into a little box in her mind and close the lid.

Almost. But not entirely. When she least expected it and her guard was down, something he said or did would remind her of the time they'd spent together, and she would feel a spike of pain before she tamped down the memory.

Now that the meeting was over, she could feel her tension seeping away, the nervous energy that had been part of her the past couple of days evaporating. She stopped at a drinking fountain near the bank of elevators and took a big drink. All that talking had left her parched.

Not that she was complaining. She grinned and punched the elevator button.

The interview had begun with the usual, expected questions: Where did you go to school? Do you have any specialized training? Here are the types of injuries we expect to see at the new clinic and have you handled similar cases?

They'd really liked the experience she had working

with athletes. She'd seen the approval on their faces when she described her internships and the job she'd held in college, working with injured athletes at the university's athletic training facility.

That was when the meeting seemed to kick into high gear. Their questions had quickly evolved into a planning discussion about equipment, organization, logistics, patients, and virtually everything else anyone would want to nail down before opening a clinic.

By the end of the interview, they'd almost guaranteed her the job. Erik had given her a look that seemed to say, *It's yours,* and she'd shaken hands all around and headed out of the meeting walking on air.

The only downside had been remembering all the lies she'd told Erik. But, to be fair to herself, she hadn't been lying about being a physical therapist or her experience treating patients, she hadn't lied about being *Nora*. The woman who went to the interview today was exactly who they had expected to meet—Nora Clark.

The elevator doors opened with a ding and she stepped into the empty car, the consummate professional. She waited serenely until the doors closed, then kicked loose, happy dancing all the way to the next floor, her reflection in the shiny metal walls dancing alongside her.

Two hours later she was leaning on her desk, daydreaming about getting the job, when her phone rang and she absently picked it up, expecting a typical call from one of her patients. Instead, she found herself talking to the hospital administrator. She sat bolt upright and tried to sound coherent. "Oh, yes, hello."

"I know this is beyond fast," he said, "but we talked everything through right after you left and the group is unanimous. We want to hire you."

Shock exploded through her. And joy. And amazement. A grin burst across her face and she laughed, tinkle tinkle. *Omigod, she had become a Nora/Tess cross.* She thrust a triumphant fist in the air. "Oh, thank you. That's great—I'm really excited about the clinic."

"I can't give you a lot of details yet," he said. "But the docs want to make sure you're involved in the whole process—from equipment purchases to space design. Let's get together next week to discuss opening up your work schedule so you have time to get going on this."

As soon as the call ended, Nora shot off a text to Tess: *I got the job!!!*

A minute later, Tess was on the phone screeching, "I knew it! I prayed to St. Jude for you all morning—well, okay, maybe not all morning, but definitely twice."

Nora leaned back in her chair, grinning. "That guy really delivers—I'm going to owe him big time."

"Just don't forget to thank him in public or he won't come through again."

"What?" Nora doodled on the notepad, writing her name and Sports Medicine Rehab Center Director several times.

"Don't you remember what Grandma always said? You have to publicly thank him. In the Want Ads," Tess said as though Nora were a moron. "You know, those little ads in the newspaper that say something like, *Thanks to St. Jude for prayers answered.*"

"What?"

"Don't you read the Want Ads?" Tess asked.

"What Want Ads? There are no Want Ads anymore."

"Maybe you could post something on Craig's List. Between *For Sale—wedding dress, never worn, fourth owner* and *John Doe, if you don't pick up your possessions this week, they will be disposed of.*"

Nora put her hand to her forehead. "I had no idea."

Tess's voice wavered and Nora couldn't make out what she was saying. "Tess, hey, I'm losing you."

"Can't you hear me now? Congratulations again—we'll celebrate when I get back." She let out a tinkle tinkle laugh. "I'll get the champagne. Hey, good thing you never told Erik the truth."

"Yeah. Good thing." Nora shut off her phone and stared at her notepad. Oh yeah. Good thing.

———

You're thinking about quitting?" Tim gaped at Erik. "We just hired the director for the clinic." The three partners were sitting around the small conference table in the corner of Erik's office. Erik wrapped his hands around his coffee mug and waited for Andy's reaction.

"The hell you're quitting!" Andy didn't even try to disguise his irritation. "What is this? A mid-life crisis?"

"Give me a break." Erik leaned back in his chair. "It's an opportunity. I've wanted to coach for years."

"Right. That's why you're coaching juniors," he replied. "This is the A team—"

"You've also wanted to open a sports medicine rehab center for years. You fought for this thing—and now you're just going to give it up?" Tim asked quietly.

Erik shook his head. He had hoped his partners would understand, but it was quickly becoming clear they didn't get it at all. "I didn't ask for both things to happen at the same time."

"But they did. Don't go back to adolescent decision

making—choosing what sounds the most exciting at the moment." Andy tapped a finger irritably on the table.

"I'm not," Erik snapped. "I've given this a lot of thought."

"Not enough, apparently, or you wouldn't have come to this conclusion." Andy sounded disgusted.

Erik tamped down his anger. Between his mother and his partners, he felt besieged. He'd expected Tim and Andy to be upset, just hadn't expected them to respond with such ferocity. "I realize this is coming as a shock. You were never on the team, so I don't expect you'll understand—"

Andy shook his head. "Nope, I understand all too well. What you're doing is that impulsive, fly-down-a-mountainside-get-an-immediate-rush thing. *And you know it*. Except this mountainside is your life. And you're about to throw it away."

"I'm with Andy," Tim said. "Five years ago, the three of us formed a partnership—we're a team. You don't get to quit now just because someone else wants you."

"This isn't kickball." Andy pushed back his chair and stood. "And we're not the scrubs. You're already on the A team, Erik. And you're a blind fool if you can't see that." He headed into the hall, then wheeled around and stepped back into the room. "And what about that woman—Tess—you've been talking about? You're going to blow off the first woman you've met in years that you actually like?" He shook his head and went into his own office.

"Don't rush this decision," Tim said. "Give it some more thought before you make up your mind. Obviously, we'll accept whatever you decide. We'll even get by without you —we just don't want to. Just make sure it's really what you want."

24

An hour later, Erik remained at his desk, staring through the open doorway at the ski painting in the hall—and not even seeing it. He mentally hashed over all the thoughts that had consumed him lately—coaching, moving, the pros, the cons, what his partners had said, what his mother had said ... Tess.

Tim was gone for the day, had stuck his head in the door before he left and told Erik to call over the weekend if he wanted to talk. Andy, though, was still in his office. Probably brooding. Probably debating whether to come in and broach the subject again.

He and Erik had become friends during their residency, discovered their goals were the same, and gone into business together not long afterward. Andy had great business sense and tremendous drive—he knew how to make things happen and he was almost never wrong. He also hated to lose—especially when he was convinced he was right.

But was he right about Erik? Was this just an impulsive get-an-immediate-rush kind of decision?

He didn't think so. He was truly excited about working with the skiers—coaching, traveling, spending the upcoming years traveling the world. He was really looking forward to the sense of belonging that came with being part of the team, something he hadn't felt since—*he was with Tess.*

He shook his head. No. This wasn't about Tess. It was about wanting to coach the A team. He wanted this as much as he'd wanted anything—including getting the rehab center going.

He flashed back to his trip to Park City, when he'd met with USSA officials. It had been great on all fronts. Well, until his flight had been delayed and he'd gotten stuck at the airport.

There would probably be plenty of delayed flights to come.

For all the benefits of this job, there were downsides, too: being away from home nine months of the year, a massive pay cut, days that began at five-thirty in the morning and didn't end until he fell into bed, setting training courses and inspecting courses when the sun came up, videotaping from the hill and analyzing technique at night, tight quarters, driving, hauling, checking ski waxes, airport food ...

What the hell was he thinking?

Nothing. There was nothing wrong with his thinking. He wanted this job. He liked doing all of that stuff. But considering that most of the time he and the team would be somewhere else in the world, it sure didn't seem crucial that he move to Utah. His home base could be anywhere ... like here.

Besides, if he kept his home in San Francisco he could still see Tess. Once in a while, anyway. Especially when they were practicing at Mammoth in May and June.

His mother's words stole into his thoughts: *The question is, do you ever want a truly intimate relationship? And if so, what part of your identity are you willing to give up for it?*

Nothing, apparently.

The reality stunned him. He was willing to give up everything—his career, the new clinic, a relationship with an incredible woman—just to coach, to belong to the ski team again. And yet, what he wanted most right now was to call Tess and find out what she thought about it.

And if he did that, and she asked him not to go, what would he do?

The answer came to him before he'd finished forming the question, his conviction so strong, he knew without a doubt it was truth. He would stay.

He considered his mother's question again. What was he willing to give up to have an intimate relationship with Tess?

Whatever she wanted.

He stood, knowing then that he was going to turn down the coaching job, that it was what he wanted to do. His heart felt lighter than it had in a week. As he passed Andy's doorway, he leaned into the room and said with a grin, "Not saying you're right, but you did make some good points. You want to go walk through our new space? I've got a couple of ideas."

Andy threw back his head and laughed. "I knew you'd figure out the right answer eventually."

Nora wandered through the gutted space that would soon become the new sports medicine rehab center. Her happiness over getting the job had quickly been tempered by unease. She remembered what it had been like to look into Erik's eyes during the interview after having made love with him the weekend before. She thought of him moving away, and the very real probability that she might never see him again. And her heart broke with the knowledge that he didn't even know the woman he'd gone away with for the weekend, the woman he'd made love with, was her.

Once her workday had ended, she'd come to the clinic space to try to regain her equilibrium, her focus, to try to figure out what it was she really wanted, to come to grips with what was right and what was just easy.

Everything was so complicated because it was built on a foundation of lies. She could almost hear her grandmother lecture many years ago, could still feel the old woman's disappointment as she quietly reprimanded her ten-year-old granddaughters: *Tell a lie once and all your truths become questionable.*

How had she let this happen? This behavior wasn't her —she was honest, trustworthy. She believed in truth. My God, she taught Danny not to lie—and yet, somehow, she'd let herself get roped into the biggest fabrication of her life.

Erik deserved to know the truth. But once he did, things could go downhill fast. Her new job offer would probably be rescinded; the hospital might even fire her. Not to mention, Tess would undoubtedly lose her largest account —Camille Lamont. Money could get pretty tight in the household.

And yet, did all that justify what they'd done?

She didn't even have to ask the question to know the answer. Erik had been honest enough to tell her he was looking at a new job that would take all his time. He'd told her the truth—and she'd kept on lying.

He deserved to know the truth. Even if she never saw

him again, even if he would have never discovered what she and Tess had done, even if the consequences were devastating, she owed him honesty.

She stared out the bank of windows at the parking lot filled with cars. Margo's words about the difference between life and living made so much sense to her now. No matter how great this job would be—and it would be wonderful—it was just life. Living, on the other hand, involved actually trusting people enough to let them into your life—and heart.

Without the shadow of a doubt, the night she'd made love with Erik marked the moment she'd stepped back into living. She wanted to tell him the truth because he deserved it. But, selfishly, she also wanted him to know that the person he had connected with was Nora, not Tess. She wanted him to know that the woman he'd made love to was Nora. She wanted him to know that Danny was Nora's son. And she wanted the chance, however slim, to see if there was anything between them.

St. Jude might have gotten her this far. The rest of the way she had to go herself. She couldn't carry on with this pretense any longer. Erik deserved the truth.

She wanted him to have it.

Her eyes filled with tears. And the sooner she told him, the better.

———

Erik spotted Nora across the empty office space, staring out a window. "Looks like our new director can't stay away either," he said in a lighthearted voice.

Nora looked up, startled, then a smile broke her face. "I was a million miles away."

"Sorry," he said as Andy said, "Welcome aboard."

"Oh, thanks."

He spotted tears in her eyes. "You okay?"

"I—" She glanced at Andy and stopped. A tear slipped over her lower lashes and she dashed it away.

He hesitated, unsure. "Is this about the job?"

She shook her head, looking so much like her sister it almost felt like Tess were hurting and not Nora. "It's nothing really …"

"We're here to help," Andy said. "Former Boy Scouts, both of us."

She shifted her gaze between them as though debating whether to reveal a great secret. "I have to tell you something …" She drew a breath. "I am—" Her eyes darted toward Andy again. "I am—" She stopped as though searching for the right words and let out a sigh. "Upset about my washing machine. It's not working right."

"Your washer?" Erik blinked.

"It's leaking."

"Have you called a repairman?" Andy asked in the nicest possible voice.

"No." She almost seemed to wince. "They can be so expensive." Her tears were gone.

A series of thoughts started to merge into an idea in Erik's mind—that Tess wasn't returning his calls, that the sisters needed a repairman, that the repairman would be welcomed into where Tess lived and probably have direct contact with her …

"I know how silly this sounds," Nora was saying. "I looked up washer repair on the Internet. Then I took the back panel off the machine yesterday hoping I'd be able to see where the leak was ... but, no luck."

Andy shook his head. "We didn't learn washer repair in the Scouts. I think you're going to need a repairman—"

"I could take a look at it," Erik said quickly.

"What do you know about fixing washers?" Andy asked.

Not much, but he knew how to use Google. "Oh, you'd be surprised."

"I bet," Andy muttered.

Nora's eyes were wide. "Oh, no. Not necessary. Really."

"You don't want to be stuck paying some exorbitant repair bill," Erik said.

Andy was staring at him, slack-jawed. So was Nora.

"Will you and Tess be around tomorrow?"

She seemed mortified. Probably just embarrassed. "Um, you mean Saturday?" she asked.

"That would be tomorrow," Andy said.

"I—ah—I—well, it's Memorial Day weekend."

"Do you have plans?" Erik pressed.

She shook her head.

"Tell you what. I've got some time in the morning. I'll swing by and see if I can figure out what's wrong," he said. *And have a face-to-face with your sister.* He couldn't wait to tell her he'd turned down the job to coach the A team.

"No, really. You don't have to," Nora said.

"No problem. I'm happy to do it." He let his insistence show in his voice.

"You'd better let him." Andy gestured with one hand. "When he gets on a path, it can be a bear to change his mind. And after the day I've had today, I don't have the strength to help you out here, Nora."

From the kitchen where she was unloading the dishwasher, Nora heard the front door open and a familiar voice yell, "Honey, I'm home!"

She dropped a handful of clean silverware into the open drawer. Oh. My. God. No. Tess was back. *Seriously?* Erik would be here any minute. This was going to screw everything up. She charged into the living room. "What are you doing here?" she asked, eyes darting from Tess to the front door. "I thought your flight didn't get in until tonight."

"Nora!" Tess set her suitcases on the floor and wrapped Nora in a hug. "A fine hello to you, too! Yes, I know it's hard to believe, but I really did take everything you said seriously. I tried to call but couldn't get a connection, so I decided to surprise—"

"This isn't a good time to chat. Get your suitcases and—"

Tess plopped into the blue chair and put her feet up on the ottoman. "I'm exhausted. I changed my flight, took the red-eye so I could get home as soon as possible." She let her head fall back against the chair cushion. "I was practically up all night."

"No, I mean it. Grab your bags and get this stuff upstairs." Nora waved both hands like she was a mad conductor in front of an orchestra. "Things are happening today. Erik—"

"Cool it, sister. I just need a few minutes. Keegan's coming over and I—"

"What?" Nora screeched. "Keegan? Why would you invite him over? We don't have a few minutes!" Waves of heat rolled over her. She picked up one of Tess's suitcases.

"Come on, we need to get your stuff off the first floor. Hurry up. Why is Keegan coming over? Tess?"

Her sister didn't move. "Why are you so nuts this morning?"

"The washer's leaking." A thousand thoughts sprinted through her mind, one stumbling over the next and none making it past her lips.

Tess looked at her like she was insane. "You think the water's going to rise from the basement and drown us all?"

"Don't be stupid." She lugged the suitcase up the stairs. "What's in here? Ice chunks? Tess get up here!" Just as she reached her sister's room, the doorbell chimed. *Oh, God, Erik was here.* "Don't answer it," she shouted from the second floor. "Don't open the—" She charged down the stairs and shoved Tess's other suitcase behind a chair at the exact moment Tess pulled open the front door. "—door!" She skidded to a stop right behind her sister.

Willa charged into the room wagging her tail, while Erik smiled broadly at Tess and said, "Hi, Tess."

Tess turned toward Nora, her brows pulled together in the center as if to seeking the answer to an unspoken question. Nora gave what she hoped was an imperceptible nod.

Tess turned stiffly back toward Erik. "Nora. I'm—Nora." She let out a light laugh—a tinkle tinkle failure as far as Nora was concerned.

"Right. I'm Tess." Nora leaned around her sister to give a little wave. "Come on in."

"Sorry about that," Erik said. "You two really look a lot alike."

They both laughed—chortled, choked, whatever. Just not light and easy, that was for sure.

As they stood in the living room looking awkwardly at

one another and taking turns petting the dog, Nora tried to figure out how to explain why Erik was here. She couldn't just come out about the washer because ... if Tess was Nora, then she would already know why he was here because she was the one who told him about the washer yesterday. Or at least that's what he thought.

Her brain hurt.

She knew she should just tell him the truth. She had planned to tell him today. But not now and not like this—not with them standing here in the midst of chaos already lying right to his face.

She restrained the urge to press her fingers into the pain that was throbbing in her temple. Finally, she gave up on subtlety and said, "I'm so glad Nora told you about the washer yesterday because we've been at wit's end not being able to figure out what's wrong with it. Thanks for coming over." *Sounded sort of fake, but not the worst considering the circumstances.*

Tess's head bobbed up and down. "Right."

Right? Nora wanted to strangle her. That was the best she could do when she must have figured out by now that, as Nora, she was responsible for him coming over?

"What exactly is it doing again?" Erik asked Tess.

Tess looked at Nora, and Nora tried to send her a telepathic message. *I told you it was leaking,* she shouted in her head. Tess smiled as though the message had gotten through, and Nora felt a rush of relief.

"Oh, you know," Tess said, "the clothes don't get so clean."

Nora shook her head slightly.

Tess cleared her throat. "What I mean is, the clothes don't get so clean because—"

"Water's leaking out of it," Nora said flatly.

"Oh, right," Tess said. "I just mean, the leak is probably causing there not to be enough water in the machine to get the clothes clean. Or properly rinsed ... or ... so they come out dirty."

Nora willed her sister to disappear.

25

———

THIS WAS SO UNBELIEVABLE. AFTER ALL THE TIMES she'd insisted Tess come home early ... and now, when she finally did, disaster broke out. She gestured toward the kitchen. "Would you like something to drink? A Coke? Water?"

"Water's great. Thanks."

"I'll have a Coke. I'm really beat," Tess said.

Nora gave her stiff smile, went into the kitchen, leaned her head against the refrigerator door and begged St. Jude to help her survive this latest debacle. She was truly beginning to understand Erik's point about celebrating the mere act of survival—even at the lowest level.

Pulling a Coke and a couple of bottles of water from the fridge, she returned to the living room and handed them out.

Tess started upstairs. "Hey, Tess, can you show him the washer?" she asked. "Nice meeting—seeing—you again, Erik."

"Sure, yeah, it's in the basement. This way." Nora couldn't wait to get him hidden away downstairs.

Before they'd taken more than a couple of steps, the front door flew open and smashed against the opposite wall. Danny raced into the living room, yelling, "Hey, Mom!"

"What?" Both women answered in unison. Nora mentally cringed and hoped Erik didn't notice.

Danny spotted Willa and his eyes widened. "Is that Willa?"

Erik nodded. "Thought you'd like to meet her."

Danny threw his arms around Willa's neck and was rewarded with several wet kisses across the cheek. "Mom, can we get a dog, can we, can we?"

"We'll talk about it later. What did you come in for?"

Danny giggled as the dog cuddled against him and licked his face. "Can I go over to Zach's?"

Please. Oh, yes, please go. Stay there all day if you'd like. "Sure, go ahead."

Tess was eyeing her from the stairway, her expression asking, *If I'm Nora, how come you're acting like Danny is your son?*

She lifted one shoulder in a small shrug as if to answer, *Sorry. Just roll with it."*

Danny gazed at Erik. "Guess what. I can ride my two-wheeler by myself now. Want to see?"

"Okay with you?" Erik asked Nora.

"Absolutely."

As soon as they were outside, Tess ran back down the stairs. "Why didn't you tell me Erik was coming over?"

Willa ran over to greet her, and she gently pushed the dog away.

"Why is Keegan coming over?" Nora asked.

They stared at each other a long moment. Finally Nora said, "I started to tell you about Erik, but I was so stressed about you being here, all I could think of was hauling your luggage upstairs and getting you out of sight."

"Is this a date?" Tess grinned wickedly. "Why's he fixing the washer?"

Nora threw her hands in the air in frustration. "Of course not. He's fixing the washer because he volunteered to fix it."

"An orthopedic surgeon is fixing our washer?"

"He insisted," Nora replied, frazzled.

"Also, I'm a little confused. Whose kid is Danny—Tess's or Nora's?"

"Tess's. I forgot I was you and ended up giving him my background instead of yours."

"So we each have our own backgrounds—all we switched is each other's names?" Tess asked.

"Right. And jobs. We switched jobs." Nora winced. "I'm Tess. I have Tess's job. But I have Nora's background and Nora's kid."

"Omigod. Okay, got it," Tess said.

"Except for Keegan. Keegan used to be engaged to Nora now."

Tess groaned. "Except on Tuesdays, right? On Tuesdays, Keegan was engaged to me. God, Nora could you make this any worse? What happens when Keegan gets here?"

"Why's he coming here anyway? The last I remember, you said, *don't worry about Keegan, by the time this is done, he'll be putty in my hands.* So, where's the putty?"

"Don't worry, I'm handling it. He's been leaving messages on my phone almost every day. Got kind of demanding—"

"That jerk. Imagine wanting his money back."

"Yeah, well, now he wants the engagement ring back, too," Tess said.

"I thought you gave it to him already."

"The ring represented a promise—one that he broke. Since he never asked for it, I wasn't going to offer it up," Tess said with a sniff.

"Okay, whatever, just get upstairs. Maybe we'll be lucky enough that I can tell him who I really am before you ever have to talk to him again."

"Wait, what? You're doing that now?"

Nora nodded. "As soon as I can. Which should help explain why I'm half insane right now." She peeked around the curtain on the front window to make sure Danny was still demonstrating his bike riding skills for Erik. "So get ready to call his mother."

"Ho-hold on, I've been up all night. I can't even think straight. I can't just call his mother without preparing," Tess said frantically. "I've got notes to review. On the cruise, Liza helped me write a script, everything I wanted to say in a way that, cross your fingers, will maybe keep me from getting fired. Thank God Liza's a journalist."

"So dig it out."

"And I need to practice once or twice. Just because Liza gave me the words to say doesn't mean I'm good at them."

Nora rolled her eyes. "Omigod, this isn't an audition."

"Yes, in a sense it is, I'm auditioning to save my business." Tess took hold of Nora's arm. "Sister, give me a little more time. There's a lot riding on my presentation."

"Fine," Nora said on an exhale. "You've got until he's done with the washer."

"That could be five minutes!"

"All the more reason for you to get moving." She

checked on Erik and Danny again. "Ugh, here comes Erik. Get out of here."

Tess was up the stairs in seconds. Nora drew in a slow breath, then went to meet Erik at the door, the dog right beside her. As long as Danny stayed at the neighbors and Tess stayed on the second floor, everything should be fine.

She showed Erik the washer in the basement, then made an excuse about forgetting her bottle of water upstairs and dashed all the way to the second floor. Bursting into Tess's room, she panted out, "If Keegan wants the ring back, it must be worth something."

Tess was stretched out on her back on the bed, a sheaf of papers in one hand. She opened her eyes. "What?"

"How long are you planning to keep Camille on the phone? Three days?" Nora gestured at Tess's pages.

"Very funny. Each page is a different approach, depending on her response."

"As long as one works. Anyway the ring—"

"He won it in a poker game. Somehow, I don't think it's going to be worth much."

"He won it in a poker game?"

"Yeah. I didn't find out until just before we broke up. And he only let it slip because he was drunk."

Nora snorted. "So much for romantically choosing a ring for your beloved."

"When you consider the effort he put into it—or rather, lack of effort—not to mention the money he *didn't* put into it, I don't know why he's so hot to get it back."

"Which only reinforces what I said. If he wants it back that bad, it's got to be worth something."

"Or whoever lost it in that game is desperate to get it back and ready to ante up big money."

"Either way, it's worth something." Nora perched on the edge of the bed.

"I'm way ahead of you. Why do you think I came back on the red-eye?" Tess asked, sitting up.

"I thought you were being responsible."

Tess had the good sense to look embarrassed. "Well, that too. But the thing is, Keegan insisted that he had to have the ring by tonight. So I cut a deal. I give him the ring and he forgets all about the cruise tickets."

"And he went for it?"

"In a heartbeat. You want to hear the cherry on the sundae? Liza and I were talking about this very thing on the cruise—selling the ring. She tried to resell some ugly jewelry that she inherited from an aunt on her other side. And the most anyone would offer was ten cents on the dollar."

"Ten percent?"

"Yeah, even for diamonds. She checked all over and it was the same. So he can have the ring, but good luck getting cash for it," Tess said, lying down again.

"Sounds like a fitting ending for a blackmailer. Are you ready to talk to Camille?"

"Don't rush it. I need a little more time."

"Why? To lie on the bed some more?"

"I'm practicing in my head."

Nora sighed. "Fine. I'd better get back downstairs before Erik comes looking for me."

"I think he really likes you." Tess nudged Nora's arm.

"No. If there's anyone he likes, it's you. And that's a big part of our problem."

———

Before half an hour passed, Erik had determined the source of the leaking water was a loose hose. "I checked those," Nora said, embarrassed. "They didn't feel loose and there wasn't any moisture around them."

"Probably because it had dried on the hose by the time you noticed the water on the floor." He glanced at her for a moment as he tightened the hose. "I left you a couple of messages."

"I know, sorry ... I've been really busy. Work ... Danny ... client shopping ..." She tried to sound sincere even though it was all a lie. *Now. Right now. She needed to tell him the truth now.*

"I know the feeling," he said before she could begin. "That rush trip to Utah threw the rest of my week out of whack."

"I can see why. How'd it go?" she asked.

"Got the job."

"Must be a lucky week for job offers," she said too brightly.

He stopped what he was doing and faced her. "I turned it down."

She caught her breath and met his eyes, her mind fumbling to come up with a response. "You turned down your dream job?"

"Mom! Hey, Mom!" Danny came pounding down the stairs, rounding the corner to the laundry area at full speed, his friend, Zach, on his heels with Willa close behind. "Mom! I want to show Zach—" Danny pulled up short at the sight of Erik with a wrench in his hand. "Mom! Why didn't you tell me you were going to fix things today? I could've helped."

"It wasn't much of a fix, buddy," Erik said. "Just tightened up a hose."

Nora felt her panic return. If Erik called her Tess in front of Danny, her son would probably blow the top off this charade without even knowing he was doing it.

"Did you see my spider back there?"

"No."

"I think he moved out," Nora said. "Boys, you should go back outside—"

"He's gone?" Danny asked, incredulous. He peered behind the washer.

"I think he took off right after we saw him that night," Nora said. *Yep, right down the toilet.* "Haven't seen him since."

Danny acted dejected for about five seconds. Then he punched Zach in the ribs and looked up at Erik. "That's him," he said proudly.

"He's taller than *my* dad." Zach stared up at Erik.

"So did you two need something, sweetie?" Nora asked.

Danny shifted from foot to foot. "I need to say it in your ear."

Nora tousled his hair and bent low so her head brushed against his.

"Zach wants to meet Erik 'cause he might be my new dad," Danny whispered loud enough for the people in the next block to hear. "And then Willa will be our dog too."

The expression on Erik's face told her he'd heard every word. Her face flamed. "Danny, Erik is a friend. That's all." She took him by the shoulders and turned him toward the doorway. "You two go outside and play."

He didn't budge. "But, Mom—" He moved closer to Erik.

"Go on now." She gave him a little shove and he walked from the room with his chin on his chest. Seriously? If anything more went wrong in her life, she was moving to a deserted island.

She looked at Erik, her face on fire. "I'm really sorry. Remember how I told you he thinks every available man is a potential father? He doesn't understand that the guys may not think it's as good an idea as he does."

"No problem. I totally get it." He put the panel on the back of the washer and began to tighten the screws.

The doorbell chimed faintly in the distance and she headed upstairs, grateful for the escape. By the time she reached the front hall, she wasn't feeling so grateful anymore. Keegan was in the house, and he and Tess were deep in discussion.

"Well, hello Nora," Keegan said smarmily. "Or should I say, *Tess*."

"Very funny. Can you go talk about this somewhere else?"

"Nothing to talk about. I just need your sister to give me what's mine." Keegan snapped his fingers twice.

"You agreed to get the ring back and that's all," Tess said.

"Go talk about this out—"

"All set!" Erik's voice sounded from the kitchen. "Good as new."

"I'm Nora," Tess hissed at Keegan. "Go with it or you get nothing."

Nora turned as Erik came into the room. Her brain felt ready to pop. "Erik, you remember Keegan?" she asked as the two men shook hands.

Keegan rocked back on his heels and cast an appraising gaze over Erik. "I was working with the band at your mother's party. The one that you took—" He looked from Nora to Tess. "The party you took Tess to."

"Good to see you again," Erik said.

Keegan put an arm around the real Tess and pulled her close. "Nora and I used to be engaged. Now we're just good friends. The best of friends."

Oh, for God's sake, he was laying it on thick. If Erik had any brains at all—and of course he did—he was going to realize something wasn't right here. Tess twisted out from under Keegan's arm and began to tug him toward the door. "Keegie, hon, let's finish this conversation later."

"I think we should finish it now." He resisted her pull.

"We have a guest," she said in her perfect hostess voice. She tried to drag him onto the porch. "How about you run some errands, and I'll give you a call when I'm free?"

"How about I take Erik with me?" he said.

Erik's brows pulled together, and he glanced at Nora. An asylum. She lived in an asylum.

"Nora," Nora said through gritted teeth. "Why don't you just get that *thing* for him that he came to pick up?" She looked at Keegan. "Then everything's square, right?" She skewered him with her eyes until he nodded agreement.

Nora leaned into Erik and whispered, "He wants the engagement ring back."

Erik nodded as though weird conversations like this were just a normal occurrence.

Tess dashed upstairs and returned a minute later. She held out a fisted hand toward Keegan. "With this ring ... I keep the tickets."

As soon as he nodded, she uncurled her fingers to reveal a big solitaire diamond in a thick gold setting. Keegan lifted the ring to the light and watched it sparkle. "This baby's worth ten thousand big ones. Thank you, ladies. Sayonara." He shoved the ring in his pocket and sauntered onto the front porch.

Tess shoved the door closed behind him. "Good riddance. Enjoy your ten percent."

Nora threw an apologetic smile at Erik. "It usually isn't so chaotic around here."

"No problem. Makes me realize how dull my life is." He looked between Nora and Tess. "You know, I think I'm finally beginning to see a bit of difference between you two."

Tess pushed her hair back with both hands. "People say that all the time—and they still mix us up. So don't be surprised if you're wrong again later." She grimaced at Nora. "Right?"

"She's right." *And we're both liars.*

"I'll take your word for it. Anybody here up for lunch? I'll buy."

Tess shook her head. "Not me. I'm exhausted. I just got home from—" She froze for a moment as if suddenly remembering she was Nora, and Nora had been at work all week. "—the —laundromat."

Nora gaped at her.

"Because ..." Tess gulped. "The washer, you know wasn't working." She made circles in the air with one finger. "What was wrong with the washer again?"

"A loose water hose," Nora managed to get out.

"No wonder my clothes weren't getting clean, probably not enough water was getting into the machine."

Stop, Tess. Know when to stop.

"So anyway," Tess said. "I got everything clean at the Laundromat ... but like I said, it was exhausting." She lifted the suitcase from behind the chair where Nora had tried to hide it earlier. "And here are my clean clothes," she said. "Suitcases work so much better than laundry baskets, don't you think, to keep clothes neatly folded. So, I'll just go upstairs and put everything away and then, um, catch up on my ... physical therapy reading."

Nora could hardly breathe. What must Erik think of the woman he'd just hired to run the sports medicine rehab center? Tess pretending to be Nora, couldn't have made Nora seem any more of an idiot if she'd tried.

Erik nodded, seemingly unfazed. "Enjoy your reading. So, how about it, Tess? You and Danny want to catch some lunch?"

"He's at the neighbors ..."

"Don't worry about Danny, I'll be here," Tess said from the staircase.

Tess smiled. Sometimes when you took too long to act, life forced your hand. It was doing that right now, pushing her forward toward the truth. For whatever reason, Erik had decided not to take the new job. For whatever reason, he was staying in San Francisco. And now it was time for her to clear the air.

"Thanks," she said over her pounding heart. She slung her purse crossways over her chest. "Let's walk the beach up to Margo's Bistro. The food is great and Willa can sit out on the patio with us." *And when all hell breaks loose after I tell you the truth, I'll have Margo to hold me up.*

"Have fun. See you later, Erik." Tess ascended the staircase, suitcase bumping on nearly every step.

"That's a different Nora than I've ever seen at work," Erik said.

"Funny. That's a different Nora than I've ever seen at home, either."

26

———

"So did I hear you right? You turned down the job?" Tess asked as they walked barefoot along the beach toward the bistro. Willa bounded though the surf beside them.

He nodded, glad she'd brought it up again. The subject had gotten lost in all the commotion at her house. "Got a pretty good reality check from my partners and ..." There was no need to tell her about his mom's input.

"They convinced you the rehab center was a better long-term choice?"

He stopped and turned to look at her. A wave of longing swept through him. "Something like that," he said.

She watched him, her gorgeous eyes full of question. And he knew that if he touched her now, he would never let go of her again. His heart rate sped up. He felt like he was at the top of an untested ski run, ready to hurl himself down without any idea what lay ahead.

Shoving away the trepidation, he pushed off. He took her by the shoulders and bent to cover her mouth with his. She leaned into him and he drew her closer, kissing her more thoroughly than he'd ever kissed anyone in the middle of the day, in the middle of the beach.

As they pulled apart, he watched her eyes slowly open. He brushed a thumb across her lips and touched her cheek. He wanted to bury his head in her hair and kiss the nape of her neck, wanted to feel her beneath him again, loving him until they both were sated.

Then he wanted to lie in bed with her and talk until morning was just few hours away and they fell asleep wrapped in each other's arms.

And then he wanted to do it all over again.

How had he gone all these years without knowing this feeling?

———

Nora wanted to cry. His eyes were so blue, the light in them so warm ... the sun was glinting in his dark hair ... and his face, damn, but she wanted to drown in his face.

Oh, God, she could lose him today.

At the thought, the pain that seared through her was almost unbearable.

He slung an arm around her shoulders, and they walked the rest of the way like that, his arm around her, her arm around him, their bodies touching from shoulder to hip— and every step taking her closer to her moment of truth.

They brushed the sand off their feet and slipped back into their shoes, then hooked the dog's leash to a chair on the patio and went inside to order. Nora introduced Erik to Margo, and they all grinned like they were sharing a secret.

Nora's stomach flopped; she was the only one with a secret, and it was a big one. Suddenly the space seemed overly bright, the warm colors, harsh. Every detail felt like it was being etched in her memory.

"I'll wait for the food," Erik said. "Why don't you go keep Willa company?"

Outside, Nora set her purse on the table and sat down to wait, her stomach churning over the discussion to come. She reached a distracted hand down to touch the dog.

Unbidden, her thoughts turned to Kevin. Theirs had been a relationship of trust. They'd been friends first, lovers later. Had been able to talk openly about everything. Knew they could speak their mind and be accepted, regardless of what was said. They had lived trust. She knew how important it was to a relationship. And yet, she had let this lie go on and on with Erik.

She spotted him coming out the door with their sandwiches. Her heart tumbled at the sight of him, all dark hair and blue eyes and grin happy to see her.

Happy to see Tess.

Here he was, beginning a relationship based on trust. And here she was, lying every step of the way.

She couldn't bear the thought of how those eyes would look at her once she told him how long she'd been deceiving him. She couldn't bear the thought that, as soon as she told him the truth, the trust would be gone.

He set their food on the table and slide into the opposite seat. God only knew how she was going to eat anything with her stomach tumbling like this. Out of sheer nervousness, she took a bite of her sandwich. The food stuck partway down her throat. She swallowed again to try to force it down, then reached for her lemonade.

"Are you okay?" Erik set down his own sandwich and started to stand.

She nodded and took a big swallow of lemonade. Today

was bad enough already—no way were they going to be adding the Heimlich maneuver to the festivities. The lump of food dropped into her stomach and landed with a thud. Okay, no more food—not until she got the truth out.

"You sure you're okay?"

"Yeah. I've got something to tell you."

He looked at her expectantly, and she pushed herself forward. "Remember when your mother called to get personal shopping help for you?" Her pulse began to pound in her ears. "She called when Tess was off on a cruise through the Inside Passage. Up in Alaska."

His brow furrowed.

"You see, Tess was engaged to Keegan—"

"I thought Nora was engaged to Keegan. And why are you talking about yourself in the third person?"

She shook her head and held up one finger. "Give me a minute. Tess was engaged to Keegan and he called it off. So Tess traded in their honeymoon tickets for an earlier cruise and took our cousin, Liza."

"I'm confused—"

"You won't be much longer. Tess was on that cruise when her largest client—Camille Lamont—called and asked her to do a job for her son, Erik." Her voice felt distant, like she was listening to someone else talking, not her. "Tess was afraid that if she didn't do the job, she might lose Camille's business." Nora glanced away, unable to look him in the eye when she said, "So, I did the job for her."

She brought her gaze back to Erik and waited, hoping that he would laugh, that he would think it was just a silly prank ... that he would forgive her.

"You ... did the job?" He cocked his head. "You're not a personal shopper?"

She shook her head.

"You're ... Nora?"

She nodded.

He sat back in his chair. "You're Nora? I've been meeting with, seeing, *Nora* all this time?"

She couldn't speak for the lump in her throat.

"I ... and Nora ..." He squinted at her. "At the ski resort?"

She nodded again.

He said nothing for a very long moment. "Why didn't you tell me?"

She scrunched up her face. "Tess didn't want to lose the account. And I didn't want her to lose it. She's been living with me, but once she can support herself, she'll be able to move into her own place."

"I get that. But it's been a while since our first meeting. Why didn't you say something when you and I ... when things began to happen between us?" Erik sounded like he was trying to understand, and she felt a glimmer of optimism.

"I tried." Her voice quivered. "I planned to tell you when we went skiing, but then you said you were taking that new job ... And I was going to tell you on Friday when I ran into you at the rehab space, but Andy was there—" The expression on his face made her stop. He didn't believe her.

"Whose son is Danny—Tess's or yours?"

"Mine. It was my husband who died—not Tess's." Her voice broke. "I'm sorry, Erik. I never meant it to go this far. I wanted to end it. I just couldn't figure out when ... or how."

"*You should have ended it before it began.*" His eyes narrowed. "Wait. Was this about getting the director job in the new clinic?"

She shook her head vehemently. "No. I was afraid to

tell you because I didn't want you to think it *was* about the job."

"Really. Did it cross your mind at all that maybe you owed me the truth before the interview?"

"I was afraid you might—I wanted you to judge me in the interview as Nora Clark, physical therapist. Not as the person who had been—" Her voice dropped to almost a whisper. "The person deceiving you. And then, when you said you were going to be coaching, somehow it seemed like, if you were going to be gone, would it really matter if you knew?"

"*Would it really matter?*"

"I don't mean it like that." Her throat tightened. This conversation probably couldn't be headed in a worse direction.

"What *do* you mean it like?"

She looked down. "Erik, you don't know how sorry I am. I wish I'd never agreed to help Tess. Is there anything I can do to fix it?"

He shoved his plate to the side. "Let's see, you've been lying to me about who you are since the day we met. Have had numerous opportunities to tell me what was going on and chose not to. Knew that I shouldn't even have been interviewing you if I was *sleeping with you.* And the only reason you have for keeping the lie going is that you wanted to get the job based on your own merits?"

She could tell he was about to walk out of her life. "Erik—"

"Merits that I have a little trouble seeing right now." He shoved his chair back and stood, resting both hands on the table to lean toward her. "Frankly, I don't see that there's anything you can do to fix it." He straightened and reached for the dog's leash, accidentally knocking her purse to the floor.

Everything inside spilled out in a mess—Chapstick, change, hairbrush, tampons, grocery lists, movie ticket stubs, and a hundred other things she had shoved in her purse at one time or another and never bothered to clean out. It was as if a synopsis of her life had been strewn across the floor for all the world to see.

Mortified, Nora dropped to her knees and began to shove everything back into her purse. A quick glance around told her that everyone else on the patio was oblivious to the drama that had just unfolded at their table. Thank God for small favors.

"Sorry." Erik knelt to help, retrieving a comb, some change, and a wrinkled sheet of paper from under his chair. "What the hell is this?" he asked, staring at the paper. "*Perfect Dad Possibilities?*"

27

———

TIME HAD TO HAVE STOPPED. NORA WAS SURE OF IT. Nothing moved, all she could hear was buzzing in her ears. She wanted to say something, but could think of absolutely nothing that wouldn't sound like another lie. After all, how many people kept lists titled, *Perfect Dad Possibilities* in their purse?

How could she still have that? Why hadn't she thrown it away? She reached for the sheet. Erik jerked it away and headed off the patio and around the side of the bistro toward the front sidewalk.

She shoved the rest of her things in her purse and caught up with him just in time to hear him read aloud, "Athletic, likes kids, patient, reads bedtime stories, good income." He looked at her in disgust. "So that's why Danny introduced me to Zach as his new dad. I guess it wasn't all about getting the job, huh?"

"That list was a joke, something my coffee group did because Danny was so fixated on finding a father." She knew she sounded pathetic, like a pathological liar. "I told you about that," she said desperately.

"Let me just run through this multipurpose scam you had going and make sure I have it right. Find a well-heeled guy to marry, get a father for your kid in the process ... oh, and land yourself a higher-level, better-paying job. All by impersonating your sister."

She touched his arm and he shook her off. "I know what it looks like," she said. "But, I swear to you, the women I meet for coffee thought it would be a good thing to do since Danny wanted a dad." *She sounded pitiful.*

"Just an easy way to narrow the field," he said. "I rest my case."

"It was just an exercise—"

"Cut your losses, Tess—Nora. I've known plenty of women like you. Sometimes it's better not to say anything at all." He crumpled the paper into a ball and tossed it in the trash can near the bistro's front door. A moment later, he and Willa were gone.

Numbness overtook her. She didn't know why she'd expected any other response from him—had known that he wouldn't take it well. Who would? That's why she'd kept putting off telling him the truth. But having him find the daddy list was the worst twist of all.

Pain welled up in her chest, and she went back into the bistro. Margo met her at the door. "I left Sandy in charge— it's too crowded for us to talk in there right now," Margo said. "Let's walk to the corner."

In a halting voice, Nora recounted everything that had transpired during past week. "He asked me not to tell anyone about the coaching job until it was official. So I didn't. But now, Margo, he's decided not to take it. *He's staying in San Francisco.* And, I've blown it completely."

"You probably have."

"Oh, thanks for the support."

Margo gave her a hug. "Well, no. We knew you were getting in too deep with the charade. But him finding that stupid daddy list ..." She groaned. "I really think there's only one thing to do—"

"He already said it. *Cut my losses.*"

"No. Go after him."

"Are you kidding?" Nora snorted out a laugh. "I told the truth—he didn't believe me. I said my apologies—he didn't care. I do have some level of pride. There are limits to how low I'll sink."

Margo took hold of Nora's shoulders and faced her. "You made decisions these past weeks—to move forward, to take a chance again. You and Erik found something together. You can't just let it go. *Go after him.*"

"I can't handle any more pain." Nora took a step back. "I'm not putting myself out there to get hurt even worse." She wanted to go home, to be with her son, to envelope herself in her little family again and forget that she'd let her heart out of its cage for a while.

———

Back home, she dropped onto the couch, and kicked her feet up on the coffee table. The afternoon sun filtered through the window, casting bright squares on the rug. Music wafted down from upstairs; Tess was probably still unpacking.

She knew she had to tell her sister what had happened so Tess could call Camille Lamont and try to save the account. But telling her felt like she was imposing a death sentence. Because after today with Erik, there wasn't a prayer in hell that Camille would want to keep working with Tess.

A minute later, Tess came bouncing down the stairs. "Hey. I didn't hear you come in. How was lunch?"

"Danny still at Zach's?"

"Yeah. Came home for a while, moping about that thing you said to him about Erik. So I tried to distract him and asked if he'd found any other new dad candidates—"

"Don't! I just gave him a talk about *not* doing that," Nora said.

"Let me finish. He told me that one of these days you were going to meet someone and fall in love and then he'd get a new dad."

Nora smiled. "Really? Good. I said that a few days ago."

"So, then he went over to his Spider Man calendar and started pointing at the dates and asking if I knew which one was *one of these days*."

Nora blew out her breath. "At least he's sort of getting it. Too bad, *one of these days* isn't ever going to include Erik." She swallowed down the lump in her throat. "I told him the truth at lunch."

"I figured you would—"

"Oh, and did I mention that this morning, as he was fixing the washer, he said he'd decided against taking the coaching job?" She pulled her feet off the coffee table and sat up.

"Seriously? Stay tuned, the story is changing hourly." Tess threw herself onto the couch next to Nora. "How'd he take it when you told him?"

Nora let out a sharp laugh. "He was furious. Thinks it was all about getting the job and finding a rich husband." She stood and crossed the room. "My purse spilled and he found this chart that my coffee group made at Margo's one night ... a list of all the eligible men I know and their attributes for fatherhood."

"You did that?" Tess's voice rose a notch.

"Not me. They did it. All because of Danny's obsession with getting a dad." She rolled her eyes.

"Oh my God. Nails in the coffin. Why don't you tell him *I* made the list and you had nothing to do with it?"

"Too late. Anyway, I'm done with this lying/changing places thing." She stared out the window, unseeing. "Margo thinks I should have gone after him when he left."

"And say what?"

She frowned. "Tell him how I feel. Beg forgiveness—again. Don't let a good thing get away. You know, that stuff."

"Maybe you should."

"No. He knows where I live. The decisions are all his now—he's the one who has to decide if I'm worth forgiving." Nora returned to the couch, dropped her head down onto one hand, and started to cry.

Tess pulled her into her arms. "It'll work out. Really. Remember what Grampa used to say? It's always darkest before the storm."

"Dawn," Nora said.

"Dawn?"

"It's always darkest before the *dawn*. Grampa always got it wrong."

"No wonder it never made any sense."

A sound escaped her, half laugh, half sob. "I finally decided to let go, move forward, say goodbye. I finally decided to take a risk and I got exactly what I was afraid of getting—a broken heart. And I've got no one to blame but me."

"And me," Tess said quietly. "You can blame me."

Nora rested her head on her sister's shoulder. "Yeah. But I love you anyway."

She closed her eyes and mentally relived the last couple

of weeks. Every possible *What If?* popped into her mind. What if she'd never changed places with Tess? What if she'd actually told Erik the truth when they went skiing? What if she hadn't applied for the rehab center job? What if he hadn't found the daddy list?

It was too late for *What ifs*. She'd already lost any hope of having Erik's respect, his friendship, *his love*. He thought she wanted a new job, a father for her son, a rich husband. And if their roles were reversed, she had to admit, she'd think the same thing.

She opened her eyes. "Don't you want to call Camille?"

"Already did. Figured you'd tell everything at lunch, so I called her while you were gone."

"Did you lose the account?"

Tess shook her head. "It was the weirdest conversation. I asked if I could meet with her to explain some recent developments and she said something like *these things happen* and I should stop by tomorrow morning."

"That's not weird. She just didn't know the truth yet because Erik was still with me at the bistro."

"Wanna bet? She told me to bring you along."

———

Erik stood at the top of a double black diamond ski run on Mammoth Mountain and took in the view stretching before him—snow-covered mountains, evergreens, early morning sun sparkling on fresh powder and all of it framed by an endless blue sky.

For the first time in his life he couldn't appreciate it. All he could feel was anger, betrayal ... and loss.

This mountain was almost more home than home to

him. He'd driven half the night thinking that just being here would ease the pain. And it wasn't working.

He'd felt like this once before—like he'd been hit in the stomach with a front-end loader and couldn't catch his breath. Fifteen years ago when he'd blown out his knees. Then, his whole world had been torn out from under him. Skiing had always been what grounded him, gave him a place to belong. And then suddenly it was gone and he was facing more than a year of recuperation—and decisions. What should he do if he couldn't be a world-class skier? The pain of so suddenly losing something he loved came back to him almost as fresh as if it had just happened.

Yesterday he'd planned to tell Tess—Nora—that she was the main reason he had turned down the coaching job. But once she'd unloaded her bombshell and he'd found that damn list, he'd wanted to get as far away from her as possible. His mother had been wrong—giving up Tess didn't mean he was giving up some great chance at happiness.

Oh, hell. His mother was expecting them for dinner tonight. He took his phone from the inside pocket of his jacket and called her number, relieved when it kicked into voice mail and he didn't have to talk to her.

"Hey, Mom, just wanted to let you know I'm out at Mammoth for the holiday weekend—so don't expect me for dinner tonight. As for all that shit you said the other day, I'm thinking there's merit to hanging on to your own identity." He let his gaze travel the panoramic view again. "And, speaking of identities, you might want to have a little talk with your personal shopper about hers."

He shoved the phone back in his pocket and set off down the mountain. All his life, he'd been able to rely on skiing to clear his head. He would take off alone, immerse himself in what he loved, push himself to his limits. Today would be no different. By the end of the day, he was confident that skiing would refocus his mind on what was really important. This mountain would erase the sting of betrayal.

By late afternoon, though, he had to admit that what always worked for him in the past wasn't working today. Being alone only served to make him dwell all the more on Tess ... and Nora. He wished he had someone to talk to, someone to hash over what he was feeling, someone to validate how wronged he'd been. Which is why, in the middle of riding the chairlift, during the usual small talk about the great weather and where you were from and which runs were your favorites, he found himself starting to tell strangers about Tess.

Catching himself a couple of times, he managed to rein himself in before he said too much. Finally, he just gave in and told the whole sordid story to a gray-haired grandmotherly woman sharing his chairlift. He couldn't help thinking that he'd become one of those people who tell the intimate details of their life to a stranger on the bus thinking they'll never see that person again. Only to later discover they were telling their deepest secrets to their new gossipy next-door neighbor.

With his luck, someone would figure out he was Erik Morgan, former Olympic skier, and the story would end up in the tabloids. Either that, or he'd learn later he was telling his woes to one of Tess's—Nora's—relatives.

And even those possibilities didn't shut him up.

"No one can blame you for being upset," the woman said when he finished.

Erik felt a measure of vindication. He watched the skiers flying down the hill below him as the chairlift slid smoothly upward.

"But what does it gain you?" she asked. "Stay mad and all you have is your anger for company. You still lose the girl. Doesn't sound very fun to me."

Her logic seemed a bit convoluted. "Well, yeah, but this lying says something about character."

"It also says something about loyalty ... that she would agree to do something so ridiculous to help her sister."

"What about that list of prospective fathers?" He shifted his ski poles to his other hand.

She let out a laugh. "So she made a list of men who had something positive going on, and you made the cut. Be flattered. Life is short. Don't take offense where none is intended."

This wasn't exactly the sympathetic backrub he'd been hoping to get. As they neared the getting off point, the woman sat forward a bit on the seat and Erik suddenly felt like he still didn't have an answer. "But what about trust? Doesn't this speak to trust?" he pressed.

"Maybe. But she did eventually tell you the truth. If I heard the story right, she told you at a point when she had a lot more to lose than she had to gain. That speaks to something, too. Integrity."

They each pushed away from the lift. "Good luck," she called as she skied off toward one of the intermediate runs.

Good luck. He needed it. He'd just given up the chance to coach the U.S. ski team. He was integrally involved in creating a new sports medicine rehab center. And he'd been taken for a ride by the woman they'd hired to run the center, a woman he would soon have to work with on a daily basis.

No damn way. Something was going to have to change with that situation. His partners would probably be on board with a change once they heard the whole story.

Although ... he didn't relish letting them in on how he'd been duped by the sisters.

How had he not noticed the difference between the two women? Now that he knew the truth, he'd be able to tell the two apart at a glance.

He shook his head. Amazing. He'd come here to forget about Tess—Nora—and instead, he'd been fixated on her all day. The more he tried to push her away, the more she seemed to take over his thoughts.

And then there was Danny. He really liked her son, had already promised to take him skiing again. That wasn't going to happen now. He hated that he was going to be the one to disappoint the kid, hoped Danny wasn't too hurt. But he didn't see any other choice.

He stretched his back. Between the seven-hour drive to get here, a less-than-ideal night's sleep, and the treacherous runs he'd been taking all day, he was feeling a little beat up. Probably a good time to call it quits. This was when skiing got dangerous—at the end of the day with tired muscles.

Dangerous for average skiers anyway. He took a breath, pulled his goggles down and set off down Dragon's Back.

28

Nora perched on a chair in Camille Lamont's very formal living room and waited for Tess or Camille to say something. Tess's hands were clasped gracefully in her lap, belying the anxiety that Nora knew she was feeling. Camille was the picture of graciousness, making small talk, and pouring each of them a glass of iced tea. Nora felt ready to jump out of her skin. *Get on with it,* she mentally urged the two of them. *Let's get this over with.*

Suddenly as if the telepathic message had, for once, gotten through, Tess began to calmly explain what she and Nora had done—and why they'd done it. She described her mental devastation after Keegan called off their wedding, how she'd needed to get away to regroup, and how she'd expected Nora to take over her personal shopping responsibilities for only one meeting. "Two at the most."

Her words were swallowed by the elegant room and replaced with absolute quiet. Nora swallowed.

Camille set her glass on the glass coffee table. "Oh, girls, I knew you switched places that first night I stopped at Erik's."

Nora blanched.

Tess choked on her iced tea.

They both gaped at Camille.

After all the efforts they'd made to keep their switch a secret so Tess didn't lose the account, and Camille was onto them the first night?

"You knew?" Tess asked.

"I suspected. Give me some credit for knowing my own personal shopper. I tried to confirm my suspicions by reminding Nora—Tess—of something I told her when she and Keegan first broke up. That sometimes the perfect person is right in front of you and you don't realize it until you clear away the debris."

Tess frowned. "Did you say that?"

"No. But since Nora had no idea it wasn't true, I hoped her response would give her away." Camille serenely sipped her iced tea. "Unfortunately, her reply was so vague I couldn't be sure. Wasn't sure until the night of the party, when Erik mentioned Tess's son. Of course, I knew she didn't have a son." She smiled and shook her head. "I had no idea what you two were up to ... but Erik seemed so taken by Nora I decided to keep my mouth shut and let nature take its course."

At the mention of the connection between Erik and Nora, Tess dipped her chin at Nora as if urging her to step up and say something. *Absolutely not.* She took a long drink of her iced tea as if to tell her sister, *You're not dragging me into another thing.*

But the silence went on too long, and finally she gave a mental huff and said, "You pretty much know the rest—" at the same moment Tess said, "It sort of snowballed—"

Nora let Tess have the lead.

"Erik and Nora really hit it off and then he asked her

out and Nora wasn't quite sure just what to do," Tess said in rush. "Because, first of all, she was pretending to be me. But also because it's been a long time. She's been a widow five years. And, I, for one, was really happy she had met someone, so we just didn't know how to get the truth out without jeopardizing their—" She smiled at Nora. "—budding relationship."

Nora pressed her lips together. Did Camille really need to know all this? "We were just friends, really," she hastily interjected.

"I think it was more than just friends for my son." Camille's voice had the self-assurance of a woman who knew far more than she was letting on.

Nora blushed. "Well, maybe a bit more. But it's over—yesterday I told Erik everything. You don't have to worry that he doesn't know the truth." Saying the words out loud put a deadening finality on the whole experience. Suddenly she just wanted to go home.

"And how did he take it?"

"Not very well," Tess said quickly. "He might have taken it better except he found a list that Nora's coffee group made." Tess described the daddy list and how it had come to be. "That's when things went from bad to worse. It sealed everything because Erik thought all Nora wanted was a rich husband and a father for Danny."

Blabber, blabber, blabberhead. Nora clenched her teeth together. When would her sister learn to keep her mouth shut?

"That explains why he's gone skiing to Mammoth. He does that when he needs to clear his mind. I wasn't sure what sent him there this time." Camille looked down at her clasped hands.

Tess cleared her throat and sat up straighter. "I'd like to

say how sorry I am that we did this. I should have told you I was on a cruise. Should never have asked Nora to take my place—"

"Apologies accepted."

Tess's expression brightened a little. "And, if it would be possible, I would really appreciate a second chance ... to keep working with you."

"Of course. That goes without saying."

"Oh, thank you!" Tess looked like she'd just won the lottery. "Rest assured, I will make sure I find the best of everything for—"

"I know you will. You always do." Camille turned to Nora. "Have you ever been to Mammoth, dear?"

No. No. No. They were not going to get into a conversation about Mammoth, which would lead to a conversation about Erik, which would somehow lead back to a conversation about Erik and Nora. They'd gotten exactly what they wanted today; now they needed to get out.

"Oh, sure, years ago. We've both been there," Tess said cheerily. "Great skiing."

"Not for a long time," Nora interjected. She glanced at her watch. "I'm sorry, but I have a meeting I'm supposed to ... do you mind—"

"Absolutely. Thank you both for coming," Camille said and waved them on their way.

Tess was positively giddy as she backed her car out of the driveway. "St. Jude has been working overtime for us. Look at today. I get to keep Camille Lamont as a client. You know where Erik is. Could we ask for more?"

"Could you ever shut up?" Nora asked. "Did you have to tell Camille everything?"

"I didn't tell her *everything*." Tess tossed her head.

"Anyway, I'm beginning to think Margo had the right idea about Erik. Go after him. Now that you know he's at Mammoth, drive up there ... recreate what you two had last weekend. I'll babysit Danny."

"Are you crazy? I'm not chasing him to the ski resort."

"Why do you think his mother told us where he is?"

Nora tapped two fingers against her forehead. "Figure it out. She was making conversation."

"No, she wants you to follow him there."

"And do what? Wrap myself in Saran Wrap and knock on his door? Because that's about the only way he's going to let me in his room."

"Now there's an idea—"

Nora blew out a breath. "Don't be a moron."

"I think you should go—"

"Stop, Tess. Just stop. I don't even know who I am anymore. And I'm not sure I like who I think I've become. I know for a fact that Erik doesn't." She made a slashing motion with one hand. "I'm not chasing him to a ski resort. Don't bring it up again."

As soon as they pulled up in front of the house, Nora jumped out hurried up the walk alone, past Danny and the babysitter making chalk drawings on the driveway. "Ashley, I'll run over with your money in a few minutes," she said.

She took the stairs two at a time and went into her bedroom, putting her back against the door to close it. Anger fought with sadness inside her. She'd tried to move on, she really had. She'd met a guy who was kind and sweet and fun. Who wasn't afraid to say what he meant, who went after what he wanted ... who took risks. It had been so long since she'd let herself take any risk at all. And she missed it.

She went to the window and pushed aside the curtain to watch her son slaying a blue chalk-drawn fire-breathing dragon on the driveway with a stick. "It happened just like I said it would, Danny," she said softly. "I met someone and we felt a connection. And I fell in love." She drew a shaky breath. "But I blew it."

She thought about her conversation with Erik, how she'd said she wanted him to judge her in the interview on her own merits—and not be influenced by knowing she'd been lying to him. Except ... one of the most important traits she could bring to the job was integrity. And she'd displayed a shocking lack of it. Even her decision to finally tell the truth was too little, too late.

Erik believed she kept lying in order to improve her chances of becoming director of the new clinic. Maybe he was right. Things had gotten so complicated the past couple of weeks she didn't know up from down anymore.

She'd pulled back from revealing the truth on the ski trip because he'd sprung his new plan on her—he was going after a coaching job that would take him everywhere in the world but here. The pain had been so strong she'd mentally run away, unable to face how much more it might hurt if she told him who she really was and he rejected her outright.

She'd promised Margo she would quit running. Then she'd run herself into the biggest mess of her life.

Oh sure, she'd landed the job she wanted, but if Erik had known all her lies before the interview, she probably wouldn't have gotten the offer. Losing him was nothing compared to knowing he thought she cheated to get the job, that he believed she had no integrity. This was an ache so deep it made her soul hurt.

She had run to avoid pain. And she got pain anyway.

Telling Erik the truth hadn't taken the tilt out of her life. In order to do that, she had to right one last wrong. She had to show him that she hadn't kept lying just to become the rehab center director. There was really only one way to right this wrong—she had to refuse the job. And she had to do it now.

She drew a long, slow breath and exhaled, more calm than she'd been in days. No one would be in the office over the Memorial Day three-day weekend—least of all the head administrator. But she could leave him a message turning down the job, and let Erik fill in all the gory details when everyone was back in the office on Tuesday.

She went downstairs to get her phone from her purse. Tess sat at the dining table eating a bowl of ice cream.

"Do me a favor. Be quiet during my call," Nora said, tapping through the hospital directory until she found the head administrator's number. "I don't need any chaos in the background."

Tess made a face. "Why would I do that? Who are you calling anyway?"

"Just don't, okay?" Nora punched in the phone number.

"Fine." Tess shoved a spoonful of ice cream in her mouth.

She waited through six rings, waited for voice mail to kick in, waited for her mind to finish forming exactly what she wanted to say. Then she left a succinct message; with each word she spoke, the weight on her heart lifted a bit more.

Tess's mouth had dropped open and she was waving her spoon in the air.

As soon as Nora swiped off her phone, Tess exploded. "You quit the job? You've only had it two days! It was everything you wanted!"

"If Erik had known the truth, I doubt I would have even gotten an interview, let alone the job." She shook her head. "He thinks the worst of me and I can't live with that. Jobs come and go. But there's only one Erik. Even if I can't have him, what he believes about me is more important than any job." She pulled a spoon from the drawer and took a scoop of her sister's ice cream.

Tess shoved the bowl toward Nora. "You can have the rest."

"I don't have germs."

"I have to go. I forgot to pick up some stuff for a client." She looked at the clock on the microwave. "God, look how late it is already. I'll probably be late."

"Fine." More than fine actually. Her life had been in turmoil since Tess got home yesterday, and a few hours without her would probably feel like peace on earth.

———

Erik watched the late news from the bed in his hotel room, his swollen right knee packed in ice, his dog lying beside him. Been here, done this ... damn, he probably aggravated the cartilage he tore when he blew out his knee fifteen years ago.

He couldn't be sure until he had an MRI, but having seen plenty of these in the office, and having experienced it himself, he was fairly confident of his diagnosis. At least the injury wasn't as bad when he was twenty-two—then he'd also had multiple fractures and torn ligaments.

He shook his head. He knew better than to ski tired. But he'd kept going, kept forcing his muscles beyond fatigue to keep his brain from thinking about Tess. *Nora.*

Leave it to a woman to screw up his life.

If he was right about this injury, he'd probably need arthroscopic surgery. Then it would be six or eight weeks before he was up to speed again. He clenched a fist. He'd been counting on working round the clock to keep him so busy he would forget all about Nora. Now that would be impossible.

"We need to forget about her, Willa," he said, running a hand down the dog's back. The thought actually hurt. *This was ridiculous.*

He pointed the controller at the TV and flipped through the channels, looking for something other than Nora and his knee to occupy his thoughts.

A firm rap sounded at the door and he frowned. He wasn't expecting anyone, hadn't ordered room service. What the hell did housekeeping want at this time of night?

He pushed himself to his feet, limped to the door and yanked it open.

Tess stood in the hall outside his door.

"What do you want, Tess?"

"Oh, good," she said. "You *can* tell the difference. I thought I might have just wasted seven hours on the road." She pushed past him into the room. "Or, God forbid, I would have had to impersonate Nora and seduce you."

He shut the door and limped after her. "What the hell are you doing here? It's ten o'clock on a Sunday night."

"Don't I know it? I've been driving since three. And I might ask you the same thing—what the hell are you doing here?" She sank onto an upholstered chair in the corner. Willa leaned against her legs and she rubbed the top of the dog's head.

Erik returned to the bed and elevated his right leg again, gently repositioning the ice pack on his knee. "I'm skiing. Your turn."

"I'm coming after you."

"One sister was enough, thanks," he said. "You might however, consider going after my mother, because when she finds out what the two of you pulled, it just may mean the end of—"

"She already knows. She doesn't care," Tess said smugly.

"She doesn't?" he asked, shocked.

Tess shook her head. "Apparently she's known the truth since the first meeting Nora had with you."

His mom was in on the scam, too? "No way. She would have said something."

"She's a romance novelist. Spotted a glimmer of attraction between you and Nora and figured it was worth waiting to see if it meant anything."

So his mother had been matchmaking even when he thought there wasn't a snowball's chance in hell of her doing it again? No wonder she'd given that little speech a few days ago. He scowled at Tess. "Which still doesn't explain why you're here."

"What did you do to yourself?" She pointed at his knee.

"Probably tore the meniscus—cartilage. I'll know better once I have an MRI."

"You going to be laid up for a while?" she asked.

"Could be. So why are you here?"

"I'd love to explain, but I'm a little parched." She lifted the lid on the ice bucket. "I see you have plenty of ice."

He gestured at his knee. "I kind of have a need for it."

"Have you got anything to drink?"

"Check the bar. Underneath."

Tess took a bottle of Snapple and a bag of peanuts from the bar. "Anything for you?"

"Yeah, give me one of those, too—mix some vodka in it. And while you're at it, don't forget to tell me why you're here."

"I think that's called a Snapple Spike," she said as she

mixed it up. She handed him the drink and settled into the chair again. "So, why am I here?" She took a long drink. "Huh. Well, it seemed like a good idea when I started out. Now, I don't know. Nora thinks I'm shopping for clients." She gave a light, easy laugh. "On a Sunday night. Late." She took another sip of Snapple, then tore open the bag of peanuts. Her voice grew serious. "Actually, I thought it might be helpful if you heard the truth from the person who started it all."

"You might have called," he said. "Save a little time, gas."

"Too impersonal. You need to understand that this whole switch was my idea," she said. "I was afraid if I wasn't available to help your mom, I would lose her account to someone else."

He frowned. *Heard this already.* "You know, Tess, I don't really care—"

"You don't get to say that until you've heard the whole story. Not after I just drove seven hours to tell it. If, when you've heard the whole story, you still want to say *I don't really care,* then I will get in my car and drive seven hours back to San Francisco and we'll never speak of this again. Agreed?" She raised her eyebrows at him.

He was taken aback. So this was the real Tess. "Okay."

"Now, where was I?" she said. "Oh, yeah. Nora really, really didn't want to take my place. But I begged her. Told her she had to help me. Convinced her it would only be for one or two meetings." She popped a handful of peanuts in her mouth and chewed thoughtfully. "Of course, then your mother had to ask her to speak at the garden club. And you had to ask her to the party. And skiing ..."

"Are you saying I'm partially responsible for this?"

"In some ways, the shoe does seem to fit don't you think?" she said.

No. He didn't see it that way at all. But he was starting to gain an understanding of how Nora got corralled into impersonating her sister in the first place.

"Anyway, then she ran into Keegan, who knew she wasn't me, and he started blackmailing her with the information—"

"What?"

"Well, not quite blackmail. There's a whole other story about the cruise tickets and the engagement ring—we can talk about that later. The thing is, Nora agreed to do the personal shopping gig for you—and then you and your mother kept asking her to do other stuff and she couldn't figure out how to say no."

"She wanted to say no?" He sat up straighter, wincing as he tweaked his swollen knee.

Tess laughed in a tinkling sort of way. "Not to you. But certainly to your mother."

Oh, well, that was understandable. He wanted to say no to his mother a lot, too.

"But then you got under her skin—in more ways than one," Tess continued.

"I did?" A warmth started in his chest.

"Yeah. You don't know this ... but Nora and her husband had a really good marriage. She pretty much figured she'd never love again. And then you came along." She screwed up her face. "Not that she's in love with you. I mean, she hasn't said that to me or anything. She could be, I suppose, but I don't know. Anyway ... there was the potential ..."

The potential? He knew all about the potential. He'd just turned down coaching the A team for *the potential*.

Tess finished off her peanuts and went to the cabinet to grab a bag of Cheetos. "She decided she was going to tell you the truth on that ski trip. But then you, um ... *did it* ... and right after that you told her you were going to take this all-year, around-the-world coaching job." She shook her head. "Not the best bedside manner, doc, if I do say so myself."

"I told her I wanted to keep seeing her."

"Sorry, but after first saying you aren't going to be around for four years, telling a woman you still want to see her feels a lot like, *Thanks for the good time, I'll call you when I'm horny.*"

He stared at her. How had he ever thought Nora was Tess?

29

"LIKE I SAID, WORK ON THAT BEDSIDE MANNER." TESS walked across the room eating Cheetos. Willa followed her, step for step, hoping to snag a dropped piece or two. "So she didn't tell you on the ski trip because, well, shock. But she hated lying. So even if you were leaving for a new job, she wanted you to know the truth. Would have told you that day she saw you in the rehab center but your partner was there."

"She said her washer was broken."

"Seriously, get a clue. Do you really think she was walking around the new space crying about her washing machine?"

He hadn't given it much thought before now. "Probably not."

Tess nodded knowingly and gestured with her bottle of Snapple. "As for that daddy list? It really was *nothing*. Did you even check out who was on it? It was a joke. One name was the guy who pushes the coffee cart at the hospital. And half of the other names were guys she didn't even know—

they were just names the women in her group threw on the list. Women do stupid things like that—usually when they're sixteen, not in their thirties—but it doesn't mean *anything*." She sat on the edge of the bed near him. "Anyway, she's sort of devastated that you don't believe her."

"She got the job she wanted. So all is not lost," he said with more bite than he intended. He took a swallow of his drink.

"That's why I'm here. You're right. She got the job of her dreams," Tess said softly. "And this afternoon, she turned it down."

What kind of game were these two playing? "What the hell does that mean?"

"She called the top dog at the hospital this afternoon and said she didn't want the job."

He twisted his head to look directly at her. "It's Sunday. He's not in."

"She left a message on his voice mail."

"But—she was really sick of doing hospital physical therapy. You should have seen her excitement about this new clinic." He struggled to find the logic in what Tess was telling him.

"I saw it. That's why I'm here. She turned it down because of you. Because she wanted to prove that everything she'd done wasn't about getting the job."

"Oh, hell." He drank some more. Earlier today he'd been planning to talk to his partners about rescinding Nora's offer. Now, all he could think was what a loss for the clinic it would be if she left. "She's the best person for the job, the most qualified. She gets our vision for it. She's exactly who we need to run the place—"

"Well, she's not going to," Tess said matter-of-factly.

"What that woman needs is—"

"What she needs is for you to accept her apology and tell her you still want her in the job. Even then, I'm not sure she'll take it."

This is why he didn't get involved with women—they were so damn difficult. He grabbed his phone from the nightstand and punched in Nora's number.

Music started playing across the room and Tess held it up her phone. "Hey, genius, that's my number. You've been working with The Shopping Goddess ... so you've been calling me all this time."

He scowled. "You were passing the messages to her?" he asked as Tess nodded. "So, when she said she was using Nora's phone because her phone was dead—"

"Yeah, another lie. But that's the number you need to call."

"I can't believe you two could keep all this straight." He scrolled through his recent calls and pressed redial on Nora's number.

Her voice mail kicked in, and he shut off the phone. "Where is she?"

Tess shook her head. "At this time of night? Probably in bed."

"Great. The best person for the job and we're going to lose her." An hour ago he wanted to fire her, now all he wanted was to make her stay. "Do you have any idea how incredible this center is going to be?"

Tess shook her head. "But then, this isn't my field. If you want to talk shopping, though, I could hold my own."

"It's the kind of place most docs dream of. It was for me anyway. My partners and I have been after the hospital to do this for a long time." He called Nora again, once more reaching voice mail.

"Her ringer may be off," Tess said.

"Hell." He tossed down the rest of his Snapple Spike. "Come on, we're going back." He took the ice bag off his knee and swung his legs over the side of the bed, exhaling sharply as he stood. "No way can I drive. My right leg is totally out of commission. I'll ride with you and leave my car behind." He grimaced. "Sorry, but you'll have to do the driving."

"Maybe you should go to an emergency room—"

"Nope. I'm pretty sure I know what's hurt. And if I'm right, I know what doctor I want to see." He snapped his fingers. "Let's go, it's a long drive."

Tess gave him a patronizing look. "I know it is. I just made it. And now you want me to turn around and go back? Seven hours here, seven back. You want me to drive fourteen hours in a row?" She popped some Cheetos in her mouth and licked the orange off her fingers.

"I'd drive if I could."

"Boy oh boy, you are going to owe me big."

He threw back his head and laughed, wincing as the motion shifted his balance and sent pain shooting through his knee. "Owe you? All this might do is make us even." He hobbled around the room gathering his stuff and shoving it into his duffel bag. Then he leashed Willa. "Okay, I'm ready. Grab my skis. And get us some of those Cokes out of the refrigerator—the caffeinated ones so we can stay awake."

Fifteen minutes later they were flying down the highway headed toward San Francisco, Tess driving, the dog riding shotgun, and Erik stretched out in the backseat with his leg up.

"Estimated arrival time, six a.m.," Tess said. "Wake up merry sunshine."

"We can do better than that. No one's on the road so you can just lay on the gas."

She snorted. "And you'll pay the speeding ticket?"

"The pleasure will be all mine." He shifted to make his knee more comfortable.

Tess tossed a glance over her shoulder. "Maybe we should stop at a hospital first. At least you could get some pain meds."

"I can write my own damn prescription if I want. Just drive. I took some over-the-counter stuff right before you arrived."

She did that laugh of hers again. "Okay, you're the expert."

They engaged in small talk for a while, then settled in, listening to the radio, the black road rolling out in front of them, the miles passing as slowly as the hours. He didn't want Tess to fall asleep, and he didn't want to fall asleep and leave her to stay awake on her own, so every now and then, they'd engage in one discussion or another, then let it lapse.

He closed his eyes and let his thoughts drift. After listening to Tess for the last hour, he completely understood how Nora had gotten roped into the whole fiasco. Tess was a lot like his mother—a steam roller on a mission. He almost laughed out loud remembering how, when he'd first met Tess—Nora, actually—he'd thought she didn't seem like a personal shopper his mother would hire. Now that he'd met the real Tess, he saw that she and Mom were a perfect match.

Shit. And now, because of all this, they were about to lose the best person for the director's job. He couldn't believe Nora had withdrawn her acceptance. Not only was it the kind of work she wanted to do, but she really was the best person for it.

Sure, she'd lied to him about who she was. In the big picture, there really was no harm done by the Shopping Goddess switch—nothing that happened would affect how she would do her job. And now that he'd decided to stay, he was more determined than ever to make the new center as good as it possibly could be. Nora Clark as the director would ensure that. She was right for the job.

By the time they reached San Francisco, his knee was throbbing, he was bone-tired, and his patience was at an end. Tess pulled into the driveway. "I'm thinking Nora might not be happy to learn I drove out to Mammoth and talked to you. So here's my plan."

"Five-thirty in the morning and we have to follow a plan?"

She nodded. "I'll go in and get into my pajamas. You wait out here a few minutes, then ring the bell. I'll answer the door and tell Nora you're here. That way she'll think I just got out of bed—and never know I had anything to do with your arrival."

Five-thirty in the morning and she was concocting schemes. Nora never had a chance. He would have to profusely apologize to her for doubting her. No wonder she agreed to take Tess's place—he would have too, if it meant she'd move out of his house. "Okay," he said.

"Then—"

"There's more?"

"Well, yeah." She put the car into Park and shut off the lights. "There's no way you could know she quit the job. She left the guy a voice mail—and he sure didn't go into work this afternoon and track you down at the ski hill to tell you. You have to come up with some other reason for being here, and then get Nora to tell you she quit."

"Some other reason for stopping by at the crack of dawn with my dog? Hell, that should be easy."

Tess ran to the back door. He limped to the front and waited on the porch in the darkness a few minutes before pressing the bell. His knee ached and his head wasn't far behind. When no one answered, he rapped the door with his knuckles. "Plan's working well, Tess," he muttered.

He rang the bell again, and finally pounded the door with his fist a couple of times. If she didn't get the door soon, one of the neighbors would probably call the police.

Finally the porch light flipped on, blinding him. He blinked several times to adjust to the sudden brightness.

Nora stood in the doorway in short pajamas, her hair mussed, her eyes heavily lidded and sultry, her face flushed from sleep. *Nora.*

He wanted to kiss her.

"Erik?"

"Nora." Leave it to a woman to screw up his life.

"Do you know what time it is?" she asked.

Where the hell was Tess? "Ah, yeah. It's around five ... thirty."

She glanced at Willa, sitting patiently at his side. "What are you doing?"

He wanted to kiss away the confusion on her face. "I hurt my knee. Can I come in?"

She hesitated just long enough that he thought she was going to refuse. Then she gave him a strange look and held the door open.

Tess bounded down the stairs. "Oh, Erik!" she said gleefully. "And Willa! How nice to see you. I was upstairs.

In bed. Sleeping. Soundly." She raised her voice a notch. "*Very soundly.*"

"Can I sit down?" Erik held up his ice pack.

"How'd you do it?" Nora asked.

"Skiing."

She winced and led him to the living room, stopping to turn on a lamp to its lowest setting. He eased himself onto the couch, favoring his bad knee as he put his legs up.

From the kitchen came the sound of pans clanking and water running. Willa's ears pricked up and she tilted her head, then padded into the kitchen to investigate.

"Tess sure is energetic for this time of morning," Nora muttered. "So now, why are you here?"

"My knee. It's killing me. I can't sleep. Not sure—think I might have torn the cartilage again." He hoped he sounded convincing—at least he knew everything he was saying was medically accurate.

She frowned at him, then stepped to the window and looked outside. "You drove back from the ski hill in the middle of the night? Where's your car?"

Tess stepped into the room. "I'm making coffee," she said brightly. "And some of those refrigerated cinnamon rolls. I know how everyone gets hungry in the middle of the night."

"Tinkle tinkle, sister, isn't going to cut it. Where's his car?" Nora asked.

"How should I know? I just got up," Tess said. "I've been sleeping for hours."

"I took a cab."

Nora turned to face him. "From Mammoth? That must have cost a fortune."

"What's money?" He was starting to get a good sense of how easy it was to get sucked into a big charade.

Nora bit her lower lip as she mulled over his words, and he was hit by a realization so hard, it almost took away his breath. When he was with Nora, he had a team. Just the two of them in one boat, rowing in the same direction. He inhaled slowly. *He hadn't come here because she was right for the job. He'd come here because she was right for him.*

———

The simple nearness of him made her weak. She tried to still the racing of her heart, to stay detached. "So ... you've come about your knee? In the middle of the night?"

He nodded. "I've been to the best doc I know and he ordered up physical therapy. I didn't want to wait another minute and have it stiffen up."

"What doc?" she asked suspiciously.

He grinned and his blue eyes sparkled. "Me. So I've come to the best physical therapist I know to get some help. The person who's going to head up the new sports medicine rehab center."

"At five-thirty in the morning." She broke eye contact. She didn't want to touch him, didn't want to feel the warmth of his skin under her hands, didn't want to be close enough to smell his aftershave ... didn't want to feel the pain in her heart.

"Humor me. Just check it over ..."

"Fine. Lay back."

As soon as he was flat on his back, she did a manual test to check for a cartilage tear in the knee—a test that was impossible for anyone to do on themselves. Taking hold of his right leg, she moved it into a full bent position, rotated the foot inward, then straightened the leg again. She didn't hear any clicking. "Any pain with that?" she asked as professionally as possible.

He looked overjoyed. "No. Quick, do it the other way." She repeated the test, rotating the foot outward this time.

He pushed himself up on his elbows and grinned at her, so cute she could hardly stand it. "No pain. No tear," he said. "Nora, you are truly a gifted therapist."

She laughed. "It probably swelled up so badly because your knee was compromised already." She sat on the edge of the coffee table and touched her fingers to the big scar that ran down his knee and shin. He'd really done a number on himself. Multiple scars surrounded that big one, so many that his knee looked like a jigsaw puzzle. For a moment, she could almost feel the pain he must have experienced when he blew out his knee and lost future, how the loss of skiing must have devastated him. She ran a finger over the scars again, then began to gently work the muscles.

Erik lay back and shut his eyes. "Maybe a little higher."

She moved her fingers up his strong, solid quad muscle and wished he would kiss her. "There?"

"Yeah, that's good," he said, eyes still closed. "Maybe a little more on the inside."

She eyed him suspiciously and slipped her fingers onto his inner thigh. He sucked in a breath.

"Does that hurt?"

"Ah ... no." He opened his eyes. "You can't turn down the job at the clinic."

"Word gets around fast." She moved her hands away.

"You are far and away the best person for the job," he said, sitting up.

"I let the ends justify the means. I should have told you the truth much earlier, but I rationalized everything." Out of need to do something, she began to work his knee again.

"Rationalization is an interesting thing," he said. "I

completely rationalized that giving up my career in order to coach was a good thing to do. I thought being part of the team would make me whole." He rubbed a hand across his jaw. "Only a funny thing happened on Friday afternoon. I realized there was something else that made me more whole than being part of the ski team."

She looked at him, at his eyes watching her with intensity, and waited.

"You," he said.

This wasn't happening. It was five in the morning and she had to be dreaming. She wanted to say something but her brain was refusing to function. Finally she whispered the only word she could find: "What?"

"You. You make me whole."

Contentment washed through her, that sensation you get after wanting something so badly, after waiting and waiting and waiting and thinking it will never happen. And then, suddenly, it does. She felt a quiet joy, a gentle relief, like a sigh, an exhale of breath that one can't hold in because life is so good and moments like these are so rare. A knot formed in her throat.

"I realized I didn't want to spend years on the road, years getting up at dawn and going to bed at midnight ... and never having you. Nora, when I'm with you, I have a team." He smiled wryly. "I was going to tell you Saturday. But then all that other stuff got in the way." He grasped her by the arms and pulled her toward him, until their faces were inches apart. "Stay."

"With the clinic?" she asked.

"With the clinic. With me."

Tears sprang to her eyes.

"I love you," he said. "Will you stay?"

She nodded and leaned into him, kissed him then and let all the tension of the past three weeks leave her.

"Hey, everyone, here's the sweet rolls, hot from the oven. Who wants coff—" Tess sang from the doorway.

They broke apart and looked at her.

"Am I interrupting something?" she asked innocently.

"A meeting. We're working on the business plan for the center," Erik said.

Tess chortled. "That's just what I thought. I so knew that fourteen-hour drive would be worth it."

Nora looked from one to the other. "What fourteen-hour drive?"

"Oh, nothing," Tess said.

"You went to Mammoth today," Nora said.

"Someone needed to get the train back on the tracks." Tess bit into a cinnamon roll.

"I feel like I've been set up."

"Join the club. Your sister has a way about her. Next thing you know, you're in so deep you can't find your way out," Erik said.

Nora rolled her eyes. "Don't I know it. It's light and easy laughter, tinkle tinkle. Works every time." She gave her own version of Tess's signature laugh.

A child's giggle echoed from the stairway. Danny was sitting on the top step, grinning as Willa ran up to see him.

"I think that's my cue to call it a night," Tess said heading for the stairs. "Come on, urchin, back to bed with you."

Erik bent to kiss Nora once more. "And my cue to pick up right where we left off."

———

If you enjoyed this book, could I ask a favor?
I would be forever grateful if you would post a review on the site where you got it.

———

The fourth book in the *Bachelor Next Door* series, **ROMANCE ON THE ROAD**, is Liza's story. Please enjoy the following excerpt.

Excerpt from
ROMANCE ON THE ROAD
The Bachelor Next Door, book four

Chapter One

Dear Cordelia,

Freud had if all wrong. He should have asked: What do men want? Why is it that saying the L word practically gives men hives? Why does the merest hint of the word "commitment" catapult men into flight? Why will a man relentlessly pursue a woman, only to change his mind about her once she yields to his advances? I'm beginning to believe men think of women as they do fishing trips. Catch and release. Thank God it's January—the lakes are frozen over just like my heart.

Shivering in Chicago

Dear Shivering,

Things could be worse. You could still be dating a commitmentphobe. At least now you're free to find the right guy. In the famous words of Mae West, "A woman has to love a bad man once or twice in her life to be thankful for a good one." Don't give up yet. Cordy predicts that if you let the ice in your heart melt a little, you'll soon land the keeper you've been looking for.

Cordelia

All she wanted was to be part of *breaking news* instead of *baking news*. The chance to write about murders instead of menus. A little more pizazz and a little less pizza. Was it really so much to ask?

Liza Dunnigan scrolled through the three story ideas her editor had sent over—fast and tasty tortilla treats, winter dinners guaranteed to warm the soul, and waffle mania (whatever that meant). She let out a sigh.

Seven years of quick easy dishes and happy holiday entertaining and cool low-carb cooking and blah, blah, blah. *Enough.* She'd been working in the same job at the Chicago Sentinel since the day she graduated college—the small, private girls' school her parents insisted she attend when she'd really wanted to go to the University of Wisconsin with its wild parties and Big Ten football games. Instead, it had been sherry with the dean, charcoal blazers, and discussions of Thomas Hardy.

Well, no more.

She glanced up as one of her food section coworkers slid into the chair next to her desk. Kristin Coulter, every man's dream woman—tall, thin, blond, blue-eyed. She wore clothing effortlessly, making everything she put on look like a *Vogue* cover. Good thing she was as nice a person as was ever born. Because it kind of made her hard to despise.

"You look different today," Kristin said.

Liza looked down at herself. "Navy skirt. White shirt. Ballet flats. I don't think so." She reached behind her back to give a quick roll to the waistband of her skirt. Kristin probably never had to roll her waistband to make her skirt length fashionable. *Probably because Kristin had the good sense to buy new clothes when styles changed.*

The thought took her aback. Until this moment, she'd

always considered Kristin's attention to fashion a frivolous waste of money.

"Not your clothes," Kristin was saying. "Your face. Seven years together in the food section and I can tell these things. You're hiding something."

Liza grinned.

"I knew it! What are you up to?"

Liza glanced at her watch with its plain black leather band. *How very mundane.* "In half an hour I'm going upstairs for an interview—"

"You're leaving the food section?" Kristin gaped at her.

A thrill ran through Liza that her announcement came as such a shock. Kristin's reaction was reinforcement of just how predictable she'd become. It was definitely time to put her new plan into action. As of today, her motto was: *Throw caution to the wind.*

Kristin leaned forward and waggled a finger at her. "This has something to do with Mark, doesn't it?"

Damn. "No. It's about me. I'm twenty-nine years old, in a rut twenty feet deep and a mile wide."

Kristin pushed herself up, put her hands on her hips and faced Liza, eyes sparkling. "It's about Mark."

Liza exhaled in defeat. "Fine. If it makes you feel better, I admit, Mark is the catalyst. But all he did was open my eyes. When he called me *practical and predictable*, it made me realize just how boring I really am."

"Honey, that was months ago. Just because he dumped you doesn't mean he's right. The world could use a few more practical people."

"Let it be someone other than me. I'm changing my life."

"Because of Mark."

"No. Because of me. All my life I've followed the rules, taken the safe route even when I didn't want to. And what has it gotten me? Don't answer that. It's too late for sales pitches about yesterday's life. I've thought about this for months. It's *time* to shake things up. I'm going after the kind of job I've always wanted, the kind of job I should have applied for years ago."

"You're leaving the food section," Kristin repeated, almost dumbfounded.

"Cross your fingers," Liza said airily. "There's an opening upstairs for an investigative reporter and I'm going for it. With any luck, I'll soon be saying goodbye meatballs and hello mystery."

Forty-five minutes later she was seated across a large beat-up metal desk from Bill Klein, managing editor, a paunchy and wrinkled middle-aged man who looked as if he had left investigative reporting behind years ago. While his desktop was virtually empty, fat manila files and stacks of paper covered almost every other flat surface in the room. Behind him, high-tech laser beams shot across his black computer screen.

He hadn't cracked a smile since the interview began, hadn't seemed impressed by her resume. And now, as she watched his bald head bent over her portfolio of sample articles, it was painfully clear that he wasn't impressed by her writing either.

"You've been with the food section for seven years," he said in a monotone. "Tell me about that."

Liza cleared her throat. The job hunting websites said to sell yourself, make your experience match the skills needed for the job. Food—investigative reporting. Now *there* was a match if she'd ever seen one.

"I get story ideas from almost anywhere. I might read something that inspires a concept for a series. Or a meal in a restaurant will trigger an idea. Then my first step is—" She paused for emphasis. "—*research and investigation*. I'll look into the history of a certain dish or the uses of a particular spice. I dig in, search to find the truth, and expose it to—"

A loud screech from the interoffice buzzer on his desk phone stopped her midsentence.

Mr. Klein sighed and picked up the phone. "Yes?"

Liza shifted in her seat so she could look through the glass wall behind her at the newsroom, awash in activity. She could picture herself there, phone squeezed between shoulder and ear as she typed the finishing touches of a gripping exposé into the computer. Her heart beat a little faster. This was where the action was, the excitement, the pulse of the newspaper. She had to get this job. She just had to. This was about as far from predictable as you could get.

After a long pause, Klein said, "You tell him the deadline is nine o'clock. If he's not finished by then, the story doesn't go in. It's not a big enough scoop to hold the presses. Got that? And Mary, hold my calls, I'm doing an interview right now."

He banged the phone onto the base and shook his head. "Sorry. We're using a freelancer until we can fill this position. The guy doesn't understand the meaning of the word *deadline*."

"I've never missed a deadline in the food section. I'd bring that same conscientiousness to investigative reporting. A reporter needs to know when the story is finished. I guess it's sort of an intuitive thing." An intuitive thing? Oh, please, she needed to learn when to quit talking.

He raised an eyebrow. "Tell me, does this intuitive thing

help at all when you can't get anyone to confirm information on the record that someone has leaked off the record?"

A thrill of excitement rushed through her. Never once in all her years on the food section had anyone ever had to go off the record to answer her questions. *Off the record.* Let alone talking about leaking secrets. The very thought made her all the more determined to get the job. She sat up straighter.

"I guess ... intuition would help me choose just the right persuasive argument to get the source to go on the record. Or even help me decide whether I can push that person to give me names of people to contact who could confirm the information."

She leaned forward and felt the waistband at the back of her skirt unroll a bit. "Mr. Klein, I think I could do a good job for you and I'd do whatever needs to be done to—make sure I do just that." Babbling, babbling.

He drew a long breath and sat back in his chair. "I'm sure you work hard—"

"And I can even work harder—"

"But this isn't an entry-level job. You've no experience in this type of journalism. And you're used to the pace of the food section—we've got tight deadlines. We'll get breaking news late in the afternoon and you'd have to investigate it and submit your story in a few hours." He closed her portfolio and shoved it gently toward her.

"I can do that. If you look at the back of my portfolio there are some stories I wrote for my college newspaper. They're much more investigative. I didn't start writing about food until I graduated." Her words tumbled out in a desperate rush. "My goal has always been to write about something more meaningful, something more important to life than food. Not that food isn't important to life ..." She felt her dream slipping away with her prattling.

"I need someone who can hit the ground running. And with so many seasoned journalists out of work these days because people aren't getting the paper anymore ..." He shook his head. "Well, let's just say your competition is fierce. I'm sorry." He stood, signaling the interview's end.

Liza stared at him dumbly. It was over? Her one chance to break out, change her life, prove to herself that she wasn't so predictable after all? Defeated, she lifted her portfolio off his desk and stood to shake his hand. "Thank you for talking with me," she said.

He pulled open the office door and stepped back to let her pass, then followed her out. For a brief heart-stopping moment she thought he wanted to talk with her further, then she realized his attention was focused on a man heading across the newsroom in their direction.

"Are you getting anywhere on the interview with Dear Cordelia?" Klein asked when the reporter neared.

Liza hesitated, curious. Dear Cordelia, the advice columnist? She bent over a nearby drinking fountain and let the water run over her lips, swallowing every now and then so it looked as if she was actually taking a drink—a very long one. The back of her waistband unrolled a little more.

"Nope," came the reply. "Can't get near her. What a recluse. Her publicist says she doesn't want publicity. Just wants to be left alone to write her column and help people find *true love*. So if that's true, what does she need a publicist for?"

"True love for me would happen on the day she finally grants us an interview."

"At this rate, we won't have it by Valentine's Day ... and you know I'll be off for two weeks—"

"Yeah, yeah. Hell, let it rest until you're back from your honeymoon."

Still bent over the water fountain, Liza tipped her head slightly and watched Mr. Klein step back into his office. She straightened and dabbed at the water that trickled over her lower lip and down her chin. Reaching one hand behind her back, she surreptitiously rerolled her waistband to even out her skirt length.

So, he wanted an interview with Dear Cordelia, the purveyor of advice about romance and marriage, the author of the bestselling *Dear Cordelia's Authoritative Guide to Finding Love and Keeping It Alive.*

Well, well. This certainly presented possibilities. The practical, predictable person would go back to her office and write a story on the many uses of the lowly tortilla. Right. And Mr. Klein had already made it clear she belonged in the food section—not in investigative reporting. Uh-huh. She knew where her place was, where her skills were valued.

Before she could second guess herself, she spun on her heel and marched back into his office. "Mr. Klein?"

He raised his head; surprise flickered across his face.

"I couldn't help overhearing the conversation you just had ... about Dear Cordelia?"

He looked at her, silent, and a heat wave of mortification swept over her. She pushed forward.

"I love her column. I've been reading it for years."

He lifted an eyebrow.

"What I'm trying to say is ... I'd like to—I could—I mean —how about letting me try to get the interview for you?" The words rushed out of her, not at all professional like the websites advised. "I could do it on spec, to show you my investigative abilities, while that other reporter is on vacation. If I don't succeed, he can take over where I leave off."

The corners of his mouth twitched, the first sign all morning that she'd made any type of impression at all. Great. He was going to laugh at her.

"What about your responsibilities for the food section?"

Oh. "Well, you know ... vacation," she blurted out. "The new year just started. I could—I've got two weeks—I could take them off now to track down Dear Cordelia and get the interview." She mentally winced. Showing desperation was a definite no-no in the job hunting book.

He steepled his fingers. "I've been trying to get an interview with Dear Cordelia for ten years. She's never, by the way, given an interview to anyone, anywhere. In all my years of reporting, this is the only story I never got. I've assigned a dozen reporters at various times to get an interview with Cordelia. And everyone has failed."

Her heart dropped into her stomach.

"In other words, Liza Dunnigan, what makes you think you can succeed where nobody else could?"

Because this is the most impulsive thing I've ever done in my life and if I don't try, then Mark is right about me. "Because I want this interview as much as you do," she said. "Because if I succeed, we agree that you'll hire me for the investigative reporter position, which is really what I want." Good God, did she just say what she heard herself say?

A slow grin slid across his face. He threw back his head and laughed. "Kid, you just might have what it takes."

"I know I can do it." She gripped the handle of her portfolio tightly to keep her hands from shaking at the enormity of her lie. Any moment the ceiling was going to open and a lightning bolt would shoot down from above and take her out.

Close the sale, the book said. *Ask for the job.* "Do we have a deal?"

"Oh, what the hell." He reached a hand across the desk and she grasped it with her own. "Deal. Let's go get the file so you can get up to speed on the first lady of the lovelorn, Dear Cordelia."

———

"You've got to be kidding me." Jack Graham shifted the telephone to his other ear and spun his chair round so he could stare out the window at the gray, blustery January afternoon. Today was one of those days that earned Chicago the nickname, the Windy City. "The caretaker kicked off before the dog?"

"Happened yesterday morning," Diane Cooper, his grandmother's neighbor, said with precision. "Heart attack right after church in the parking lot. Like the good Lord just didn't want Billy to leave, wanted to call him home right then and there. I'll go feed CJ and let her out, but you know I can't bring her over here. I have allergies ... and at my age even allergies can be dangerous."

Just what he needed—one more damn thing to take care of. Halfway across the country, in Maine no less. *Happy Monday.* He sighed.

As a publicist, he always had one fire or another to put out. And on top of all his usual work, next week he had an appointment with a wide receiver for the Chicago Bears who wanted to talk about Jack becoming his agent. Representing this guy would be a huge step toward realizing a dream he'd had since college.

Except, the dog's caretaker had died. And now—hold the presses, stop the train—he had to drop everything and go to Maine to find a new caretaker for his late grandmother's basset hound.

"Jack? Are you still there? Did you say something? Speak up—I don't hear so well anymore. What do you want me to do? You'll be coming out, won't you?" Diane asked.

Guilt washed through him; his grandmother had loved that dog. She'd taken it in as a mangy, moth-eaten stray and given it a home—just like she'd done over the years with so many other dogs and cats, and a little boy named Jack. Before she died three years ago, she'd set up a trust fund to cover the cost of a caretaker for CJ so the dog could live out the rest of her days in her home.

"Uh, yeah, I'm here. Can you keep taking care of CJ for a few days? I have to clear my calendar, then I'll get out there as soon as I can."

"At some point, Billy's daughter is going to want to get his stuff."

"Maybe she'll want the job," he said hopefully.

"Hmmph. I know you always *see* her when you come back. And it's none of my business who you hire, but she's got all those boys—four wild—"

"Right. Forget I said it. Just let her in if she wants to pick up his things before I get there." He paused, thinking.

It had been hard enough to find the guy who took the job three years ago. Now, who the hell was going to want to take care of a fat, old, shedding, slobbering basset hound that had one bulging eye from glaucoma?

"You know it might speed things up if ... Can you put an ad on Craig's List for me? Something like ... *Live-in caretaker needed for twelve-year-old basset hound. Single person preferred. If interested, leave message at ...*" He paused, wondering if he could get Diane to field the calls.

"Craig's List? I can call the shopper paper and put something in the classifieds but I've never used Craig's—"

"Yeah, okay. You do the shopper, I'll set up Craig's List. Put in my phone number as the contact."

Jack's new administrative assistant stepped into the room and dropped a note on his desk, smiling prettily in her clingy little sweater and short skirt. He grinned back at her. She might be a bit light on gray matter, but she sure improved the office scenery. Maybe he should take her with him to Maine to interview candidates. They could call it a business retreat.

As she strolled gracefully from his office, he gave his head a shake. Not a good idea. Years ago, he'd given himself a rule to live by—never get involved with employees. Too much risk that the woman would learn more about him than anyone needed to know. If that ever happened, he stood to lose way too much—his income, his lifestyle, his reputation, his future.

He finished up the call with Diane, setting the phone back in its cradle as he scanned the note. A reporter from the *Chicago Sentinel* had called asking for an interview with Cordelia. This was the third call from that guy in as many weeks. He was just one of several reporters who had called.

"Not going to happen," he muttered, crumbling the paper into a ball and tossing it in his garbage can.

The month before Valentine's Day always brought the most requests for interviews with Cordelia. As her publicist, all the requests came to him. After so many years of turning them down, he'd have thought the media would have accepted that Cordy just didn't give interviews. Instead, the clamor seemed to be increasing.

"The worst thing you can do is run from the media," he said aloud, repeating the advice he typically gave other clients. Unfortunately, that advice didn't help in this situation at all.

Because Cordelia didn't exist.

He'd started the damn column himself in a local shopper paper to make some extra money in college. His grandmother's dog, Cordelia Jane, had provided his nom de plume—and he'd named himself Cordelia's publicist. Dear Cordelia had been a short-term financial solution—not a career plan.

But the column had taken off. A bestselling book followed. The more successful he got, the more important it became to make sure no one learned that Cordelia was a man. So he'd doubled down on his efforts to roadblock the media, and shoved his dream of being a sports agent into a dark corner.

Until now.

After ten years as Cordelia, he'd finally begun to go after his original goal. In the last year he'd become the agent for a couple of up and coming athletes. Now he just had to build his clientele until he was doing well enough that Cordy could quietly retire. He didn't want to risk the truth ever getting out, didn't want to take the chance that athletes might not want to be represented by him because they were afraid a guy who wrote a column for the lovelorn wouldn't be a tough enough at contract negotiations.

He walked over to the window to watch Mother Nature bluster outside as she tried to make it snow. In order to go to Maine, he'd have to reschedule his appointment with that football player.

As for the rest of his business, he could easily handle everything via cell phone from Maine for a week or two. His primary work still involved writing the column, and he was behind on that because he'd been putting so much energy into building his sports agenting business. At least in Maine he'd have no excuses not to get the column written.

ROMANCE ON THE ROAD *excerpt*
Copyright © 2017 by Pamela Ford

ABOUT THE AUTHOR

PAMELA FORD is the award-winning author of contemporary and historical romance. She grew up watching old movies, blissfully sighing over the romance; and reading sci-fi and adventure novels, vicariously living the action. The combination probably explains why the books she writes are romantic, happily-ever-afters with plenty of plot—and often, lots of laughter.

After graduating from college with a degree in Advertising, Pam spent many years as a copywriter and freelance writer before inserting a plot twist in her career path and writing her first book.

Pam has won numerous awards including the Booksellers Best, the Laurel Wreath, and a gold medal IPPY in the Independent Book Publisher Awards. She is a National Readers' Choice Awards finalist, a Maggie Awards finalist, a Kindle Book Awards finalist, and a two-time Golden Heart Finalist.

Sign up for Pam's mailing list at: www.pamelaford.net
Contact: pamelafordbooks@gmail.com
Facebook.com/pamelafordbooks
Instagram.com/pamelafordbooks

www.ingramcontent.com/pod-product-compliance
Lightning Source LLC
Chambersburg PA
CBHW032046180726
48284CB00008B/2776